New York Times bestseller **LINDA HOWARD** says that books have long played a profound role in her life. She cut her teeth on Margaret Mitchell, and from then on continued to read widely and eagerly. In recent years her interest has settled on romance fiction, because she's "easily bored by murder, mayhem and politics." After twenty-one years of penning stories for her own enjoyment, Ms. Howard finally worked up the courage to submit a novel for publication—and met with success! Happily, the Alabama author has been steadily publishing ever since.

* * *

New York Times bestselling author **LINDA LAEL MILLER** started writing at age ten and has made a name for herself in both contemporary and historical romance. Her bold and innovative style has made her a favorite among readers. Named "The Most Outstanding Writer of Sensual Romance" by *Romantic Times,* Linda Lael Miller never disappoints.

* * *

A master storyteller with over 10 million copies of her books in print around the world, **HEATHER GRAHAM POZZESSERE** describes her life as "busy, wild and fun." Surprisingly, with all her success, Heather's first career choice was not writing but acting on the Shakespearean stage. Happily for her fans, fate intervened and now she is a *New York Times* bestselling author. Married to her high school sweetheart, this mother of five spends her days picking up the kids from school, attending Little League games and taking care of two cats. Although Heather and her family enjoy traveling, southern Florida—where she loves the sun and water—is home.

LINDA HOWARD
LINDA LAEL MILLER
HEATHER GRAHAM POZZESSERE

SUMMER SENSATIONS

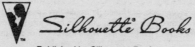

Published by Silhouette Books

America's Publisher of Contemporary Romance

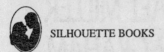

SILHOUETTE BOOKS

ISBN 0-373-48363-5

Copyright © by 1998 Harlequin Books S.A.

The publisher acknowledges the copyright holders of the individual works as follows:

OVERLOAD
Copyright © 1993 by Linda Howington

THE LEOPARD'S WOMAN
Copyright © 1992 by Linda Lael Miller

LONESOME RIDER
Copyright © 1993 by Heather Graham Pozzessere

CONTENTS

OVERLOAD
Linda Howard

Chapter One

It was hot, even for Dallas.

The scorching heat of the pavement seared through the thin leather of Elizabeth Major's shoes, forcing her to hurry even though it was an effort to move at all in the suffocating heat. The sleek office building where she worked didn't have its own underground parking garage, the builders having thought it unnecessary, since a parking deck was situated right across the street. Every time Elizabeth crossed the street in the rain, and every time she had risked being broiled by crossing it since this heat wave had begun, she swore that she would start looking for other office space. She always changed her mind as soon as she got inside, but it made her feel better to know she had the option of relocating.

Except for the parking situation, the building was perfect. It was only two years old, and managed to be both charming and convenient. The color scheme in the lobby was a soothing mixture of gray, dark mauve and white, striking the precise balance between masculine and feminine, so both genders felt comfortable. The lush greenery so carefully tended by a professional service added to the sense of freshness and spaciousness. The elevators were both numerous and fast and, so far, reliable. Her office having previously been in an older building where the elevator service had been cramped and erratic, Elizabeth doubly appreciated that last quality.

A private guard service handled the security, with a man stationed at a desk in the lobby for two shifts, from six in the morning until ten at night, as none of the businesses located in the building currently worked a third shift. Anyone wanting to come in earlier than six or stay later than ten had to let the guard service know. There was a rumor that the data processing firm on the tenth floor was considering going to three full shifts, and if that happened there would be a guard on duty around the clock. Until then, the building was locked down tight at 10:00 p.m. on weekdays and at 6:00 p.m. on weekends.

She pushed open the first set of doors and sighed with relief as the cool air rushed to greet her, washing over her hot face, evaporating the uncomfortable sweat that had formed in the time it had taken her to park her car and cross the street. When she entered the lobby itself through the second set of heavy glass doors, the full benefit of air conditioning swirled around her, making her shiver uncontrollably for just a second. Her panty hose had been clinging uncomfortably to her damp legs, and now the clammy feel made her grimace. For all that, however, she was jubilant as she crossed the lobby to the bank of elevators.

A big, unkempt man, a biker from the looks of him, entered the elevator just ahead of her. Immediately alert and wary, Elizabeth shifted her shoulder bag to her left shoulder, leaving her right hand unencumbered, as she stepped in and immediately turned to punch the button for the fifth floor, only to see a big, callused hand already pressing it. She aimed a vague smile, the kind people give each other in elevators, at the big man, then resolutely kept her gaze on the doors in front of her as they were whisked silently and rapidly to the fifth floor. But she relaxed somewhat, for if he was going to the fifth floor, he was undoubtedly involved, in some way, with Quinlan Securities.

She stepped out, and he was right on her heels as she marched down the hallway. Her offices were on the left, the chic interior revealed by the huge windows, and she saw that her secretary, Chickie, was back from lunch on time. Not only that, Chickie looked up and watched her coming down the hall. Or rather, she watched the man behind her. Elizabeth could see Chickie's big dark eyes fasten on the big man and widen with fascination.

Elizabeth opened her office door. The biker, without pausing, opened the door to Quinlan Securities, directly across the hall from her. Quinlan Securities didn't have any windows into the hallway, only a discreet sign on a solid-looking door. She had been glad, on more than one occasion, that there were no windows for more than one reason. The people who went through that door were ...*interesting*, to say the least.

"Wow," Chickie said, her gaze now fastened on the closed door across the hall. "Did you see that?"

"I saw it," Elizabeth said dryly.

Chickie's taste in men, regrettably, tended toward the unpolished variety. "He wore an earring," she said dreamily. "And did you see his hair?"

"Yes. It was long and uncombed."

"What a *mane!* I wonder why he's going into Quinlan's." Chickie's eyes brightened. "Maybe he's a new staffer!"

Elizabeth shuddered at the thought, but it was possible. Unfortunately the "Securities" in Quinlan Securities didn't refer to the financial kind but the physical sort. Chickie, who didn't have a shy bone in her body, had investigated when they had first moved into the building and cheerfully reported that Quinlan handled security of all types, from security systems to bodyguards. To Elizabeth's way of thinking, that didn't explain the type of people they saw coming and going from the Quinlan offices. The clientele, or maybe it was the *staff*, had a decidedly rough edge. If they were the former, she couldn't imagine them having enough money to afford security services. If they were the latter, she likewise couldn't imagine a client feeling comfortable around bodyguards who looked like mass murderers.

She had dated Tom Quinlan, the owner, for a while last winter, but he had been very closemouthed about his business, and she had been wary about asking. In fact, everything about Tom had made her wary. He was a big, macho, take-charge type of man, effortlessly overwhelming in both personality and body. When she had realized how he was taking over her life, she had swiftly ended the relationship and since then gone out of her way to avoid him. She would *not* lose control of her life again, and Tom Quinlan had overstepped the bounds in a big way.

Chickie dragged her attention away from the closed door across the hall and looked expectantly at Elizabeth. "Well?"

Elizabeth couldn't hold back the grin that slowly widened as her triumph glowed through. "She loved it."

"She did? You *got* it?" Chickie shrieked, jumping up and sending her chair spinning.

"I got it. We'll start next month." Her lunch meeting had been with Sandra Eiland, possessor of one of the oldest fortunes in Dallas. Sandra had decided to renovate her lavish hacienda-style house, and Elizabeth had just landed the interior-design account. She had owned her own firm for five years now, and this was the biggest job she had gotten, as well as being the most visible one. Sandra Eiland loved parties and entertained often; Elizabeth couldn't have paid for better advertising. This one account lifted her onto a completely different level of success.

Chickie's enthusiasm was immediate and obvious; she danced around the reception area, her long black hair flying. "Look out, Dallas, we are cooking now!" she crowed. "Today the Eiland account, tomorrow—tomorrow you'll do something else. We are going to be *busy*."

"I hope," Elizabeth said as she passed through into her office.

"No hoping to it." Chickie followed, still dancing. "It's guaranteed. The phone will be ringing so much I'll have to have an assistant. Yeah, I like the idea of that. Someone else can answer the phone, and I'll chase around town finding the stuff you'll need for all the jobs that will be pouring in."

"If you're chasing around town, you won't be able to watch the comings and goings across the hall," Elizabeth pointed out in a casual tone, hiding her amusement.

Chickie stopped dancing and looked thoughtful. She considered Quinlan's to be her own secret treasure trove of interesting, potential men, far more productive than a singles' bar.

"So maybe I'll have *two* assistants," she finally said. "One to answer the phone, and one to chase around town while I stay here and keep things organized."

Elizabeth laughed aloud. Chickie was such an exuberant person that it was a joy to be around her. Their styles complemented each other, Elizabeth's dry, sometimes acerbic wit balanced by Chickie's unwavering good nature. Where Elizabeth was tall and slim, Chickie was short and voluptuous. Chickie tended toward the dramatic in clothing, so Elizabeth toned down her own choices. Clients didn't like to be overwhelmed or restrained. It was subtle, but the contrast between Elizabeth and Chickie in some way relaxed her clients, reassured them that they wouldn't be pressured into a style they weren't comfortable with. Of course, sometimes Elizabeth wasn't comfortable with her own style of dress, such as today, when the heat was so miserable and she would have been much happier in shorts and a cotton T-shirt, but she had mentally, and perhaps literally, girded her loins with panty hose. If it hadn't been for the invention of air conditioning, she never would have made it; just crossing the street in this incredible heat was a feat of endurance.

Chickie's bangle bracelets made a tinkling noise as she seated herself across from Elizabeth's desk. "What time are you leaving?"

"Leaving?" Sometimes Chickie's conversational jumps were a little hard to follow. "I just got back."

"Don't you ever listen to the radio? The heat is *hazardous.* The health department, or maybe it's the weather bureau, is warning everyone to stay inside during the hottest part of the day, drink plenty of water, stuff like that. Most businesses are opening only in the mornings, then letting their people go home early so they won't get caught in traffic. I checked around. Just about everyone in the building is closing up by two this afternoon.''

Elizabeth looked at the Eiland folder she had just placed on her desk. She could barely wait to get started. "You can go home anytime you want," she said. "I had some ideas about the Eiland house that I want to work on while they're still fresh in my mind."

"I don't have any plans," Chickie said immediately. "I'll stay."

Elizabeth settled down to work and, as usual, soon became lost in the job. She loved interior design, loved the challenge of making a home both beautiful and functional, as well as suited to the owner's character. For Sandra Eiland, she wanted something that kept the flavor of the old Southwest, with an air of light and spaciousness, but also conveyed Sandra's sleek sophistication.

The ringing of the telephone finally disrupted her concentration, and she glanced at the clock, surprised to find that it was already after three o'clock. Chickie answered the call, listened for a moment, then said, "I'll find out. Hold on." She swiveled in her chair to look through the open door into Elizabeth's office. "It's the guard downstairs. He's a substitute, not our regular guard, and he's checking the offices, since he doesn't know anyone's routine. He says that almost everyone else has already gone, and he wants to know how late we'll be here.''

"Why don't you go on home now," Elizabeth suggested. "There's no point in your staying later. And tell the guard I'll leave within the hour. I want to finish this sketch, but it won't take long.''

"I'll stay with you," Chickie said yet again.

"No, there's no need. Just switch on the answering machine. I promise I won't be here much longer.''

"Well, all right." Chickie relayed the message to the guard, then hung up and retrieved her purse from the bottom desk drawer. "I dread going out there," she said. "It might be worth it to wait until after sundown, when it cools down to the nineties.''

"It's over five hours until sundown. This is July, remember.''

"On the other hand, I could spend those five hours beguiling the cute guy who moved in across the hall last week.''

"Sounds more productive.''

"And more fun." Chickie flashed her quick grin. "He won't have a chance. See you tomorrow.''

"Yes. Good luck." By the time Chickie sashayed out of the office, scarlet skirt swinging, Elizabeth had already become engrossed in the sketch taking shape beneath her talented fingers. She always did the best she could with any design, but she particularly wanted this one to be perfect, not just for the benefit to her career, but because that wonderful old house deserved it.

Her fingers finally cramped, and she stopped for a moment, noticing at the same time how tight her shoulders were, though they usually got that way only when she had been sitting hunched over a sketch pad for several hours. Absently she flexed them and was reaching for the pencil again when she realized what that tightness meant. She made a sound of annoyance when a glance at the clock said that it was 5:20, far later than she had meant to stay. Now she would have to deal with the traffic she had wanted to avoid, with this murderous heat wave making everyone ill-tempered and aggressive.

She stood and stretched, then got her bag and turned off the lights. The searing afternoon sun was blocked by the tall building next door, but there was still plenty of light coming through the tinted windows, and the office was far from dark. As she stepped out into the hall and turned to lock her door, Tom Quinlan exited his office and did the same. Elizabeth carefully didn't look at him, but she felt his gaze on her and automatically tensed. Quinlan had that effect on her, always had. It was one of the reasons she had stopped dating him, though not the biggie.

She had the uncomfortable feeling that he'd been waiting for her, somehow, and she glanced around uneasily, but no one else was around. Usually the building was full of people at this hour, as the workday wound down, but she was acutely aware of the silence around them. Surely they weren't the only two people left! But common sense told her that they were, that everyone else had sensibly gone home early; she wouldn't have any buffer between herself and Quinlan.

He fell into step beside her as she strode down the hall to the elevators. "Don't I even rate a hello these days?"

"Hello," she said.

"You're working late. Everyone else left hours ago."

"You didn't."

"No." He changed the subject abruptly. "Have dinner with me." His tone made it more of an order than an invitation.

"No, thank you," she replied as they reached the elevators. She punched the Down button and silently prayed for the elevator to hurry. The sooner she was away from this man, the safer she would feel.

"Why not?"

"Because I don't want to."

A soft chime signaled the arrival of a car; the elevator doors slid open, and she stepped inside. Quinlan followed, and the doors closed, sealing her inside with him. She reached out to punch the ground-floor button, but he caught her hand, moving so that his big body was between her and the control panel.

"You do want to, you're just afraid."

Elizabeth considered that statement, then squared her shoulders and looked up at his grim face. "You're right. I'm afraid. And I don't go out with men who scare me."

He didn't like that at all, even though he had brought up the subject. "Are you afraid I'll hurt you?" he demanded in a disbelieving tone.

"Of course not!" she scoffed, and his expression relaxed. She knew she hadn't quite told the truth, but that was her business, not his, a concept he had trouble grasping. Deftly she tugged her hand free. "It's just that you'd be a big complication, and I don't have time for that. I'm afraid you'd really mess up my schedule."

His eyes widened incredulously, then he exploded. "Hellfire, woman!" he roared, the sound deafening in the small enclosure. "You've been giving me the cold shoulder for over six months because you don't want me to interfere with your *schedule?*"

She lifted one shoulder in a shrug. "What can I say? We all have our priorities." Deftly she leaned past him and punched the button, and the elevator began sliding smoothly downward.

Three seconds later it lurched to a violent stop. Hurled off balance, Elizabeth crashed into Quinlan;

his hard arms wrapped around her as they fell, and he twisted his muscular body to cushion the impact for her. Simultaneously the lights went off, plunging them into complete darkness.

Chapter Two

The red emergency lights blinked on almost immediately, bathing them in a dim, unearthly glow. She didn't, couldn't move, not just yet; she was paralyzed by a strange mixture of alarm and pleasure. She lay sprawled on top of Quinlan, her arms instinctively latched around his neck while his own arms cradled her to him. She could feel the heat of his body even through the layers of their clothing, and the musky man-scent of his skin called up potent memories of a night when there had been no clothing to shield her from his heat. Her flesh quickened, but her spirit rebelled, and she pushed subtly against him in an effort to free herself. For a second his arms tightened, forcing her closer, flattening her breasts against the hard muscularity of his chest. The red half-light darkened his blue eyes to black, but even so, she could read the determination and desire revealed in them.

The desire tempted her to relax, to sink bonelessly into his embrace, but the determination had her pulling back. Almost immediately he released her, though she sensed his reluctance, and rolled to his feet with a lithe, powerful movement. He caught her arms and lifted her with ridiculous ease. "Are you all right? Any bruises?"

She smoothed down her skirt. "No, I'm fine. You?"

He grunted in reply, already opening the panel that hid the emergency phone. He lifted the receiver and punched the button that would alert Maintenance. Elizabeth waited, but he didn't say anything. His dark brows drew together, and finally he slammed the receiver down. "No answer. The maintenance crew must have gone home early, like everyone else."

She looked at the telephone. There was no dial on it, no buttons other than that one. It was connected only to Maintenance, meaning they couldn't call out on it.

Then she noticed something else, and her head lifted. "The air has stopped." She lifted her hand to check, but there was no cool air blowing from the vents. The lack of noise had alerted her.

"The power must be off," he said, turning his attention to the door.

The still air in the small enclosure was already becoming stuffy. She didn't like the feeling, but she refused to let herself get panicky. "It probably won't be long before it comes back on."

"Normally I'd agree with you, if we weren't having a heat wave, but the odds are too strong that it's a system overload, and if that's the case, it can take hours to repair. We have to get out. These lights are battery operated and won't stay on long. Not only that, the heat will build up, and we don't have water or enough oxygen in here.'' Even as he spoke, he was attacking the elevator doors with his strong fingers, forcing them open inch by inch. Elizabeth added her strength to his, though she was aware that he could handle it perfectly well by himself. It was just that she couldn't tolerate the way he had of taking over and making her feel so useless.

They were stuck between floors, with about three feet of the outer doors visible at the bottom of the elevator car. She helped him force open those doors, too. Before she could say anything, he had lowered himself through the opening and swung lithely to the floor below.

He turned around and reached up for her. ''Just slide out. I'll catch you.''

She sniffed, though she was a little apprehensive about what she was going to try. It had been a long time since she had done anything that athletic. ''Thanks, but I don't need any help. I took gymnastics in college.'' She took a deep, preparatory breath, then swung out of the elevator every bit as gracefully as he had, even encumbered as she was with her shoulder bag and handicapped by her high heels. His dark brows arched, and he silently applauded. She bowed. One of the things that she had found most irresistible about Quinlan was the way she had been able to joke with him. Actually there was a lot about him that she'd found irresistible, so much so that she had ignored his forcefulness and penchant for control, at least until she had found that report in his apartment. She hadn't been able to ignore that.

"I'm impressed," he said.

Wryly she said, "So am I. It's been years."

"You were on the college gymnastics team, huh? You never told me that before."

"Nothing to tell, because I *wasn't* on the college team. I'm too tall to be really good. But I took classes, for conditioning and relaxation."

"From what I remember," he said lazily, "you're still in great shape."

Elizabeth wheeled away and began walking briskly to the stairs, turning her back on the intimacy of that remark. She could feel him right behind her, like a great beast stalking its prey. She pushed open the door and stopped in her tracks. "Uh-oh."

The stairwell was completely dark. It wasn't on an outside wall, but it would have been windowless in any case. The hallway was dim, with only one office on that floor having interior windows, but the stairwell was stygian. Stepping into it would be like stepping into a well, and she felt a sudden primal instinct against it.

"No problem," Quinlan said, so close that his breath stirred her hair and she could feel his chest brush against her back with each inhalation. "Unless you have claustrophobia?"

"No, but I might develop a case any minute now."

He chuckled. "It won't take that long to get down.

We're on the third floor, so it's four short flights and out. I'll hold the door until you get your hand on the rail.''

Since the only alternative was waiting there until the power came back on, Elizabeth shrugged, took a deep breath as if she were diving and stepped into the dark hole. Quinlan was so big that he blocked most of the light, but she grasped the rail and went down the first step. "Okay, stay right there until I'm with you," he said, and let the door close behind him as he stepped forward.

She had the immediate impression of being enclosed in a tomb, but in about one second he was beside her, his arm stretched behind her back with that hand holding the rail, while he held her other arm with his free hand. In the warm, airless darkness she felt utterly surrounded by his strength. "I'm not going to fall," she said, unable to keep the bite from her voice.

"You're sure as hell not," he replied calmly. He didn't release her.

"Quinlan—"

"Walk."

Because it was the fastest way to get out of his grasp, she walked. The complete darkness was disorienting at first, but she pictured the stairs in her mind, found the rhythm of their placement, and managed to go down at almost normal speed. Four short flights, as he had said. Two flights separated by a landing constituted one floor. At the end of the fourth flight he released her, stepped forward a few steps and found the door that opened onto the first floor. Gratefully Elizabeth hurried into the sunlit lobby. She knew it was all in her imagination, but she felt as if she could breathe easier with space around her.

Quinlan crossed rapidly to the guard's desk, which was unoccupied. Elizabeth frowned. The guard was always there—or rather, he had always been there before, because he certainly wasn't *now*.

When he reached the desk, Quinlan immediately began trying to open the drawers. They were all locked. He straightened and yelled, "Hello?" His deep voice echoed in the eerily silent lobby.

Elizabeth groaned as she realized what had happened. "The guard must have gone home early, too."

"He's supposed to stay until everyone is out."

"He was a substitute. When he called the office, Chickie told him that I would leave before four. If there were other stragglers, he must have assumed that I was among them. What about you?"

"Me?" Quinlan shrugged, his eyes hooded. "Same thing."

She didn't quite believe him, but she didn't pursue it. Instead she walked over to the inner set of doors that led to the outside and tugged at them. They didn't budge. Well, great. They were locked in. "There has to be some way out of here," she muttered.

"There isn't," he said flatly.

She stopped and stared at him. "What do you mean, 'there isn't'?"

"I mean the building is sealed. Security. Keeps looters out during a power outage. The glass is reinforced, shatterproof. Even if we called the guard service and they sent someone over, they couldn't unlock the doors until the electricity was restored. It's like the vault mechanisms in banks."

"Well, you're the security expert. Get us out. Override the system somehow."

"Can't be done."

"Of course it can. Or are you admitting there's something you can't do?"

He crossed his arms over his chest and smiled benignly. "I mean that I designed the security system in this building, and it can't be breached. At least, not until the power comes back on. Until then, I can't get into the system. No one can."

Elizabeth caught her breath on a surge of fury, more at his attitude than the circumstances. He just looked so damn *smug*.

"So we call 911," she said.

"Why?"

"What do you mean, why? We're stuck in this building!"

"Is either of us ill? Hurt? Are we in any danger? This isn't an emergency, it's an inconvenience, and believe me, they have their hands full with real emergencies right now. And they can't get into the building, either. The only possible way out is to climb to the roof and be lifted off by helicopter, but that's an awful lot of expense and trouble for someone who isn't in any danger. We have food and water in the building. The sensible thing is to stay right here.''

Put that way, she grudgingly accepted that she had no choice. ''I know,'' she said with a sigh. ''It's just that I feel so…trapped.'' In more ways than one.

''It'll be fun. We'll get to raid the snack machines—''

''They operate on electricity, too.''

''I didn't say we'd use money,'' he replied, and winked at her. ''Under the circumstances, no one will mind.''

She would mind. She dreaded every minute of this, and it could last for *hours*. The last thing she wanted to do was spend any time alone with Quinlan, but it looked as if she had no choice. If only she could relax in his company, she wouldn't mind, but that was beyond her ability. She felt acutely uncomfortable with him, her tension compounded of several different things: uppermost was anger that he had dared to pry into her life the way he had; a fair amount of guilt, for she knew she owed him at least an explanation, and the truth was still both painful and embarrassing; a sort of wistfulness, because she had enjoyed so much about him; and desire—God, yes, a frustrated desire that had been feeding for months on the memory of that one night they had spent together.

"We don't have to worry about the air," he said, looking around at the two-story lobby. "It'll get considerably warmer in here, but the insulation and thermal-glazed windows will keep it from getting critically hot. We'll be okay."

She forced herself to stop fretting and think sensibly. There was no way out of this situation, so she might as well make the best of it, and that meant staying as comfortable as they could. In this case, comfortable meant cool. She began looking around; as he'd said, they had food and water, though they would have to scrounge for it, and there was enough furniture here in the lobby to furnish several living rooms, so they had plenty of cushions to fashion beds. Her mind skittered away from that last thought. Her gaze fell on the stairway doors, and the old saying "hot air rises" came to mind. "If we open the bottom stairway doors, that'll create a chimney effect to carry the heat upward," she said.

"Good idea. I'm going to go back up to my office to get a flashlight and raid the snack machine. Is there anything you want from your office while I'm up there?"

Mentally she ransacked her office, coming up with several items that might prove handy. "Quite a bit, actually. I'll go with you."

"No point in both of us climbing the stairs in the dark," he said casually. "Just tell me what you want."

That was just like him, she thought irritably, wanting to do everything himself and not involve her. "It makes more sense if we both go. You can pilfer your office for survival stuff, and I'll pilfer mine. I think I have a flashlight, too, but I'm not certain where it is."

"It's eight flights, climbing, this time, instead of going down," he warned her, looking down at her high heels.

In answer, she stepped out of her shoes and lifted her eyebrows expectantly. He gave her a thoughtful look, then gave in without more argument, gesturing her ahead of him. He relocated a large potted tree to hold the stairway door propped open, handling it as casually as if the big pot didn't weigh over a hundred pounds. Elizabeth had a good idea how heavy it was, however, for she loved potted plants and her condo was always full of greenery. She wondered how it would feel to have such strength, to possess Quinlan's basic self-confidence that he could handle any situation or difficulty. With him, it was even more than mere confidence; there was a certain arrogance, subtle but unmistakably there, the quiet arrogance of a man who knew his own strengths and skills. Though he had adroitly sidestepped giving out any personal information about his past, she sensed that some of those skills were deadly.

She entered the stairwell with less uneasiness this time, for there was enough light coming in through the open door to make the first two flights perfectly visible. Above that, however, they proceeded in thick, all-encompassing darkness. As he had before, Quinlan passed an arm behind her back to grip the rail, and his free hand held her elbow. His hand had always been there whenever they had gone up or down steps, she remembered. At first it had been pleasurable, but soon she had felt a little smothered, and then downright alarmed. Quinlan's possessiveness had made her uneasy, rather than secure. She knew too well how such an attitude could get out of hand.

Just to break the silence she quipped, "If either of us smoked, we'd have a cigarette lighter to light our path."

"If either of us smoked," he came back dryly, "we wouldn't have the breath to climb the stairs."

She chuckled, then saved her energy to concentrate on the steps. Climbing five floors wasn't beyond her capabilities, but it was still an effort. She was breathing hard by the time they reached the fifth floor, and the darkness was becoming unnerving. Quinlan stepped forward and opened the door, letting in a sweet spill of light.

They parted ways at their respective offices, Quinlan disappearing into his while Elizabeth unlocked hers. The late-afternoon light was still spilling brightly through the windows, reminding her that, in actuality, very little time had passed since the elevator had lurched to a halt. A disbelieving glance at her wristwatch said that it had been less than half an hour.

The flashlight was the most important item, and she searched the file cabinets until she found it. Praying that the batteries weren't dead, she thumbed the switch and was rewarded by a beam of light. She switched it off and placed it on Chickie's desk. She and Chickie made their own coffee, as it was both more convenient and better tasting than the vending machine kind, so she got their cups and put them on the desk next to the flashlight. Drinking from them would be easier than splashing water into their mouths with their hands, and she knew Chickie wouldn't mind if Quinlan used her cup. Quite the contrary.

Knowing that her secretary had an active sweet tooth, Elizabeth began rifling the desk drawers, smiling in appreciation when she found a six-pack of chocolate bars with only one missing, a new pack of fig bars, chewing gum, a honey bun and a huge blueberry muffin. Granted, it was junk food, but at least they wouldn't be hungry. Finally she got two of the soft pillows that decorated the chairs in her office, thinking that they would be more comfortable for sleeping than the upholstered cushions downstairs.

Quinlan opened the door, and she glanced at him. He had removed his suit jacket and was carrying a small black leather bag. He looked at her loot and laughed softly. "Were you a scout, by any chance?"

"I can't take the credit for most of it. Chickie's the one with a sweet tooth."

"Remind me to give her a big hug the next time I see her."

"She'd rather have you set her up on a date with that biker who came in after lunch."

He laughed again. "Feeling adventurous, is she?"

"Chickie's *always* adventurous. Was he a client?"

"No."

She sensed that that was all the information he was going to give out about the "biker." As always, Quinlan was extremely closemouthed about his business, both clients and staff. On their dates, he had always wanted to talk about *her,* showing interest in every little detail of her life, while at the same time gently stonewalling her tentative efforts to find out more about him. It hadn't been long before that focused interest, coupled with his refusal to talk about himself, had begun making her extremely uncomfortable. She could understand not wanting to talk about certain things; there was a certain period that she couldn't bring herself to talk about, either, but Quinlan's secretiveness had been so absolute that she didn't even know if he had any family. On the other hand, he had noticed the gap in her own life and had already started asking probing little questions when she had broken off the relationship.

There was a silk paisley shawl draped across a chair, and Elizabeth spread it across the desk to use

as an upscale version of a hobo's pouch. As she began
piling her collection in the middle of the shawl, Quinlan casually flicked at the fringe with one finger. "Do
people actually buy shawls just because they look
good draped across chairs?"

"Of course. Why not?"

"It's kind of silly, isn't it?"

"I guess it depends on your viewpoint. Do you
think it's silly when people spend hundreds of dollars
on mag wheels for their cars or trucks, just because
they look good?"

"Cars and trucks are useful."

"So are chairs," she said dryly. She gathered the
four corners of the shawl together and tied them in a
knot. "Ready."

"While we're up here, we need to raid the snack
machines, rather than rely on what you have there.
There's no point in making extra trips upstairs to get
more food when we can get it now."

She gave him a dubious look. "Do you think we'll
be here so long that we'll need that much food?"

"Probably not, but I'd rather have too much than
too little. We can always return what we don't eat."

"Logical," she admitted.

He turned to open the door for her, and Elizabeth
stared in shock at the lethal black pistol tucked into
his waistband at the small of his back. "Good God,"
she blurted. "What are you going to do with that?"

Chapter Three

He raised his eyebrows. "Whatever needs doing," he said mildly.

"Thank you so much for the reassurance! Are you expecting any kind of trouble? I thought you said the building was sealed."

"The building *is* sealed, and no, I'm not expecting any trouble. That doesn't mean I'm going to be caught unprepared if I'm wrong. Don't worry about it. I'm always armed, in one way or another. It's just that this is the first time you've noticed."

She stared at him. "You don't usually carry a pistol."

"Yes, I do. You wouldn't have noticed it now if I hadn't taken my coat off."

"You didn't have one the night we—" She cut off the rest of the sentence.

"Made love?" He finished it for her. His blue eyes were steady, watchful. "Not that night, no. I knew I was going to make love to you, and I didn't want to scare you in any way, so I locked the pistol in the glove compartment before I picked you up. But I had a knife in my boot. Just like I do now."

It was difficult to breathe. She fought to suck in a deep breath as she bypassed the issue of the pistol and latched on to the most shocking part of what he'd just said. "You *knew* we were going to make love?"

He gave her another of those thoughtful looks. "You don't want to talk about that right now. Let's get finished here and get settled in the lobby before dark so we can save the batteries in the flashlights."

It was another logical suggestion, except for the fact that night wouldn't arrive until about nine o'clock, giving them plenty of time. She leaned back against the desk and crossed her arms. "Why don't I want to talk about it now?"

"Just an assumption I made. You've spent over half a year avoiding me, so I didn't think you would suddenly want to start an in-depth discussion. If I'm wrong, by all means let's talk." A sudden dangerous glitter lit his eyes. "Was I too rough? Was five times too many? I don't think so, because I could feel your climaxes squeezing me," he said bluntly. "Not to mention the way you had your legs locked around me so tight I could barely move. And I know damn good and well I don't snore or talk in my sleep, so just what in hell happened to send you running?"

His voice was low and hard, and he had moved closer so that he loomed over her. She had never seen him lose control, but as she saw the rage in his eyes she knew that he was closer to doing so now than she had ever imagined. It shook her a little. Not because she was afraid of him—at least, not in that way—but because she hadn't imagined it would have mattered so much to him.

Then she squared her shoulders, determined not to let him take charge of the conversation and turn it back on her the way he had so many times. "What do you mean, you *knew* we would make love that night?" she demanded, getting back to the original subject.

"Just what I said."

"How could you have been so sure? *I* certainly hadn't planned on it happening."

"No. But I knew you wouldn't turn me down."

"You know a damn lot, don't you?" she snapped, incensed by that unshakable self-confidence of his.

"Yeah. But I don't know why you ran afterward. So why don't you tell me? Then we can get the problem straightened out and pick up where we left off."

She glared at him, not budging. He ran his hand through his dark hair, which he kept in a short, almost military cut. He was so controlled, it was one of the few gestures of irritation she could ever remember him making. "All right," he muttered. "I knew you were hiding things from me, maybe because you didn't trust what was between us. I thought that once we'd made love, once you knew you belonged to me, you'd trust me and stop holding back."

She forgot to glare. Her arms dropped to her sides, and she gaped at him. "I *belong* to you? I beg your pardon! Do you have a bill of sale that I don't know about?''

"Yes, belong!" he barked. "I had planned on marriage, kids, the whole bit, but you kept edging away from me. And I didn't know why. I still don't.''

"Marriage? Kids?" She could barely speak, she was so astounded. The words came out in a squeak. "I don't suppose it ever occurred to you to let me in on all of this planning you were doing, did it? No, don't bother to answer. You made up your mind, and that was it, regardless of how *I* felt.''

"I knew how you felt. You were in love with me. You still are. That's why it doesn't make sense that you ran.''

"Maybe not to you, but it's crystal clear to me.'' She looked away, her face burning. She hadn't realized her feelings had been so obvious to him, though she had known fairly early in their relationship that she loved him. The more uneasy she had become, however, the more she had tried to hide the intensity of her feelings.

"Then why don't you let me in on the secret? I'm tired of this. Whatever it is I did, I apologize for it. We've wasted enough time.''

His arrogance was astonishing, even though she had recognized that part of his character from the beginning. Quinlan was generally a quiet man, but it was the quietness of someone who had nothing to prove, to himself or anyone else. He had decided to put an end to the situation, and that was that, at least from his viewpoint.

But not from hers.

"You listen to me, Tom Quinlan," she said furiously. "I don't care what plans you've made, you can just write me out of them. I don't want—"

"I can't do that," he interrupted.

"Why not?"

"Because of this."

She saw the glitter in his eyes and immediately bolted away from the desk, intent on escape. She was quick, but he was quicker. He seized her wrists and folded her arms behind her back, effectively wrapping her in his embrace at the same time. The pressure of his iron-muscled arms forced her against the hard planes of his body. Having seen him naked, she knew that his clothing disguised his true strength and muscularity, knew that she didn't have a prayer of escaping until he decided to release her. She declined to struggle, contenting herself with a furious glare.

"Cat eyes," he murmured. "The first time I saw you, I knew you were no lady. Your eyes give you away. And I was right, thank God. The night we spent together proved that you don't give a damn about what's proper or ladylike. You're wild and hot, and we wrecked my bed. You should have known there's no way in hell I'd let you go."

He was aroused. She could feel his hardness thrusting against her, his hips moving ever so slightly in a nestling motion, wordlessly trying to tempt her into opening her thighs to cradle him. It *was* tempting. Damn tempting. She couldn't deny wanting him, had never tried to, but he was right: she didn't trust him.

"It won't work," she said hoarsely.

"It already has." The words were soft, almost crooning, and his warm breath washed over her mouth a second before his lips were there, firm and hot, his head slanting to deepen the kiss and open her mouth to him. She hadn't meant to do so, but she found herself helpless to prevent it. Right from the beginning, his kisses had made her dizzy with delight. His self-confidence was manifested even in this; there was no hesitancy, no awkwardness. He simply took her mouth as if it were his right, his tongue probing deep, and a deep shudder of pleasure made her quake.

Held against him as she was, she could feel the tension in his body, feel his sex throbbing with arousal. He had never made any effort to disguise his response to her. Though it had been obvious even on their first date, he hadn't pressured her in any way. Maybe she had started falling in love with him then, because he had been both amused and matter-of-fact about his frequent arousal, his attitude being that it was a natural result of being in her company. She hadn't felt threatened in any way; in fact, looking back, she realized that Quinlan had gone out of his way to keep from alarming her. He had been remarkably unaggressive, sexually speaking, despite the per-

sistent evidence of his attraction. She had never felt
that she might have to face a wrestling match at the
end of an evening. Even the night they had made love,
she hadn't fully realized the seriousness of his kisses
until she had somehow found herself naked in bed
with him, her body on fire with need. Then she had
discovered that he was very serious, indeed.

The memory made her panic, and she tore her
mouth away from his. She had no doubt that if she
didn't stop him now, within five minutes he would be
making love to her. The hot sensuality of his kisses
was deceptive, arousing her more and faster than
she'd expected. It had been the same way that one
night. He had just been kissing her; then, before she
knew it, she had been wild for him. She hadn't known
such intense heat and pleasure had existed, until then.

"What's wrong?" he murmured, reclaiming her
mouth with a series of swift, light kisses that nevertheless burned. "Don't you like it? Or do you like it
too much?"

His perceptiveness alarmed her even more, and despite herself she began to struggle. To her surprise,
he released her immediately, though he didn't step
back.

"Tell me what went wrong, babe." His tone was
dark and gentle. "I can't make it right if I don't know
what it is."

She put her hands on his chest to force him away
and was instantly, achingly aware of his hard, warm

flesh covered only by a thin layer of cotton. She could even feel the roughness of his hair, the strong, heavy beat of his heart pulsing beneath her fingers. "Quinlan—"

"Tell me," he cajoled, kissing her again.

Desperately she slipped sideways, away from him. Her body felt overheated and slightly achy. If she didn't tell him, he would persist in his seductive cajoling, and she didn't know how long she could resist him. "All right." She owed him that much. She didn't intend to change her mind about dating him, but at least he deserved an explanation. She should have told him before, but at the time all she had wanted was to stay as far away from him as possible. "But...later. Not right now. We need to get everything gathered up and get settled in the lobby."

He straightened, amusement in his eyes. "Where have I heard that before?"

"It isn't polite to gloat."

"Maybe not, but it's sure as hell satisfying."

She was nervous. Quinlan was surprised at the depth of her uneasiness, because that wasn't a trait he associated with Elizabeth. He wondered at the cause of it, just as he had wondered for the past six months why she had run from him so abruptly after spending the night in his arms. She wasn't afraid of him; that was one of the things he liked best about her. For him to find women attractive, they had to be intelligent,

but unfortunately that intelligence tended to go hand
in glove with a perceptiveness that made them shy
away from him.

He couldn't do anything about his aura of danger-
ousness, because he couldn't lose the characteristics,
the habits or the instincts that made him dangerous.
He didn't even want to. It was as much a part of him
as his bones, and went as deep. He had made do with
shallow relationships for the sake of physical gratifi-
cation, but inside he had been waiting and watching.
Though the life he had led sometimes made him feel
as if only a few people in this world really *saw* what
went on around them, that most people went through
life wearing blinders, now that he was mostly out of
the action he wanted the normalcy that the average
person took for granted. He wanted a wife and family,
a secure, settled life; as soon as he had met Elizabeth,
he had known that she was the one he wanted.

It wasn't just her looks, though God knew he broke
out in a sweat at the sight of her. She was a little over
average height, as slim as a reed, with sleek dark hair
usually pulled back in a classic chignon. She had the
fast lines of a thoroughbred, and until he had met her,
he hadn't known how sexy that was. But it was her
eyes that had gotten him. Cat eyes, he'd told her, and
it was true, but though they were green, it was more
the expression in them than the color that made them
look so feline. Elizabeth's nature shone in her eyes.
She had given him a warning look that had said she

wasn't intimidated by him at all, underlaid by a cool disdain that was certainly catlike.

Excitement and arousal had raced through him. The more he'd learned about her, the more determined he had been to have her. She was sharply intelligent, witty, sarcastic at times and had a robust sense of humor that sometimes caught him off guard, though it always delighted him. And she burned with an inner intensity that drew him as inexorably as a magnet draws steel.

The intensity of his attraction had caught him off guard. He wanted to know everything there was to know about her, even her childhood memories, because that was a time in her life that would be forever closed to him. He wanted to have children with her and was fascinated by the possibility of a daughter in Elizabeth's image, a small, strong-willed, sharp-tongued, dimpled cherub. Talking about Elizabeth's own childhood made that possibility seem tantalizingly real.

At first Elizabeth had talked openly, with that faint arrogance of hers that said she had nothing to hide and he could like it or lump it. But then he had begun to sense that she *was* hiding something. It wasn't anything he could put his finger on; it was more of a withdrawal from him, as if she had built an inner wall and had no intention of letting him progress past that point.

Both his training and his nature made it impossible

for him just to let it pass. Her withdrawal didn't make sense, because he *knew*, knew with every animal instinct in him that she felt the same way he did. She wanted him. She loved him. If she were truly hiding something, he wanted to know about it, and he had both the skill and the resources to find out just about anything in a person's life. His inquiries had turned up the fact that she had been married before, but the marriage had seemed to be fairly typical, and fairly brief, the sort of thing a lot of college graduates drifted into, quickly finding out they didn't suit. He'd had his own short fling with marriage at that age, so he knew how it happened. But the more he'd thought about it, the more he'd noticed that the period of her marriage was the one period she didn't talk about, not even mentioning that she'd ever been married at all. He was too good at what he did not to realize the significance of that, and he had begun to probe for answers about those two missing years. At the same time, feeling her slipping away from him, he had made a bold move to cement their relationship and taken her to bed, trusting in the bonds of the flesh to both break down the barriers and hold her to him until she learned to trust him completely.

It hadn't worked.

She had fled the next morning while he was still in the shower, and this was the first time he'd gotten her alone since then.

Over half a year wasted. Almost seven long damn

months, endless nights spent in burning frustration, both physical and mental.

But he had her now, all alone, and before they left this building he intended to know just what the hell happened and have her back where she belonged, with him.

Chapter Four

"Let's get those snack machines raided," she muttered, grabbing up her ditty bag of goodies and heading for the door. Quinlan had been standing there, staring at her for what seemed like several minutes but had probably been less than thirty seconds. There was a hooded, predatory expression in his gleaming blue eyes, and she just couldn't stand there, like a tethered goat, for another second.

He sauntered out in her wake, and she relocked the office door, then looked up and down the dim hallway. "Just where *are* these snack machines?" she finally asked. "I'm not a junk food junkie, so I've never used them."

"There's a soft drink machine at this end of the hallway," he said, pointing, "but there are snack machines in the insurance offices. They have a break room for their employees, but they let us use them." He set off down the long hallway, away from the bank of elevators, and Elizabeth trailed after him.

"How are we going to get in?" she asked caustically. "Shoot the lock off?"

"If I have to," he replied, lazy good humor in his voice. "But I don't think it will come to that."

She hoped not. From what she could tell, insurance

companies tended to be rather humorless about such things. She could well imagine receiving a bill for damages, which she could certainly do without.

Quinlan knelt in front of the insurance company's locked door and unzipped the leather bag, taking from it a small case resembling the one in which she kept her makeup brushes. He flipped it open, though, and the resemblance ended. Instead of plush brushes, there was an assortment of oddly shaped metal tools. He took two of them out, inserted the long, thin, bent one into the keyhole, then slid the other instrument in beside it and jiggled it with small, delicate movements.

Elizabeth sidled closer, bending down to get a better look. "Can you teach me how to do that?" she asked in an absent tone, fascinated with the process.

The corners of his mouth twitched as he continued to gingerly work at the lock. "Why? Have you just discovered a larcenous streak?"

"Do *you* have one?" she shot back. "It just seems like a handy skill to have, since you never know when you'll accidentally lock yourself out."

"And you're going to start carrying a set of locksmith's tools in your purse?"

"Why not?" She nudged the black leather bag with her toe. "Evidently you carry one in yours."

"That isn't a purse. Ah," he said with satisfaction, as he felt the lock open. He withdrew the slender tools, stored them in their proper places in the case and replaced the case in the bag. Then he calmly opened the door.

"Explain the difference between my purse and yours," she said as she entered the dim, silent insurance office.

"It isn't a purse. The difference is the things that are in them."

"I see. So if I emptied the contents of my purse into your leather bag, it would then become a purse?"

"I give up," he said mildly. "Okay, it's a purse. Only men don't call them purses. We call them satchels or just plain leather bags."

"A rose by any other name," she murmured with gentle triumph.

He chuckled. "That's one of the things I like best about you. You're such a gracious winner. You never hesitate at all to gloat."

"Some people just ask for it more than others." She looked around, seeing nothing but empty desks and blank computer screens. "Where's the break room?"

"This way." He led her down a dark interior hallway and opened the last door on the right.

The room had two windows, so it wasn't dark. A variety of vending machines lined one wall, offering soft drinks, coffee, juice and snacks. A microwave oven sat on a counter, and a silent refrigerator stood at another wall. There was a vinyl sofa with splits in the cushions that allowed the stuffing to show, and a number of folding chairs shoved haphazardly around two cafeteria tables.

"Check the refrigerator while I open the machines," Quinlan said. "See if there's any ice. We don't need it now, but it would be nice to know that it's there just in case. Do it as fast as you can, to keep the cold air in."

"I do know about refrigerators and power failures," she said pointedly. Swiftly she opened the freezer compartment, and vapor poured out as cold air met warm. There were six ice trays there, all of them full. She shut the door just as fast as she had opened it. "We have ice."

"Good." He had the snack machine open and was removing packs of crackers.

Elizabeth opened the main refrigerator door but was disappointed with the contents. A brown paper bag sat in lone splendor, with several translucent greasy spots decorating it. She had no interest in investigating its contents. There was an apple, though, and she took it. The shelves in the door were lined with various condiments, nothing that tempted her. The thought of putting ketchup on the honey bun was revolting.

"Just an apple here," she said.

He finished loading his booty into the leather bag. "Okay, we have cakes, crackers and candy bars, plus the stuff you got from Chickie's desk. My best guess is we'll get out of here sometime tomorrow morning, so this should be more than enough. Do you want a soft drink, or juice? There's water downstairs, so we don't need to raid the drink machines. It's strictly a matter of preference.''

She thought about it, then shook her head. "Water will be enough."

He zipped the bag. "That's it, then. Let's make ourselves comfy downstairs."

"Should we leave a note?" she asked.

"No need. I'll take care of things when the power comes on and everything gets back to normal."

The trip downstairs was considerably easier with the aid of one of the flashlights, and soon they reentered the lobby, which was noticeably cooler because of the two-story ceiling. She looked out through the dark glass of the double entrance; the street was oddly deserted, with only the occasional car passing by. A patrol car crawled past as she watched. "It looks weird," she murmured. "As if everyone has been evacuated."

"If the power doesn't come back on," Quinlan said in a grim tone, "it will probably get a lot busier once the sun goes down and things cool off a little. By the way, I tried to call out from my office, just to see what was going on and let someone know where we were, but I couldn't get a call to go through. If there's a city-wide blackout, which I suspect, the circuits will be jammed with calls. But I did find a battery-operated radio, so we'll be able to listen to the news."

"Turn it on now," she suggested, walking over to a sofa to dump her load on it. "Let's find out what's going on."

He opened the leather bag and took out a small radio, not even as big as her hand. After switching it on and getting only static, he began running through the frequencies, looking for a station. Abruptly a voice jumped out at them, astonishingly clear for such a small radio. "—the National Guard has been called out in several states to help prevent looting—"

"Damn," Quinlan muttered. "This sounds bad."

"Information is sketchy," the announcer continued, "but more reports are coming in, and it looks as if there has been a massive loss of electrical power across the Southeast and most of Texas."

"I'm not an expert," a second voice said, "but the southern tier of the country has been suffering under this heat wave for two weeks, and I imagine the demands for electricity overloaded the system. Have we had any word yet from the governor?"

"Nothing yet, but the phone lines are tied up. Please, people, don't use the telephones unless it's an emergency. Folks can't get through to 911 if you're on the phone to your friends telling them that your power's out, too. Believe me, they *know*."

The second announcer chimed in, "Remember the safety precautions the Health Department has been telling us for two weeks. It's especially critical without electricity for air conditioning and fans. Stay out of the sun if possible. With the power off, open your windows for ventilation, and drink plenty of liquids. Don't move around any more than you have to. Conserve your energy.''

"We'll be on the air all night long," said the first announcer, "operating on emergency power. If anything happens you'll hear it first here on—"

Quinlan switched off the radio. "Well, now we know what happened," he said calmly. "We'll save the batteries as much as we can."

She gave him a mock incredulous look. "What? You mean you don't have replacement batteries?"

"It isn't my radio."

It wasn't necessary for him to add that if it had been, of course he would have had extra batteries. She wished it *were* his radio. And while she was wishing, she wished she had left the building on time, though she wasn't certain she wouldn't be in a worse situation at her condo. Certainly she was safer here, inside a sealed building.

The magnitude of the problem was stunning. This wasn't something that was going to be corrected in a couple of hours. It was possible they would still be locked in at this time tomorrow.

She looked at Quinlan. "Are you *sure* it won't get dangerously hot in here?"

"Not absolutely positive, but reasonably sure. We'll be okay. We have water, and that's the most important thing. Actually, we're probably as comfortable as anyone in this city is, except for those places that have emergency generators. If we start getting too warm, we'll just take off some clothes.''

Her heart literally jumped, sending her pulse rate soaring, and immediately she began to feel uncomfortably warm. Her stomach muscles clenched at the thought of lying naked in the darkness with him, but it was the tightness of desire. While her mind was wary, her body remembered the intense pleasure of his lovemaking. She turned back to the windows to keep him from reading her expression. Staring at the glass made her think of something else, and gratefully she seized on it.

''When it gets dark, will anyone on the outside be able to see us in here when we turn on a flashlight? Does the privacy glazing work at night?''

''Anyone who looked closely would be able to tell that there's a light in here, I suppose,'' he said thoughtfully. ''But no one will be able to actually *see* us.''

Just the possibility was enough. She had been about to arrange their supplies in the seating area closest to the entrance, but now she moved farther away. The lobby had several comfortable seating areas, and she chose one that was close to the middle. It was at least semiprivate, with a long, waist-high planter that created the sense of a small alcove. It was also closer to the bathrooms, making it a better choice all the way around.

She arranged their food supplies on a low table, while Quinlan shoved the chairs around to make more room. Then he collected cushions from the other chairs and stacked them close to hand, ready to make into beds when they decided to sleep. Elizabeth gave the cushions a sidelong glance. She wasn't sure she would be able to close her eyes with Quinlan so close by, or that it would be smart to sleep, even if she could.

She looked at him and started when she found him watching her. He didn't look away as he unknotted his tie and stripped it off, then unbuttoned his shirt down to his waist and rolled up his sleeves. His actions were practical, but the sight of his muscled, hairy chest and hard belly aroused a reaction in her that had nothing to do with common sense.

"Why don't you take off those panty hose?" he suggested in a low, silky voice. "They have to be damn hot."

They were. She hesitated, then decided wryly that it wasn't the thin nylon that would protect her from him. Only *she* could do that. Quinlan wasn't a rapist; if she said no, he wouldn't force himself on her. She had never been afraid of that; her only fear was that she wouldn't be able to say no. That was one reason why she had avoided him for the past six months. So leaving her panty hose on wouldn't keep him from making love to her if she couldn't say no, and taking them off wouldn't put her at risk if she did keep herself under control. It was, simply, a matter of comfort.

She got a flashlight and carried it into the public rest room, where she propped it on one of the basins. The small room felt stuffy and airless, so she hurriedly removed her panty hose and immediately felt much cooler. She turned on the cold water and held her wrists under the stream, using the time-proven method of cooling down, then dampened one of the paper towels and blotted her face. There. That was much better.

A few deep breaths, a silent pep talk and she felt ready to hold Tom Quinlan at arm's length for the duration. With her panty hose in one hand and the flashlight in the other, she returned to the lobby.

He was waiting for her, sprawled negligently in one of the chairs, but those blue eyes watched her as intently as a tiger watches its chosen prey. "Now," he said, "let's have our little talk."

Chapter Five

Her heart lurched in her chest. It strained her composure to walk over to the chairs and sit down, but she did it, even crossed her legs and leaned back as negligently as he. "All right," she said calmly.

He gave her that considering look again, as if he were trying to decide how to handle her. Mentally she bristled at the idea of being "handled," but she forced down her irritation. She knew how relentless Quinlan could be when crossed; she would need to keep her thoughts ordered, not let him trip her up with anger.

He remained silent, watching her, and she knew what he wanted. He had already asked the question; he was simply waiting for the answer.

Despite herself, Elizabeth felt a spurt of anger, even after all these months. She faced him and went straight to the heart of the matter. "I found the file you had on me," she said, every word clipped short. "You had me investigated."

"Ah." He steepled his fingers and studied her over them. "So that's it." He paused a few seconds, then said mildly, "Of course I did."

"There's no 'of course' to it. You invaded my privacy—"

"As you invaded mine," he interrupted smoothly. "That file wasn't lying out in the open."

"No, it wasn't. I looked in your desk," she admitted without hesitation.

"Why?"

"I felt uneasy about you. I was looking for some answers."

"So why didn't you ask *me?*" The words were as sharp as a stiletto.

She gave him a wry, humorless smile. "I did. Many times. You're a master at evasion, though. I've been to bed with you, but I don't know much more about you right now than I did the day we met."

He neatly sidestepped the charge by asking, "What made you feel uneasy? I never threatened you, never pushed you. You know I own and run my company, that I'm solvent and not on the run."

"You just did it again," she pointed out. "Your ability to evade is very good. It took me a while to catch on, but then I noticed that you didn't answer my questions. You always responded, so it wasn't obvious, but you'd just ask your own question and ignore mine."

He surveyed her silently for a moment before saying, "I'm not interested in talking about myself. I already know all the details."

"I'd say that the same holds true for me, wouldn't you?" she asked sweetly. "I wanted to know about *you,* and got nowhere. But I didn't have you investigated.''

"I wouldn't have minded if you had." Not that she would have been able to find out much, he thought. Great chunks of his life after high school graduation weren't to be found in public records.

"Bully for you. *I* minded."

"And that's it? You walked out on me and broke off our relationship because you were angry that I had you investigated? Why didn't you just yell at me? Throw things at me? For God's sake, Elizabeth, don't you think you took it a little far?"

His tone was both angry and incredulous, making it plain that he considered her reaction to be nothing short of hysteric, far out of proportion to the cause.

She froze inside, momentarily paralyzed by the familiar ploy of being made to feel that she was in the wrong, that no matter what happened it was her fault for not being good enough. But then she fought the memories back; she would never let anyone make her feel that way again. She had gotten herself back, and she knew her own worth. She knew she hadn't handled the matter well, but only in the way she had done it; the outcome itself had never been in question.

Her voice was cool when she replied. "No, I don't think I took it too far. I'd been feeling uneasy about you for quite a while. Finding that you had investigated me was the final factor, but certainly not all of it."

"Because I hadn't answered a few questions?" That incredulous note was still there.

"Among other things."

"Such as?"

In for a penny, in for a pound. "Such as your habit of taking over, of ignoring my objections or suggestions as if I hadn't even said anything."

"Objections to what?" Now the words were as sharp as a lash. His blue eyes were narrowed and vivid. A bit surprised, she realized that he was angry again.

She waved her hand in a vague gesture. "Any little thing. I didn't catalog them—"

"Surprises the hell out of me," he muttered.

"But you were constantly overriding me. If I told you I was going shopping, you insisted that I wait until you could go with me. If I wanted to wear a sweater when we were going out, you insisted that I wear a coat. Damn it, Quinlan, you even tried to make me change where I bank!"

His eyebrows rose. "The bank you use now is too far away. The one I suggested is much more convenient."

"For whom? If I'm perfectly happy with my bank, then it isn't inconvenient for me, is it?"

"So don't change your bank. What's the big deal?"

"The big deal," she said slowly, choosing her words, "is that you want to make all the decisions, handle everything yourself. You don't want a relationship, you want a dictatorship.''

One moment he was lounging comfortably, long legs sprawled out in front of him; the next he was in front of her, bending over to plant his hands on the arms of her chair and trap her in place. Elizabeth stared up at him, blinking at the barely controlled rage in his face, but she refused to let herself shrink from him. Instead she lifted her chin and met him glare for glare.

"I don't believe it!" he half shouted. "You walked out on me because I wanted you to change banks? God in heaven." He shoved himself away from the chair and stalked several paces away, running his hand through his hair.

"No," she shouted back, "I walked out because I refuse to let you take over my life!" She was unable to sit still, either, and surged out of the chair. Instantly Quinlan whirled with those lightning-quick reactions of his, catching her arms and hauling her close to him, so close that she could see the white flecks in the deep blue of his irises and smell the hot, male scent of his body. Her nostrils flared delicately as she instinctively drank in the primal signal, even though she stiffened against his touch.

"Why didn't you tell me you were married before?"

The question was soft, and not even unexpected,

but still she flinched. Of course he knew; it had been in that damn investigative report.

"It isn't on my list of conversational topics," she snapped. "But neither is it a state secret. *If* our relationship had ever progressed far enough, I would have told you then. What was I supposed to do, trot out my past life the minute we met?"

Quinlan watched her attentively. As close as they were, he could see every flicker of expression on her face, and he had noticed the telltale flinch even though she had replied readily enough. Ah, so there *was* something there.

"Just how far did our relationship have to go?" he asked, still keeping his voice soft. "We weren't seeing anyone else. We didn't actually have sex until that last night together, but things got pretty hot between us several times before that."

"And I was having doubts about you even then," she replied just as softly.

"Maybe so, but that didn't stop you from wanting me, just like now." He bent his head and settled his mouth on hers, the pressure light and persuasive. She tried to pull away and found herself powerless against his strength, even though he was taking care not to hurt her. "Be still," he said against her lips.

Desperately she wrenched her head away. He forced it back, but instead of kissing her again, he paused with his mouth only a fraction of an inch above hers. "Why didn't you tell me about it?" he murmured, his warm breath caressing her lips and making them tingle. With his typical relentlessness, he had fastened on an idea and wouldn't let it go until he was satisfied with the answer. The old blind fear rose in her, black wings beating, and in panic she started to struggle. He subdued her without effort, wrapping her in a warm, solid embrace from which there was no escape.

"What happened?" he asked, brushing light kisses across her mouth between words. "What made you flinch when I mentioned it? Tell me about it now. I need to know. Did he run around on you?"

"No." She hadn't meant to answer him, but somehow, caught in those steely arms and cradled against his enticing heat, the word slipped out in a whisper. She heard it and shuddered. "No!" she said more forcefully, fighting for control. "He didn't cheat." If only he had, if only his destructive attention had been diluted in that way, it wouldn't have been so bad. "Stop it, Quinlan. Let me go."

"Why did you start calling me Quinlan?" His voice remained low and soothing, and his warm mouth kept pressing against hers with quick, gentle touches. "You called me Tom before, and when we made love."

She had started calling him Quinlan in an effort to distance herself from him. She didn't want to think of him as Tom, because the name was forever linked in her mind with that night when she had clung to his naked shoulders, her body lifting feverishly to his forceful thrusts as she cried out his name over and over, in ecstasy, in need, in completion. Tom was the name of her lover; Quinlan was the man she had fled.

And Quinlan was the one she had to deal with now, the man who never gave up. He held her helpless in his grasp, taking kiss after kiss from her until she stopped trying to evade his mouth and opened her lips to him with a tiny, greedy sound. Instantly he took her with his tongue, and the sheer pleasure of it made them both shudder.

His warm hand closed over her breast, gently kneading. She groaned, the sound captured by his mouth, and desperately tried to marshal her resistance. He was seducing her just as effortlessly as he had the first time, but even though she realized what was happening she couldn't find the willpower to push him away. She loved him too much, savored his kisses too much, desired him too strongly, found too much pleasure in the stroke of those hard hands.

The pressure of his fingers had hardened her nipple into a tight nub that stabbed his palm even through the layers of fabric protecting her. He deepened the kiss as he roughly opened the buttons of her blouse and shoved a hand inside the opening, then under the lacy cup of her bra to find the bare flesh he craved. She whimpered as his fingers found her sensitive nipple and lightly pinched at it, sending sharp waves of sensation down to her tightening loins. The sound she made was soft, more of a vibration than an actual noise, but he was so attuned to her that he felt it as sharply as an electrical shock.

She was limp as he bent her back over his arm and freed her breast from the lace that confined it, cupping the warm mound and lifting it up to his hungry mouth. He bent over her, sucking fiercely at her tender flesh, wild with the taste and scent and feel of her. He stabbed at her nipple with his tongue, excited and triumphant at the way she arched responsively at every lash of sensation. She wanted him. He had told himself that there had been no mistaking her fiery response that night, but the six months since then had weakened his assurance. Now he knew he hadn't been wrong. He barely had to touch her and she trembled with excitement, already needing him, ready for him.

He left her breast for more deeply voracious kisses taken from her sweetly swollen lips. God, he wanted her! No other woman had ever made him feel as Elizabeth did, so completely attuned with and lost within her.

He wanted to make love to her, *now,* but there were still too many unanswered questions. If he didn't get things settled while he had her marooned here, unable to get away from him, it might be another six months before he could corner her again. No, by God, it wouldn't be; he couldn't stand it again.

Reluctantly he left her mouth, every instinct in him wanting to take this to completion, knowing that he could if only he didn't give her a chance to surface from the drugging physical delight, but he still wanted answers and couldn't wait, didn't dare wait, to get them. "Tell me," he cajoled as he trailed his mouth down the side of her neck, nibbling on the taut tendon and feeling the response ripple through her. Finally— *finally*—he was on the right track. "Tell me what *he* did that made you run from *me*."

Chapter Six

Frantically Elizabeth tried to jerk away, but he controlled her so easily that her efforts were laughable. Nevertheless, she lodged her hands against his heavy shoulders and pushed as hard as she could. "Let me go!"

"No." His refusal was flat and calm. "Stop fighting and answer me."

She couldn't do either one, and she began to panic, not because she feared Quinlan, but because she didn't want to talk about her marriage to Eric Landers, didn't want to think about it, didn't want to revive that hell even in memory. But Quinlan, damn his stubborn temperament, had fastened on the subject and wouldn't drop it until he got what he wanted. She knew him, knew that he intended to drag every detail out of her, and she simply couldn't face it.

Sheer survival instinct made her suddenly relax in his arms, sinking against him, clutching his shoulders instead of pushing against them. She felt his entire body tighten convulsively at her abrupt capitulation; her own muscles quivered with acute relief, as if she had been forcing them to an unnatural action. Her breath caught jerkily as her hips settled against his and she felt the thick ridge of his sex. His arousal was so familiar, and unbearably seductive. The lure of his sexuality pulled her even closer, her loins growing heavy and taut with desire.

He felt the change in her, saw it mirrored almost instantly in her face. One moment she had been struggling against him, and the next she was shivering in carnal excitement, her body tense as she moved against him in a subtle demand. He cursed, his voice thick, as he tried to fight his own response. It was a losing battle; he had wanted her too intensely, for too long. Talking would have to wait; for now, she had won. All he could think about was that she was finally in his arms again, every small movement signaling eager compliance. He didn't know what had changed her mind, and at this moment he didn't particularly care. It was enough that she was once again clinging to him, as she had the one night they had spent together, the night that was burned into his memory. He had tossed restlessly through a lot of dark, sleepless hours since then, remembering how it had been and aching for the same release, needing her beneath him, bewildered by and angry at her sudden coldness.

There was nothing cold about her now. He could feel her heat, feel her vibrating under his hands. Her hips moved in an ancient search, and a low moan hummed in her throat as she found what she had sought, her legs parting slightly to nestle his hard sex between them.

Fiercely he thrust his hand into her hair and pulled

her head back. "Do you want this?" he asked hoarsely, hanging on to his control with grim concentration. It had happened so abruptly that he wanted to make sure before another second had passed, before she moved again and launched him past the point of no return. He hadn't felt like this since he'd been a teenager, the tide of desire rising like floodwaters in his veins, drowning thought. God, he didn't care what had caused her to change; right now, all he wanted was to thrust into her.

For a second she didn't answer, and his teeth were already clenching against a curse when she dug her nails into his shoulder and said, "Yes."

Her senses whirled dizzily as he lowered her to the floor, right where they stood. "The sofa..." she murmured, but then his weight came down on top of her and she didn't care anymore. Her initial tactic had been a panicked effort to distract him, but her own desire had blindsided her, welling up and overwhelming her senses so swiftly that she had no defense against it. She had hungered for him for so long, lying awake during the long, dark nights with silent tears seeping from beneath her lids because she missed him so much, almost as much as she feared him—and herself. The relief of being in his arms again was almost painful, and she pushed away all the reasons why this shouldn't happen. She would face the inevitable later; for now, all she wanted was Tom Quinlan.

He was rough, his own hunger too intense, too long

denied, for him to control it. He shoved her skirt up
to her waist and dragged her panties down, and Elizabeth willingly opened her thighs to receive him. He
dealt just as swiftly with his pants, then brought his
loins to hers. His penetration was hard and stabbing,
and she cried out at the force of it. Her hips arched,
accepting, taking him deeper. A guttural sound vi-
brated in his wide chest; then he caught the backs of
her thighs, pulling her legs higher, and he began
thrusting hard and fast.

She loved it. She reveled in it. She sobbed aloud
at the strong release that pulsed through her almost
immediately, the staggering physical response that
she had known only with this man and had thought
she would never experience again. She had been willing to give up this physical ecstasy in order to protect
her inner self from his dominance, but oh, how she
had longed for it, and bitterly wondered why the most
dangerous traps had the sweetest bait.

Blinded by the ferocity of his own need, he an-
chored her writhing hips with his big hands and
pounded into her. Dazedly she became aware of the
hard floor beneath her, bruising her shoulders, but
even as her senses were recovering from their sensual
battering and allowing her to take stock of her surroundings, he gripped her even harder and convulsed.
Instinctively she held him, cradling him with arms
and legs, and the gentle clasp of her inner warmth.
His harsh, strained cries subsided to low, rhythmic

moans, then finally to fast and uneven breathing as he relaxed on top of her, his heavy weight pressing her to the floor.

The silence in the huge, dim lobby was broken only by the erratic intake and release of their breathing. His slowing heartbeat thudded heavily against her breasts, and their heated bodies melded together everywhere that bare flesh touched bare flesh. She felt the moisture of sweat, and the inner wetness that forcibly awakened her to the realization that their frantic mating had been done without any means of protection.

Her own heart lurched in panic; then logic reasserted itself and she calmed down. She had just finished her monthly cycle; it was highly unlikely that she could conceive. Perversely, no sooner had she had that reassuring thought than she was seized by a sense of loss, even of mourning, as if that panicked moment had been truth rather than very remote possibility.

"Elizabeth?"

She didn't open her eyes. She didn't want to face reality just yet, didn't want to have to let him go, and that was something reality would force her to do.

He lifted himself on his elbows, and she could feel the penetrating blue gaze on her face, but still she clung to the safety of her closed eyes.

She felt his muscles gathering, and briefly she tried to hold him, but he lifted himself away from her, and she caught her breath at the slow withdrawal that separated his body from hers. Despite herself, the friction set off a lingering thrill of sensation, and her hips lifted in a small, uncontrollable, telltale movement. Because there was no sanctuary any longer, she opened her eyes and silently met his gaze. That curious, sleepy blankness of sexual satisfaction was on his face, as she knew it must also be on hers, but in his eyes was a predatory watchfulness, as if he knew his prey had been caught but not vanquished.

His astuteness was disturbing, as it had always been. Her own gaze dared him to try to make anything more of what had just happened than an unadorned act of sex, without cause or future.

His mouth twisted wryly as he knelt away from her and pulled his pants up, zipping them with a faint, raspy sound. Then he got to his feet and effortlessly lifted her to hers. Her skirt, which had been bunched around her waist, dropped to the correct position. Elizabeth instinctively clenched her thighs to hold the wetness between them.

Quinlan shrugged out of his shirt and handed it to her, then leaned down and retrieved her panties from the floor. Thrusting them into her hands, too, he said, "Take off those clothes and put on my shirt. It's getting warmer in here, and you'll be more comfortable in something loose."

Silently she turned, picked up the flashlight and went into the ladies' rest room. Her knees were shaking slightly in reaction, and her loins throbbed from the violence of his possession. He hadn't hurt her, but it was as if she could still feel him inside.

She stared at her reflection in the mirror, the image ghostly with only the flashlight for illumination, making her eyes look huge and dark. Her hair had come loose and tumbled around her shoulders; she pushed it back distractedly, still staring at herself, then buried her face in her hands.

How could she go back out there? God, how could she have been so *stupid?* Alone with him for little more than an hour, and she had had sex with him on the floor like an uncontrolled animal. She couldn't even blame it on him; no, *she* had made the big move, grabbing at him, pushing her hips at him, because she had panicked when he had tried to pull back and begin asking questions again. She had gotten exactly what she had asked for.

She felt confused, both ashamed and elated. She was ashamed that she had used sex as an evasion tactic...or maybe she was ashamed that she had used it as an *excuse* to do what she had been longing to do anyway. The physical desire she felt for him was sharp and strong, so urgently demanding that stopping felt unnatural, all of her instincts pushing her toward him.

Her body felt warm and weak with satiation, faintly trembling in the aftermath. But now that he was no longer touching her, the old wariness was creeping back, pulling her in two directions. She had thought the decision simple, though it had never been easy, but now she was finding that nothing about it, either Quinlan or her own emotions, was simple.

Dazedly she stripped off her disheveled clothing and used some wet paper towels to wash; the cool moisture was momentarily refreshing, but then the close heat of the rest room made sweat form almost as fast as she could wash it off. Ironically she admitted that, no matter how reluctant she was, she had no real choice but to face him again. If she remained in here, she would have heat stroke. It was a sad day when a woman couldn't even count on a rest room for sanctuary. Ah, well, she hadn't yet found any place that was truly safe from him, for her own memories worked against her.

Just as she pulled on her panties, the door was thrust open and Quinlan loomed in the opening, his big body blotting out most of the light from the lobby but allowing the welcome entrance of relatively cooler air. The subtle breeze washed around her body, making her nipples pucker slightly. Or was that an instinctive female reaction to the closeness of her mate? She didn't want to think of him in such primitive, possessive terms, but her body had different priorities.

He noticed, of course. His gaze became smoky with both desire and possessiveness as he openly admired her breasts. But he didn't move toward her, holding himself very still as if he sensed her confusion. "Hiding?" he asked mildly.

"Delaying," she admitted, her tone soft. She didn't try to shield her body from him; such an action would seem silly, after what they had just done. It wasn't as if he hadn't seen her completely naked before, as if they hadn't made love before. Moreover, he had decided to remove his pants and stood before her wearing only a pair of short, dark boxers. Barefoot and mostly naked, his dark hair tousled and wet with both sweat and the water he had splashed on his face, he was stripped of most of the trappings of civilization. Despite the heat, a shiver ran up her spine in yet another feminine response to the primitiveness of his masculinity, and she looked away to keep him from seeing it in her face.

He came to her and took up his shirt, holding it for her to slip into; then, when she had done so, he turned her and began buttoning the garment as if she were a child being dressed. "You can't stay in here," he said. "Too damn hot."

"I know. I was coming out."

He shepherded her toward the door, his hand on her back. She wondered if the action was just his usual take-charge attitude, or if he was acting on some primitive instinct of his own, to keep the female from bolting. Probably a mixture of the two, she thought, and sighed.

He had been busy while she had been in the rest

room, and she realized she had delayed in there much longer than she had intended. He had arranged the extra cushions on the floor—in the shape of a double bed, she noticed—and gotten some cool water from the fountain, the cups ready for them to drink. The water was welcome, but if he thought she was going to docilely stretch out on those cushions, he would shortly be disillusioned. She sat down in a chair and reached for a cup, sipping it without enthusiasm at first, then more eagerly as she rediscovered how good plain water was for quenching thirst. It was a delight of childhood that tended to be forgotten in the adult world of coffee, tea and wine spritzers.

"Are you hungry?" he asked.

"No." How could she be hungry? Her nerves were so tightly drawn that she didn't think she would be able to eat until they got out of here.

"Well, I am." He tore open the wrapping on the big blueberry muffin and began eating. "Tell me about your marriage."

She stiffened and glared at him. "It wasn't a good marriage," she said tightly. "It also isn't any of your business."

He glanced pointedly at the floor where they had so recently made love. "That's debatable. Okay, let's try it this way. I'll tell you about my marriage if you'll tell me about yours. No evasion tactics. I'll answer any question you ask."

She stared at him in shock. "*Your* marriage?"

He shrugged. "Sure. Hell, I'm thirty-seven years old. I haven't lived my entire life in a vacuum."

"You have your nerve!" she flared. "You jumped down my throat for not talking about my past marriage when you've only now mentioned your own?"

He rubbed the side of his nose and gave her a faintly sheepish look. "That occurred to me," he admitted.

"Well, let me put another thought in your dim Neanderthal brain! The time for heart-to-heart confidences was over a long time ago. We aren't involved any longer, so there's no point in 'sharing.'"

He took another bite of the muffin. "Don't kid yourself. What we just did felt pretty damn involved to me."

"That was just sex," she said dismissively. "It had been a while, and I needed it."

"I know exactly how long it had been." His blue gaze sharpened, and she knew he hadn't liked her comment. "You haven't gone out with anyone else since you walked out on me."

She was enraged all over again. "Have you had me followed?"

He had, but he wasn't about to tell her that now. Instead he said, "Chickie worries because your social life, in her words, resembles Death Valley—nothing of interest moving around."

Elizabeth snorted, but she was mollified, because she had heard Chickie make that exact comment on a couple of occasions. Still, she would have to have a word with her about discretion.

"I've been busy," she said, not caring if he believed her or not, though it happened to be the truth. She had deliberately been as busy as she could manage in order to give herself less free time to think about him.

"I know. You've found a lot of lilies to gild."

Her teeth closed with a snap. "That's so people will have a reason to install your fancy security systems. I gild the lilies, and you protect them."

"I protect *people*," he clarified.

"Uh-huh. That's why you set up so many security systems for people who live in rough neighborhoods, where their lives are really in danger."

"I can see we aren't going to agree on this."

"You brought it up."

"My mistake. Let's get back to the original subject, namely our respective failed marriages. Go ahead, ask me anything you want."

The perfect response, of course, was that she wasn't interested. It would also be a lie, because she was not only interested, she was suddenly, violently jealous of that unknown, hitherto unsuspected woman who had been his wife, who had shared his name and his bed for a time, and who had been, in the eyes of the world, his mate. Elizabeth firmly kept her mouth closed, but she couldn't stop herself from glaring at him.

Quinlan sighed. "All right, I'll tell you the boring facts without making you ask. Her name was Amy. We dated during college. Then, when college was finished, it seemed like we should do adult things, so we got married. But I was away on my job a lot, and Amy found someone in the office where she worked who she liked a lot better. Within six months of getting married we knew it had been a mistake, but we held out for another year, trying to make it 'work,' before we both realized we were just wasting time. The divorce was a relief for both of us. End of story."

She was still glaring at him. "I don't even know where you went to college."

He sighed again. She was getting damn tired of that sigh, as if he were being so noble in his dealings with an irrational woman. "Cal Tech."

"Ah." Well, that explained his expertise with electronics and computers and things.

"No children," he added.

"I should hope not!" It was bad enough that he had, for some reason, concealed all the rest of the details of his life. "If you'd kept *children* hidden, I would never have forgiven you."

His eyes gleamed. "Does this mean you *have?*"

"No."

He gave a startled shout of laughter. "God, I've missed you. You don't dissemble at all. If you're grouchy, you don't feel any need at all to make nice and pretend to be sweetness and light, do you?"

She gave him a haughty look. "I'm not sweetness and light."

"Thank God," he said fervently. He leaned back and spread his hands, then stretched his long, muscular legs out before him in a posture of complete relaxation. "Okay, it's your turn. Tell me all the deep, dark secrets about *your* marriage."

Chapter Seven

"Show-and-tell was your idea, not mine." Her throat tightened at the idea of rehashing the details, reliving the nightmare even in thought. She just couldn't do it.

"You asked questions."

"I asked where you went to college, hardly the same as prying into your private life." Agitated, she stood up and longingly looked through the huge windows to the world outside. Only two thin sheets of transparent material kept her prisoner here with him, but it would take a car ramming into the glass at respectable speed to break it. The glass looked fragile but wasn't, whereas she was the opposite. She looked calm and capable, but inside she hid a weakness that terrified her.

"Don't run away," Quinlan warned softly.

She barely glanced at him as she edged out of the semicircle of sofa and chairs. "I'm not running," she denied, knowing that it wasn't the truth. "It's cooler moving around."

Silently Quinlan got to his feet and paced after her, big and virtually naked, the dark boxer shorts nothing more than the modern version of the loincloth. His muscled chest was hairy, the thick curls almost hiding his small nipples, and a silky line of hair ran down the center of his abdomen to his groin. His long legs were also covered with hair, finer and straighter, but he was undoubtedly a dominating male animal in his prime. Elizabeth gave him a distracted, vaguely alarmed look that suddenly focused on his loins, and her eyes widened.

He looked down at himself and shrugged, not pausing in his slow, relentless pursuit. "I know, at my age I shouldn't have recovered this fast. I usually don't," he said thoughtfully. "It's just my reaction to you. Come here, sweetheart." His voice had turned soft and cajoling.

Wildly Elizabeth wondered if this was going to degenerate into the stereotypical chase around the furniture. On the heels of that thought came the certain knowledge that if she ran, Quinlan would definitely chase her, instinctively, the marauding male subduing the reluctant female. She could prevent that farce by not running, thereby giving him nothing to chase. On the other hand, if she stood still things would only reach the same conclusion at a faster pace. Evidently the only real choice she had was whether or not to hold on to her dignity. If she had felt differently about him she could have said "no," but she had already faced that weakness in herself. For right now, in these circumstances, she couldn't resist him—and they both knew it.

He drew closer, his eyes gleaming. "For tonight,

you're mine," he murmured. "Let me at least have that. You can't get away from me here. You don't even want to get away, not really. The circumstances aren't normal. When we get out of here you'll have options, but right now you're forced to be with me. Whatever happens won't be your fault. Just let go and forget about it."

She drew a deep, shuddering breath. "Pretty good psychologist, aren't you? But I'm not a coward. I'm responsible for whatever decisions I make, period."

He had reached her now, one arm sliding around her back. Elizabeth looked up at him, at the tousled dark hair and intense blue eyes, and her heart squeezed. "All right," she whispered. "For tonight. For as long as we're locked in here." She closed her eyes, shivering with sensual anticipation. She would let herself have this, just for now; she would feast on him, drown herself in sensation, let the darkness of the night wrap protectively around them and hold off thought. The time would come all too soon when she would have to push him away again; why waste even one precious minute by fighting both him and herself?

"Anything," she heard herself say as he lifted her. Her voice sounded strange to her, thick, drugged with desire. "For tonight."

His low, rough laugh wasn't quite steady as he lowered her to the cushions. "Anything?" he asked. "You could be letting yourself in for an interesting night."

She put out her hand and touched his bare chest. "Yes," she purred. "I could be."

"Cat." His breathing was fast and unsteady as he swiftly stripped her panties down her legs and tossed them to the side. "You won't be needing those again tonight."

She pulled at the waistband of his shorts. "And you won't be needing these."

"Hell, I only kept them on because I figured you'd fight like a wildcat if I came after you stark naked." He dealt with his shorts as rapidly as he had her underwear.

She was already excited by the anticipation of his slow, thorough loveplay. Quinlan was a man who enjoyed the preliminaries and prolonged them, as she had learned during the one night she had spent with him. It didn't happen this time, though. He pushed her legs open, knelt between them and entered her with a heavy thrust that jarred her. The shock of it reverberated through her body; then her inner muscles clamped down in an effort to slow that inexorable invasion.

He pushed deeper, groaning at the tightness of her, until he was in her to the hilt. She writhed, reaching down to grasp his thighs and hold him there, but he slowly withdrew, then just as slowly pushed back into her.

"Did your husband make you feel like this?" he whispered.

Her head rolled on the cushions at the speed and intensity of the sensations. It was an effort to concentrate on his words. "N-no," she finally sighed.

"Good." He couldn't keep the savage satisfaction out of his voice. He didn't like the thought of anyone else pleasing her. This was something she had known only with him; he had realized it immediately when they had first made love, but he had needed to hear her say it, admit that she had given her response to no one else.

He teased her with another slow withdrawal and thrust. "What did he do to you?" he murmured, and pulled completely away from her.

Her eyes opened in protest and she reached for him, moaning low in her throat as she tried to reestablish that delicious contact. Then comprehension made her eyes flare wider, and she jerked backward, away from him, trying to sit up. "You bastard!" she said in a strangled tone.

Quinlan caught her hips and dragged her back, slipping into her once again. "Tell me," he said relentlessly. "Did he mistreat you? Hurt you in any way? What in hell did he do that you're making me pay for?"

Elizabeth wrenched away from him again. She felt ill, all desire gone. How could he have done that to her? She fought to cover herself with his shirt, all the while calling herself several harsh names for her stupidity in thinking they could have this night, that she could give herself a block of time unattached to either past or present. She should have remembered that Quinlan never gave up.

No, he never gave up. So why didn't she tell him? It wouldn't be easy for her to relive it, but at least then he would know why she refused to allow him any authority in her life, why she had denied herself the love she so desperately wanted to give him.

She curled away from him, letting her head fall forward onto her knees so her hair hid her face. He tried to pull her back into his arms, into his lovemaking, but she resisted him, her body stiff in reaction to the memories already swamping her.

"Don't touch me!" she said hoarsely. "You wanted to know, so sit there and listen, but don't— don't touch me."

Quinlan frowned, feeling vaguely uneasy. He had deliberately pushed her, though he hadn't intended to push so hard that she withdrew from him, but that was what had happened. His body was still tight with desire, demanding release. He ground his teeth together, grimly reaching for control; if Elizabeth was ready to talk, after all these months, then he was damn well going to listen.

She didn't lift her head from her knees, but in the silent, darkening lobby, he could plainly hear every soft word.

"I met him when I was a senior in college. Eric. Eric Landers. But you already know his name, don't

you? It was in your damn report. He owned an upscale decorating firm, and getting a part-time job there
was a real plum.''

She sighed. The little sound was sad, and a bit
tired. ''He was thirty-five. I was twenty-one. And he
was handsome, sophisticated, self-assured, worldly,
with quite a reputation as both a ladies' man and a
well-known professional. I was more than flattered
when he asked me out, I was absolutely giddy.
Chickie would seem grim compared to the way I felt.

''We dated for about three months before he asked
me to marry him, and for three months I felt like a
princess. He took me everywhere, wined and dined
me at the best places. He was interested in every minute of my day, in everything I did. A real princess
couldn't have been more coddled. I was a virgin—a
bit unusual, to stay that way through college, but I'd
been studying hard and working part-time jobs, too,
and I hadn't had time for much socializing. Eric
didn't push me for sex. He said he could wait until
our wedding night, that since I had remained a virgin
that long, he wanted to give me all the traditional
trappings.''

''Let me guess,'' Quinlan said grimly. ''He was
gay.''

She shook her head. ''No. His ladies' man reputation was for real. Eric was very gentle with me on
our wedding night. I'll give him that. He never mis-
treated me that way.''

"If you don't mind," Quinlan interrupted, his teeth coming together with an audible snap, "I'd rather not hear about your sex life with him, if that wasn't the problem."

Elizabeth was surprised into lifting her head. "Are you jealous?" she asked warily.

He rubbed his hand over his jaw; as late in the day as it was, his five-o'clock shadow had become more substantial and made a rasping sound as his hand passed over it. "Not jealous, exactly," he muttered. "I just don't want to hear it, if you enjoyed making love with him. Hell, *yes,* I'm jealous!"

She gave a spurt of laughter, startling herself. She had never expected to be able to laugh while discussing Eric Landers, but Quinlan's frustration was so obvious that she couldn't help it.

"I don't mind giving the devil his due," she said in a generous tone. "You can pat yourself on the back, because you know you were the first to— umm—"

"Satisfy you," he supplied. A sheepish expression crossed his face.

"I'm not very experienced. You're the only man I've gone to bed with since my divorce. After Eric, I just didn't want to let anyone close to me."

She didn't continue, and the silence stretched between them. It was growing darker by the minute as the sun set completely, and she was comforted by the shield of night. "Why?" Quinlan finally asked.

It was easier to talk now, after that little bit of laughter and with the growing darkness concealing both their expressions. She felt herself relaxing, uncurling from her protective knot.

"It was odd," she said, "but I don't think he wanted me to be sensual. He wanted me to be his perfect princess, his living, breathing Barbie doll. I had gotten used to his protectiveness while we were dating, so at first I didn't think anything of it when he wanted to be with me every time I set foot outside the door. Somehow he always came up with a reason why I shouldn't put in for this job, or that one, and why I couldn't continue working with him. He went shopping with me, picked out my clothes...at first, it all seemed so flattering. My friends were so impressed by the way he treated me.

"Then he began to find reasons why I shouldn't see my friends, why first this one and then that one wasn't 'good' for me. I couldn't invite them over, and he didn't want me visiting them, or meeting them anywhere for lunch. He began vetting my phone calls. It was all so gradual," she said in a faintly bewildered tone. "And he was so gentle. He seemed to have a good reason for everything he did, and he was always focused on me, giving me the kind of attention all women think they want. He only wanted what was best for me, he said."

Quinlan was beginning to feel uneasy. He shifted position, leaning his back against one of the chairs and stretching out in a relaxed position that belied his inner tension. "A control freak," he growled.

"I think we'd been married about six months before I really noticed how completely he'd cut me off from everyone and everything except him," she continued. "I began trying to shift the balance of power, to make a few decisions for myself, if only in minor things, such as where I got my hair cut."

"Let me make another guess. All of a sudden he wasn't so gentle, right?"

"He was furious that I'd gone to a different place. He took the car keys away from me. That was when I really became angry, for the first time. Until then, I'd made excuses, because he'd been so gentle and loving with me. I'd never defied him until then, but when he took the keys out of my purse I lost my temper and yelled at him. He knocked me down," she said briefly.

Quinlan surged to his feet, raw fury running through him so powerfully that he couldn't sit there any longer. To hell with trying to look relaxed. He paced the lobby like a tiger, naked and primitive, the powerful muscles in his body flexing with every movement.

Elizabeth kept on talking. Now that she had started, she wanted to tell it all. Funny, but reliving it wasn't as traumatic as she had expected, not as bad as it had been in her memories and nightmares. Maybe it was having someone else with her that blunted the pain, because always before she had been alone with it.

"I literally became his prisoner. Whenever I tried to assert myself in any way, he'd punish me. There was no pattern to it. Most of the time he would slap me, or even whip me, but sometimes he would just yell, and I never knew what to expect. It was as if he knew that yelling instead of hitting me made it even worse, because then the next time I *knew* he'd hit me, and I'd try, oh, I'd try so hard, not to do anything that would cause the next time. But I always did. I was so nervous that I always did something. Or he'd make up a reason.

"Looking back," she said slowly, "it's hard to believe I was so stupid. By the time I realized what he had done and started trying to fight back, he had me so isolated, so brainwashed, that I literally felt powerless. I had no money, no friends, no car. I was ashamed for anyone to know what was happening. That was what was so sick, that he could convince me it was my fault. I did try to run away once, but he'd paid the doorman to call him if I left, and he found me within half an hour. He didn't hit me that time. He just tied me to the bed and left me. The terror of waiting, helpless, for him to come back and punish me was so bad that hitting me would have been a relief, because that would have meant it was over. Instead he kept me tied for two days, and I nearly became hysterical every time he came into the room."

Quinlan had stopped pacing. He was standing motionless, but she could feel the tension radiating from him.

"He put locks on the phone so I couldn't call out, or even answer it," she said. "But one day he blacked my eye. I don't even remember why. It didn't take much to set him off. When I looked in the mirror the next morning, all of a sudden something clicked in my brain and I knew I had to either get away from him or kill him. I couldn't live like that another day, another hour."

"I'd have opted for killing him," Quinlan said tonelessly. "I may yet."

"After that, it was all so easy," she murmured, ignoring him. "I just packed my suitcases and walked out. The doorman saw me and reached for the phone...and then stopped. He looked at my eye and let the phone drop back into the cradle, and then he opened the door for me and asked if he could call a cab for me. When I told him I didn't have any money, he pulled out his wallet and gave me forty dollars.

"I went to a shelter for abused women. It was the hardest, most humiliating thing I've ever done. It's strange how the women are the ones who are so embarrassed," she said reflectively. "Never the men who have beaten them, terrorized them. *They* seem to think it was their right, or that the women deserved it. But I understand how the women feel, because I was one of them. Its like standing up in public and letting everyone see how utterly stupid you are, what bad judgment you have, what horrible mistakes you've made. The women I met there could barely look anyone in the eye, and they were the victims!

"I got a divorce. It was that simple. With the photographs taken at the shelter, I had evidence of abuse, and Eric would have done anything to preserve his reputation. Oh, he tried to talk me into coming back, he made all sorts of promises, he swore things would be different. I was even tempted," she admitted. "But I couldn't trust my own judgment any longer, so the safest thing, the only thing to do was stay away from romantic relationships in general and Eric Landers in particular."

God, it was so plain now. Quinlan could barely breathe with the realization of the mistakes he'd made in dealing with her. No wonder she had pulled away from him. Because he'd wanted her so much, he had tried to take over, tried to coddle and protect her. It was a normal male instinct, but nothing else could have been more calculated to set off her inner alarms. When she had needed space, he had crowded her, so determined to have her that he hadn't let anything stand in his way. Instead of binding her to him, he had made her run.

"I'm not like Landers," he said hoarsely. "I'll never abuse you, Elizabeth, I swear."

She was silent, and he could sense the sadness in her. "How can I trust you?" she finally asked. "How can I trust *myself?* What if I make the wrong decision about you, too? You're a much stronger man than Eric could ever hope to be, both physically and mentally. What if you *did* try to hurt me? How could I protect myself? You want to be in charge. You admit it. You're dominating and secretive. God, Quinlan, I love you, but you scare me to death."

His heart surged wildly in his chest at her words. He had known it, but this was the first time she had actually said so. She loved him! At the same time he was suddenly terrified, because he didn't see any way he could convince her to trust him. And that was what it was: a matter of trust. She had lost confidence in her own ability to read character.

He didn't know what to do; for the first time in his life he had no plan of action, no viable option. All he had were his instincts, and he was afraid they were all wrong, at least as far as Elizabeth was concerned. He had certainly bungled it so far. He tried to think what his life would be like without her, if he never again could hold her, and the bleakness of the prospect shook him. Even during these past hellish months, when she had avoided him so totally, even refusing to speak to him on the phone, he hadn't felt this way, because he had still thought he would eventually be able to get her back.

He had to have her. No other woman would do.

And he wanted her just as she was: elegant, acerbic, independent, wildly passionate in bed. That, at last, he had done right. She had burned bright and hot in his arms.

He suspected that if he asked for an affair, and only that, she would agree. It was the thought of a legal, binding relationship that had sent her running. She had acted outraged when he had mentioned marriage and kids, getting all huffy because he hadn't included her in the decision-making, but in truth it was that very thing that had so terrified her. Had she sensed he had been about to propose? Finding the file had made her furious, but what had sent her fleeing out the door had been the prospect that he wanted more than just a sexual relationship with her. She could handle being intimate with him; it was the thought of giving him legal rights that gave her nightmares.

He cleared his throat. He felt as if he were walking blindfolded through a mine field, but he couldn't just give up. "I have a reason for not talking about myself," he said hesitantly.

Her reply was an ironic, "I'm sure you do."

He stopped, shrugging helplessly. There was nothing he could tell her that wouldn't sound like an outrageous lie. Okay, that had been a dead end.

"I love you."

The words shook him. He'd admitted the truth of it to himself months ago, not long after meeting her, in fact, but it had been so long since he'd said them aloud that he was startled. Oh, he'd said them during his marriage, at first. It had been so easy, and so expected. Now he realized that the words had been easy because he hadn't meant them. When something really mattered, it was a lot harder to get out.

Elizabeth nodded her head. It had gotten so dark that all he could see was the movement, not her expression. "I believe you do," she replied.

"But you still can't trust me with your life."

"If I needed someone to protect me from true danger, I can't think of anyone I would trust more. But for the other times, the day-to-day normal times that make up a true lifetime, I'm terrified of letting someone close enough to ever have that kind of influence on me again."

Quinlan took another mental sidestep. "We could still see each other," he suggested cautiously. "I know I came on too strong. I'll hold it down. I won't pressure you to make any kind of commitment."

"That wouldn't be fair to you. Marriage is what you want."

"I want *you*," he said bluntly. "With or without the legal trappings. We're great in bed together, and we enjoy each other's company. We have fun together. We can do that without being married, if that's all that's making you shy away from me."

"You want to have an affair?" she asked, needing to pin him down on his exact meaning.

"Hell, no. I want everything. The ring, the kids, all

of it. But if an affair is all I can have, I'll take it. What do you say?''

She was silent a long time, thinking it over. At last she sighed and said, ''I think I'd be a fool to make any decision right now. These aren't normal circumstances. When the power is back on and our lives are back to normal, then I'll decide.''

Quinlan had always had the knack of cutting his losses. He took a step toward her. ''But I still have tonight,'' he said in a low tone. ''And I don't intend to waste a minute of it.''

Chapter Eight

It was much as it had been that other night, and yet it was much more intense. Quinlan made love to her until she literally screamed with pleasure, and then loved her past her embarrassment. The darkness wrapped around them like a heated cocoon, suspending time and restrictions, allowing anything to be possible. The hours seemed endless, unmarked as they were by any clock or other means that civilized man had developed. The streets outside remained dark and mostly empty; he didn't turn on the radio again, because he didn't want the outside world to intrude, and neither did she.

It was too hot to sleep, despite the high ceiling in the lobby that carried the heat upward. They lay on the cushions and talked, their voices not much more than slow murmurs in the sultry heat. Quinlan's big hands never left her bare body, and Elizabeth suspended her thoughts for this one magic night. She became drowsy, but all inclination to sleep fled when he turned to her in the thick, heated darkness, pressing down on her, his callused hands stroking and probing until she writhed on the cushions. His lovemaking was as steamy as the night, as enveloping. In the darkness she had no inhibitions. She not only let him do as he wanted with her, she reveled in it. There wasn't an inch of her body that he didn't explore.

Daylight brought sunlight and steadily increasing temperatures, but the power remained off. Even though she knew it was impossible to see inside through the glazed windows, she was glad that they could remain snugly hidden in their own little lair. They drank water and ate, and Elizabeth insisted on washing off again in the smothering heat of the rest room, though she knew it wouldn't do any good to clean up with Quinlan waiting impatiently for her outside. Did the man never get tired?

She heard other voices and froze, panicking at the thought of being caught naked in the rest room. Had the power come back on? Impossible, because it was dark in the bathroom. Or had the guard cut off the lights in here before he'd left the day before? She hadn't even thought to check the switch.

Then she heard a familiar call sign and relaxed. The radio, of course. A bit irritated, with herself for being scared and with him because he'd caused it, she strode out of the rest room. "I nearly had a heart attack," she snapped. "I thought someone had come in and I was caught in the rest room."

Quinlan grinned. "What about me? I'm as naked as you are."

He was still sprawled on the cushions, but somehow he looked absolutely at home in his natural state.

She looked down at herself and laughed. "I can't believe this is happening."

He stared to say, *It'll be something to tell our grandkids,* but bit the words back. She wouldn't want to hear it, and he'd promised he wouldn't push her. He held out his hand to her, and she crawled onto the cushions with him, sinking into his arms.

"What was on the news?"

"A relatively quiet night in Dallas, though there was some sporadic looting. The same elsewhere. It was just too damn hot to do anything very strenuous."

"Oh, yeah?" she asked, giving him a sidelong glance.

He laughed and deftly rolled her onto her back, mounting her with a total lack of haste that demonstrated how many times during the night he'd done the same thing. "The news?" she prompted.

He nuzzled her neck, breathing in the sweet woman scent. "Oh, that. The national guard has been mobilized from Texas to the East Coast. There were riots in Miami, but they're under control now."

"I thought you said things were relatively quiet?"

"That *is* quiet. With electricity off in almost a quarter of the country, that's amazingly quiet." He didn't want to talk about the blackout. Having Elizabeth naked under him went to his head faster than the most potent whiskey. He kissed her, acutely savoring her instant response, even as he positioned her for his penetration and smoothly slid within. He felt the delicious tightening of her inner muscles as she adjusted to him, the way her fingers dug into his shoulders as she tried to arch even closer to him. His feelings for her swamped him, and he found himself wishing the electricity would never come back on.

Afterward, she yawned and nestled down on his shoulder. "Did the radio announcers say when the power company officials thought the power would be back on?"

"Maybe by this afternoon," he said.

So soon? She felt a bit indignant, as if she had been promised a vacation and now it had been cut short. But this wasn't a vacation; for a lot of people, it was a crisis. Electricity could mean the difference between life and death for someone who was ill. If all they had was a few more hours, she meant to make the best of them.

It seemed that he did, too. Except for insisting that they regularly drink water, he kept her in his arms. Even when he finally tired and had to take a break from lovemaking, he remained nestled within her body. Elizabeth was too tired to think; all she could do was feel. Quinlan had so completely dominated her senses that she would have been alarmed, if she hadn't seen the same drugged expression in his eyes that she knew was in hers. This wasn't something he was doing to her; it was something they were sharing.

They dozed, their sweaty bodies pressed tightly together despite the heat.

It was the wash of cool air over her skin that woke her, shivering.

Quinlan sat up. "The power's back on," he said, squinting up at the overhead lights that seemed to be glaring after the long hours without them. He looked at his watch. "It's eleven o'clock."

"That's too soon," Elizabeth said grumpily. "They said it would be this afternoon."

"They probably gave themselves some extra time in case something went wrong."

Feeling incredibly exposed in the artificial light, Elizabeth scrambled into her clothing. She looked at her discarded panty hose in distaste and crumpled them up, then threw them into the trash.

"What do we do now?" she asked, pushing her hair back.

Quinlan zipped his pants. "Now we go home."

"How? Do we call the guard service?"

"Oh, I'll call them all right. Later. I have a few things to say. But now that the power's on, I can get us out of here."

While he tapped into the security system, Elizabeth hastily straightened the furniture, shoving it back into place and restoring all the cushions to their original sites. A blush was already heating her face at the possibility of anyone finding out about their love nest, literally in the middle of the lobby. She didn't know if she would ever be able to walk into this building again without blushing.

Quinlan grunted with satisfaction as he entered a manual override into the system that would allow him to open the side door. "Come on," he said, grabbing Elizabeth's hand.

She barely had time to snatch up her purse before he was hustling her out of there. She blinked in the blinding sunshine. The heat rising off the sidewalk was punishing. "We can't just leave the building unlocked," she protested.

"I didn't. It locked again as soon as the door closed." Taking her arm, he steered her around the corner and across the street to the parking deck.

Before she could react, he was practically stuffing her into his car. "I have my own car!" she said indignantly.

"I know. Don't worry, it isn't going anywhere. But we don't know that the electricity is on all over the city, and we don't know what kind of situation you'll find at your place. Until I know you're safe, I'm keeping you with me."

It was the sort of high-handed action that had always made her uneasy in the past, but now it didn't bother her. Maybe it was because she was so sleepy. Maybe it was because he was right. For whatever reason, she relaxed in the seat and let her eyes close.

He had to detour a couple of times to reach her apartment, but the traffic was surprisingly light, and it didn't take long, not even as long as normal. She didn't protest when he went inside with her. The electricity was on there, too, the central air conditioning humming as it tried to overcome the built-up heat.

"Into the shower," Quinlan commanded.

She blinked at him. "What?"

He put his arm around her, turning her toward her bedroom. "The shower. We're both going to take a nice, cool shower. We're in good shape, but this will make us feel better. Believe me, we're a little dehydrated."

Their bargain had been only for the night, but since it had already extended into the day, she supposed it wouldn't hurt to carry it a little further. She allowed him to strip her and wasn't at all surprised when he undressed and climbed in with her. The shower spray was cool enough to raise a chill, and it felt wonderful. She turned around to let it wash over her spine and tilted her head back so the water soaked through her sweat-matted hair.

"Feel good?" he murmured, running his hands over her. She would have thought that he was washing her, except that he wasn't using soap.

"Mmm." He bent his head and Elizabeth lifted hers. If only she could stay this way, she thought. Kissing him, being kissed by him. His hard arms locked around her. Feeling him so close, all worries pushed aside...

The cool shower was revitalizing in more ways

than one. Abruptly he lifted her and braced her against the wall, and she gasped as he drove deep into her. There was nothing slow about it this time; he took her fiercely, as wild as he had been the day before on the floor of the lobby, as if all those times in between had never been.

Later they went to bed. She could barely hold her eyes open while he dried her hair, then carried her to the bed and placed her between the cool, smooth sheets. She sighed, every muscle relaxing, and immediately went to sleep, not knowing that he slipped into bed beside her.

Still, she wasn't surprised when she woke during the afternoon and he was there. Lazily she let her gaze drift over his strong-boned features. He needed to shave; the black beard lay on his skin like a dark shadow. His hair was tousled, and his closed eyelids looked as delicate as a child's. Odd, for she had never thought of Quinlan as delicate in any way, never associated any sort of softness with him. Yet he had been tender with her, even in his passion. It wasn't the same type of gentleness Eric had displayed; Eric had been gentle, she realized now, because he hadn't *wanted* any responding passion from her. He had wanted her to be nothing more than a doll, to be dressed and positioned and shown off for his own ego. Quinlan, on the other hand, had been as helpless in his passion as she had been in hers.

Her body quivered at his nearness. Still half asleep,

she pushed at him. His eyes opened immediately, and he rolled onto his back. "What's wrong?"

"Plenty," she said, slithering on top of him and feeling the immediate response between his legs. "It's been at least—" She paused to look at the clock, but it was blinking stupidly at her, not having been reset since the power had come back on. "It's been too damn long since I've had this." She reached between his legs, and he sucked in his breath, his back arching as she guided him into place.

"God, I'm sorry," he apologized fervently, and bit back a moan as she moved on him. This was the way he had always known his Elizabeth could be, hot with uncomplicated passion, a little bawdy, intriguingly earthy. She made him dizzy with delight.

Her eyes were sultry, her lips swollen and pouty from his kisses, her dark hair tumbling over her shoulders. He watched her expression tighten with desire as she moved slowly up and down on him, her eyes closing even more. "Just for that," she murmured, "I get to be on top."

He reached overhead and caught the headboard, his powerful biceps flexing as his fists locked around the brass bars. "No matter how I beg and plead?"

"No matter what you say," she assured him, and gasped herself as her movements wrenched another spasm of pleasure from her nerve endings.

"Good." Quinlan arched, almost lifting her off the

bed. "Then I won't accidentally say something that will make you quit."

He didn't. When she collapsed, exhausted, on his chest, they were both numb with pleasure. He thrust his hand into her tangled hair and held her almost desperately close. She inhaled the hot, musky scent of his skin, and with the slightest of motions rubbed her cheek against the curly hair on his chest. She could feel his heart thudding under her ear, and the strong rhythm was reassuring. They slept again, and woke in the afternoon with the sun going down in a blaze of red and gold, to drowsily make love again.

He got up to turn on the television sitting on her dresser, then returned to bed to hold her while they watched the news, which was, predictably, all about the blackout. Elizabeth felt a little bemused, as if a national crisis had passed without her knowing about it, even though she had been intimately embroiled in this one. Intimately, she thought, in more ways than one. Perhaps that was why she felt so out of touch with reality. She hadn't spent the past twenty-four hours concentrating on the lack of electricity, she had been concentrating on Quinlan.

The Great Blackout, as the Dallas newscasters were calling it, had disrupted electrical services all over the Sun Belt. The heat wave, peak usage and solar flares had all combined to overload and blow circuits, wiping out entire power grids. Elizabeth felt as if her own circuits had been seriously damaged by Quinlan's high-voltage lovemaking.

He spent the night with her. He didn't ask if he could, and she didn't tell him that he couldn't. She knew that she was only postponing the inevitable, but she wanted this time with him. Telling him about Eric hadn't changed her mind, any more than knowing about Eric had changed Quinlan's basic character.

When morning came, they both knew that the time-out had ended. Reality couldn't be held at bay any longer.

"So what happens now?" he asked quietly.

She looked out the window as she sipped her coffee. It was Saturday; neither of them had to work, though Quinlan had already talked to a couple of his staffers, placing the calls almost as soon as he'd gotten out of bed. She knew that all she had to say was one word, "Stay," and they would spend the weekend in bed, too. It would be wonderful, but come Monday, it would make it just that much more difficult to handle.

"I don't see that the situation has changed," she finally said.

"Damn it, Elizabeth!" He got up, his big body coiled with tension. "Can you honestly say that I'm anything like Landers?"

"You're very dominating," she pointed out.

"You love me."

"At the time, I thought I loved him, too. What if

I'm wrong again?'' Her eyes were huge and stark as she stared at him. ''There's no way you can know how bad it was without having lived through it yourself. I would rather die than go through anything like that again. I don't know how I can afford to take the chance on you. I still don't know *you*, not the way you know me. You're so secretive that I can't tell who you really are. How can I trust you when I don't know you?''

''And if you did?'' he asked in a harsh tone. ''If you knew all there is to know about me?''

''I don't know,'' she said; then they looked at each other and broke into snickering laughter. ''There's a lot of knowing and not knowing in a few short sentences.''

''At least we know what we mean,'' he said, and she groaned; then they started laughing again. When he sobered, he reached out and slid his hand underneath her heavy curtain of hair, clasping the back of her neck. ''Let me give something a try,'' he urged. ''Let me have another shot at changing your mind.''

''Does this mean that if it doesn't work, you'll stop trying?'' she asked wryly, and had to laugh at the expression on his face. ''Oh, Tom, you don't even have a clue about how to give up, do you?''

He shrugged. ''I've never wanted anyone the way I want you,'' he said, smiling back just as wryly. ''But at least I've made some progress. You've started calling me Tom again.''

He dressed and roughly kissed her as he started out the door. "I'll be back as soon as I can. It may not be today. But there's something I want to show you before you make a final decision."

Elizabeth leaned against the door after she had closed it behind him. Final decision? She didn't know whether to laugh or cry. To her, the decision had been final for the past six months. So why did she feel that, unless she gave him the answer he wanted, she would still be explaining her reasons to him five years from now?

Chapter Nine

The doorbell rang just before five on Sunday morning. Elizabeth stumbled groggily out of bed, staring at the clock in bewilderment. She had finally set the thing, but surely she had gotten it wrong. Who would be leaning on her doorbell at 4:54 in the morning?

"Quinlan," she muttered, moving unsteadily down the hall.

She looked through the peephole to make certain, though she really hadn't doubted it. Yawning, she released the chain and locks and opened the door. "Couldn't it have waited another few hours?" she asked grouchily, heading toward the kitchen to put on a pot of coffee. If she had to deal with him at this hour, she needed to be more alert than she was right now.

"No," he said. "I haven't slept, and I want to get this over with."

She hadn't slept all that much herself; after he'd left the morning before, she had wandered around the apartment, feeling restless and unable to settle on anything to do. It had taken her a while to identify it, but at last she had realized that she was lonely. He had been with her for thirty-six hours straight, holding her while they slept, making love, talking, arguing, laughing. The blackout had forced them into a hothouse intimacy, leading her to explore old nightmares and maybe even come to terms with them.

The bed had seemed too big, too cold, too empty. For the first time she began to question whether or not she had been right in breaking off with him. Quinlan definitely was *not* Eric Landers. Physically, she felt infinitely safe and cherished with him; on that level, at least, she didn't think he would ever hurt her.

It was the other facet of his personality that worried her the most, his secrecy and insistence on being in control. She had some sympathy with the control thing; after all, she was a bit fanatic on the subject herself. The problem was that she had had to fight so hard to get herself back, how could she risk her identity again? Quinlan was as relentless as the tides; lesser personalities crumbled before him. She didn't know anything about huge chunks of his life, what had made him the man he was. What if he were hiding something from her that she absolutely couldn't live with? What if there was a darkness to his soul that he could keep under control until it was too late for her to protect herself?

She was under no illusions about marriage. Even in this day and age, it gave a man a certain autonomy over his wife. People weren't inclined to get involved in domestic "disputes," even when the dispute involved a man beating the hell out of his smaller, weaker wife. Some police departments were starting to view it more seriously, but they were so inundated with street crime, drug and highway carnage that, objectively, she could see how a woman's swollen face or broken arm didn't seem as critical when weighed in that balance.

And marriage was what Quinlan wanted. If she resumed a relationship with him, he might not mention it for a while—she gave him a week, at the outside—but he would be as relentless in his pursuit of that goal as he was in everything else. She loved him so much that she knew he would eventually wear her down, which was why she had to make a final decision now. And she *could* do it now—if the answer was no. She still had enough strength to walk away from him, in her own best interests. If she waited, every day would weaken that resolve a little more.

He had been silent while she moved around the kitchen, preparing the coffeemaker and turning it on. Hisses and gurgles filled the air as the water heated; then came the soft tinkle of water into the pot and the delicious aroma of fresh coffee filled the room.

"Let's sit down," he said, and placed his briefcase on the table. It was the first time she had noticed it.

She shook her head. "If this requires thinking, at least wait until I've had a cup of coffee."

His mouth quirked. "I don't know. Somehow I think I'd stand a better chance if your brain stayed in neutral and you just went with your instincts."

"Hormones, you mean."

"I have nothing against those, either." He rubbed his beard and sighed wearily. "But I guess I could use a cup of coffee, too."

He had taken the time to change clothes, she saw; he was wearing jeans that looked to be at least ten years old, and a soft, white, cotton shirt. But his eyes were circled with dark rings and were bloodshot from lack of sleep, and he obviously hadn't shaved since the morning before the blackout. The blackness of his heavy beard made him look like a ruffian; actually, he looked exactly like the type of people he hired.

When the coffee stopped dripping, she filled two mugs and slid one in front of him as she took a seat at the table. Cautiously sipping the hot brew, she wondered how long it would take to hit the bloodstream.

He opened the briefcase and took out two files, one very thin and the other over an inch thick. He slid the thin one toward her. "Okay, read this one first."

She opened it and lifted her eyebrows when she saw that it was basically the same type of file that he'd had on her, though this one was on himself. Only it seemed to be rather sketchy. *Bare bones* was more like it, and even then, part of the skeleton was missing. It gave his name, birthdate, birthplace, social security number, physical description, education and present employment, as well as the sketchy facts of his brief marriage, so many years ago. Other than that, he seemed not to have existed between the years of his divorce and when he had started his security business.

"Were you in cold storage for about fifteen years?" she finally asked, shoving the file back toward him. "I appreciate the gesture, but if this was supposed to tell me about you, it lacks a little something."

He eyed her warily, then grinned. "Not many people can manage to be sarcastic at five o'clock in the morning."

"At five o'clock, that's about all I *can* manage."

"I'll remember that," he murmured, and slid the second file, the thick one, toward her. "This is the information you wouldn't have gotten if you investigated me."

Her interest level immediately soared, and she flipped the manila folder open. The documents before her weren't originals, but were a mixture of photostats and faxes. She looked at the top of one and then gave him a startled look. "Government, huh?"

"I had to get a buddy to pull up my file and send it to me. Nothing in there is going to reveal state secrets, but the information is protected, for my sake. I could have hacked into the computer, but I'd just as soon not face a jail term, so it took some time to get it all put together."

"Just exactly what did you do?" she asked, not at all certain that she wanted to know. After being so frustrated by his lack of openness, now that his life lay open before her, she wasn't all that eager to know the details. If he had been shot at, if he had been in danger in any way...that could give her a different set of nightmares.

"No Hollywood stuff," he assured her, grinning.

"I'm disappointed. You mean you weren't a secret agent?" Relieved was more like it.

"That's a Hollywood term. In the business, it's called a field operative. And no, that isn't what I did. I gathered information, set up surveillance and security systems, worked with antiterrorist squads. It wasn't the kind of job that you talk over with your buddies in the bar after work."

"I can understand that. You got in the habit of not talking about yourself or what you did."

"It was more than just a habit, it could have meant people's lives. I still don't talk about it, because I still know people in the business. Information is the greatest asset a government can have, and the most dangerous."

She tapped the file. "So why are you showing me this?"

"Because I trust you," he said simply; then another grin spread across his face. "And because I didn't think you'd believe me if I just said, 'I can't talk about myself, government stuff, very hush-hush.' You would have laughed in my face. It's the kind of crap you hear in singles bars, hot-shot studs trying to impress the airheads. You aren't an airhead."

After flipping a few pages and scanning them, she said, "You're right. I wouldn't have believed this. Most people don't do this type of work."

He shrugged. "Like I said, I went to Cal Tech, and I was very good at what I did."

"Did?" she asked incredulously. "It's what you still do. It's just that now you do it for yourself instead of the government." An idea struck her. "The people you hire. Are they—?"

"Some of them," he admitted.

"Like the biker?"

He laughed. "Like the biker. Hell, do you think I'd hire anyone who looked like that if I didn't personally know him? He really was an operative, one mean son of a bitch."

"They come to you for jobs when they retire?"

"No, nothing like that. I'm not a halfway house for burned-out government employees. I keep track of people, contact them to see if they're interested in working for me. Most of them are very normal, and it's just a matter of moving from one computer job to another."

She closed the file and pushed it away from her. Quinlan eyed her with alarm. "Aren't you going to read it?"

"No. I don't need to know every detail of everything you've done. A brief overview is enough."

He drew a deep breath and sat back. "Okay. That's it, then. I've done all I can. I can't convince you, prove it to you in any way, that I'll never treat you the way Landers did. *I* know I won't, but you're the one who has to believe it. Elizabeth, sweetheart, will you marry me?''

She couldn't help it. She knew it wasn't the way a woman was supposed to respond to a marriage proposal, but the relentlessness of it was so typical of Tom Quinlan that she couldn't stop the sharp crack of laughter from exploding into sound. She would probably hear that question every day until she either gave him the answer he wanted or went mad under the pressure. Instead of making her feel pressured, as it would have before, there was a certain amount of comfort in knowing she could depend on him to that extent. Seeing that file had meant more to her than he could know. It wasn't just that it filled in the gaps of his life, but that he trusted her to know about him.

She managed to regain her composure and stared seriously at him. Somehow, what had happened during the blackout had lessened the grip that Eric Landers had still had on her, even after so many years. During the long hours of that hot night she had been forced to truly look at what had happened, to deal with it, and for the first time she'd realized that Eric had still held her captive. Because of him, she had been afraid to truly let herself live. She was still afraid, but all of a sudden she was more afraid of losing what she had. If it were possible to lose Quinlan, she thought, looking at him with wry fondness.

But, yes, she could lose him, if she didn't start appreciating the value of what he was offering her. It was sink or swim time.

He had begun to fidget under her silent regard. She inhaled deeply. "Marriage, huh? No living together, seeing how it works?"

"Nope. Marriage. The love and honor vows. Until death."

She scowled a little at him. He was as yielding as rock when he made up his mind about something. "Yours could come sooner than you think," she muttered.

"That's okay, if you're the one who does me in. I have an idea of the method you'd use," he replied, and a look of startlingly intense carnal hunger crossed his face. He shivered a little, then gathered himself and raised his right hand. "I swear I'll be an absolute pussycat of a husband. A woman like you needs room."

She had taken a sip of coffee, and at his words she swallowed wrong, choking on the liquid. She coughed and wheezed, then stared at him incredulously. "Then why haven't you been giving me any?" she yelled.

"Because I was afraid to give you enough room to push me away," he said. He gave her a little half smile that acknowledged his own vulnerability and held out his hand to her. "You scare me, too, babe. I'm scared to death you'll decide you can get along without me."

She crossed her arms and glared at him, refusing to take his outstretched hand. "If you think you'll get a little slave, you'll be disappointed. I won't pick up after you, I don't like cooking and I won't tolerate dirty clothes strewn all over the place."

A grin began to spread across his face as she talked, a look of almost blinding elation, but he only said mildly, "I'm fairly neat, for a man."

"Not good enough. I heard that qualification."

He sighed. "All right. We'll write it into our wedding vows. I'll keep my clothes picked up, wash the whiskers out of the sink and put the lid back down on the toilet. I'll get up with the kids—"

"Kids?" she asked delicately.

He lifted his brows at her. She stifled a smile. God, dealing with him was exhilarating! "Okay," she said, relenting. "Kids. But not more than two."

"Two sounds about right. Deal?"

She pretended to consider, then said, "Deal," and they solemnly shook hands.

Quinlan sighed with satisfaction, then hauled her into his arms, literally dragging her across the table and knocking her mug of coffee to the floor. Oblivious to the spreading brown puddle, he held her on his lap and kissed her until her knees were weak. When he lifted his head, a big grin creased his face and he said, "By the way, I always know how to bypass my own systems."

She put her hand on his rough jaw and kissed him again. "I know," she said smugly.

Over an hour later, he lifted his head from the pillow and scowled at her. "There's no way you could have known."

"Not for certain, but I suspected." She stretched, feeling lazy and replete. Her entire body throbbed with a pleasant, lingering heat.

He gathered her close and pressed a kiss to the top of her head. "Six months," he grumbled. "And it took a damn blackout to get you to talk to me."

"I feel rather fond of the blackout," she murmured. "Without it, I wouldn't have been forced to spend so much time with you."

"Are you saying we never would have worked it out if it hadn't been for that?"

"I wouldn't have given you the chance to get that close to me," she said, her voice quiet with sincerity. "I wasn't playing games, Tom. I was scared to death of you, and of losing myself again. You never would have had the chance to convince me, if it hadn't been for the blackout."

"Then God bless overloaded power grids," he muttered. "But I'd have gotten to you, one way or another."

"Other than kidnapping, I can't think how," she replied caustically.

He went very still, and the silence made her lift her

head to give him a suspicious glare. He tried to look innocent, then gave it up when he saw she wasn't buying it.

"That was what I had planned for the weekend, if you refused to have dinner with me Thursday night," he admitted a bit sheepishly.

"Ah-ha. I *thought* you waylaid me that afternoon."

"A man has to do something when his woman won't give him the time of day," he muttered. "I was desperate."

She said, "It's six-thirty."

A brief flicker of confusion crossed his face; then he glanced at the clock and grinned. "So it is," he said with satisfaction. She had just given him the time of day—and a lot more. With a lithe twist of his powerful body he tumbled her back into the twisted sheets and came down on top of her.

"I love you," he rumbled. "And I still haven't heard the 'yes' I've been waiting for."

"I agreed. We made a deal."

"I know, but I'm a little more traditional than that. Elizabeth Major, will you marry me?"

She hesitated for a second. Eric Landers had lost the power to keep her a victim. "Yes, Tom Quinlan, I certainly will."

He lowered his head to kiss her. When he surfaced, they were both breathing hard and knew it would be a while yet before they got out of bed. He gave the clock another glance. "Around nine," he murmured, "remind me to make a couple of phone calls. I need to cancel the kidnapping plans."

She laughed, and kept laughing until his strong thrust into her body changed the laughter into a soft cry of pleasure, as he turned that relentless focus to the task of bringing them both to the intense ecstasy they found only with each other. She had been so afraid of that part of him, but now she knew it was what made him a man she could depend on for the rest of her life. As she clung to his shoulders, a dim echo of thought floated through her brain: "God bless overloads!"

THE LEOPARD'S WOMAN
Linda Lael Miller

Chapter One

Olivia Stillwell's wrists were bound behind her, and the filthy, rusted floor of the Jeep bruised her anew with every jostle and bump. In that one small corner of her mind that had not yet gone numb with terror, she reflected that this adventure would surely qualify her for a generous bonus—should she survive to collect.

The fierce Mexican sun pounded down, cooking her, unhindered by her sleeveless white cotton blouse and khaki slacks. Her shoulder-length auburn hair clung to the mixture of sweat and dust covering her face and neck, and she was pretty sure she was going to throw up if she had to travel another mile taped up like a lobster on its way to the boiling pot.

Not that Olivia wanted her abductors to stop. *Or* go on to whatever horrifying destination they had in mind, for that matter.

She closed her eyes, trying to retreat into the darkness inside her head, but there was no hiding place there, either. Scenes from B-movies she'd seen years before played in her mind in vivid color.

Olivia couldn't go forward mentally from there, and she certainly found the present intolerable, so she let her thoughts slide backward to the past.

Until that morning, Olivia's life had gone very well, all things considered.

Her Uncle Errol, who wrote fantastically successful romantic adventure novels for a predominantly female audience, had hired her to work on his research staff five years before, after her graduation from college. She'd loved the job immediately and been good at it. Through attrition and a gradual accumulation of experience, Olivia had eventually earned the right to direct the other staffers and take her choice of the research assignments her uncle doled out.

She'd earned her position through a lot of hard work and innovative thinking, though of course a lot of people didn't give her credit for personal effort. Because she was Errol McCauley's only living relative, because he'd raised and educated her, almost everyone assumed her exciting career had been handed to her on the proverbial silver platter.

Even now, under these desperate circumstances, Olivia yearned for an accomplishment of her own, however modest.

For about the thousandth time, Olivia's right cheek thumped against the Jeep floor. Just then, she thought with desolate wryness, she'd have given her job to anyone who asked for it.

Tears flooded her lashes, and she was relieved to know she wasn't dehydrated to the point where she couldn't cry. She sniffled. Only that morning, she'd dined happily on the terrace of her hotel room, shielded from the cruel sun by a bright red-and-white awning. She'd finished her two-week research assignment—Uncle Errol was writing about a rich American heiress who, after many trials and tribulations, married a matador—and decided to reward herself with a few pieces of pottery from a special artists' colony she'd read about.

Olivia had a potter's wheel and a small kiln at home. In fact, she was quite good with clay, and she had aspirations to sell her own work at art shows and in galleries. As much as she loved her job and the adventures it provided, another side of her nature was developing. She wanted a new career, and a baby, not that one had much to do with the other.

After getting directions from a good-natured bellman, Olivia had set out for the compound in her rented car.

Somewhere in the desert, she'd taken a wrong turn, and the horrors that had followed would have sent Stephen King rushing for his typewriter, inspired.

First, the small sedan, which had seemed perfectly reliable when she'd left the secluded resort town of San Carlos, had overheated. The radiator had exploded, making hot water hiss against the underside of the hood, and of course there had been no starting the car again after that.

Still, Olivia had not been overly alarmed. After all, she'd been in similar predicaments in much wilder parts of the world—"soaking up atmosphere," as her uncle called it—places like Colombia and Morocco and Nepal. She'd had a canteen and there was sunscreen in her purse, along with a billed cap, and she'd never doubted for a moment that she'd find the artists' colony if she walked just a short way farther.

Someone there would take her back to the hotel.

Olivia had put on her sunglasses, slathered her face and arms with protective lotion, donned her neon-pink baseball cap and set off confidently down the rutted road. Several alarming creatures had scurried across her path, and she'd made mental notes about their coloring and size. The more details she brought home, the happier Uncle Errol would be; he liked to use a lot of vibrant description in his books.

Even after an hour, though, there was no sign of the art colony. All Olivia could see in any direction was desert and cacti and a very distant mountain range. She was doing some serious sweating by then, and her bravado turned rapidly to plain fear.

Then the Jeep had appeared, far off on the dusty ribbon of a road, flinging up brown plumes of dirt behind it.

Presently, the vehicle had come to a lurching stop beside Olivia, and she had seen instantly that these men, with their rifles and leering eyes, weren't planning to help her. She'd turned and fled into the desert, the sand so hot that it burned her feet even through the soles of her sandals, and they'd caught her easily.

Olivia had screamed and fought wildly, certain they

meant to rape her and leave her to die, and the younger of the two *bandidos* had moved to backhand her. The other man had caught hold of his partner's wrist, staying the blow, and shouted furiously in Spanish.

After that, however, they'd pulled her hands behind her back and taped her wrists together. Her ankles were hobbled in much the same way, and a gag put on her mouth. Her cap had fallen off in the scuffle.

Olivia had lost track of how long they'd been traveling; it seemed like days, but she knew no more than a few hours had passed, if that.

She turned restlessly, giving a low moan. Her throat and sinuses burned with bile, and every muscle and bone in her body ached, but it was the fear that caused her the most suffering. She couldn't forget those terrible low-budget movies about young women taken captive in Mexico.

When they came to a jolting, unexpected stop, Olivia's head crashed into the back of a seat. Her heart seemed to collide with her windpipe.

The older man came around to the back, his shirt soaked in sweat, clasped Olivia's arm and pulled her upright. For a moment he wavered, like a shimmery figure in a mirage, and Olivia felt herself slipping into the darkness.

Her captor muttered urgently, again in Spanish too rapid and colloquial for Olivia to understand, untied the bandanna gag and raised a canteen to her mouth.

She drank greedily; he scolded her and pulled the blessed water away until she realized he wanted her to sip slowly. She nodded, and the cool liquid flowed over her tongue again, metallic and sulfur-scented and more delicious than ambrosia.

When the *señor* finally withdrew the canteen, he gestured for Olivia to lie down again. She obeyed, since her options were so limited, and he covered her with a striped blanket, the kind sold to *turistas* in the marketplace, along with plaster statues, tablecloths and cheap jewelry. The Jeep set off again.

The heat underneath that thickly woven cover was excruciating in its intensity, but Olivia recognized a kindness when she saw one. Without that shelter, the brutal sun would literally have broiled her alive.

The trip went on and on, and Olivia began to drift in and out of consciousness. There was so much she hadn't done yet—making a place for herself in the art world, getting married, having babies, winning the Publisher's Clearing House Sweepstakes—she wanted to live! On the other hand, if she was about to be sold into white slavery, as she suspected, death seemed preferable.

As if anybody planned to give her a choice.

There was another water stop, but Olivia was in a dreamworld by then. She was back in Connecticut, in the attic of her uncle's wonderful old pre-Revolutionary house, happily spinning pots and vases and fruit bowls to be offered for sale at local craft shows.

The unbearable Mexican heat gradually went away and was replaced by a growing chill that finally revived Olivia, wrenching her back to bitter reality. She wasn't exactly grateful, but she *was* glad for the blanket.

Beneath her throbbing bones, the Jeep trundled mercilessly along, finding every pothole and rut, occasionally making a sudden swerve so that she was flung against the bolts that held the seats in place. She managed to wriggle enough to peer out from under the blanket with one eye, and she saw a galaxy of spectacular silver stars spread across the dark sky like a banner at some cosmic going-away party.

So long, Olivia. Too bad about all you'll be missing.

The idea of dying made her throat thicken with grief. She was only twenty-six, and the world was entirely too beautiful to leave.

The Jeep climbed, descended, climbed again. When it finally stopped and she heard new voices, all male and all speaking the native language, Olivia passed out.

When she awakened, she thought she was dead. Practically everything in the room where she found herself was covered in white linen, with the palest pastels for accent, and the place was comfortably cool. Beyond the open windows, turquoise waves capped in iridescent alabaster flirted with a sugar-white beach.

Olivia tried to speak, but her throat was too sore.

She sat up in bed, ran her hands over the coverlet, then the expensive cutwork sheets beneath. She was wearing a loose percale gown, and the skin on her arms was red and peeling, though swathed in some rich, soothing cream.

Despite the luxury surrounding her—there was a carafe of cool water on the bedside table, along with a crystal bowl brimming with fresh fruit—Olivia was terrified. This could not be a friendly place, not when she'd been brought here by *bandidos*. Maybe she was in a sort of halfway house, about to be sent to South America, or maybe somewhere like Libya....

The thing to do, of course, was to find her clothes, climb over the terrace and make a break for it. She'd travel on foot if she had to; if she was lucky, she would be able to steal a car. Fortunately, she wouldn't need a key—she'd learned to hotwire engines as part of the research for her uncle's last book.

Carefully, flinching at the pain of her bruises and sunburn, Olivia pushed back the covers and climbed out of the fancy four-poster bed. Her knees immediately folded, and she barely kept herself from toppling to the white woven rug.

Groping, she retreated back to the mattress. Her head was pounding from even that small effort, and her stomach was queasy. She had to get away—as horrible as her kidnapping had been, Olivia was certain the worst was yet to come—but she didn't have the strength.

She gasped when the door opened suddenly, but the visitor was only a mild-looking Mexican woman in her late fifties or early sixties. Neither fat nor thin, she was wearing a pale pink cotton dress and no shoes, and her smile was reassuring.

If this woman was involved in white slavery, she certainly didn't look the part. She said hello in Spanish—the first bit of conversation Olivia had understood since leaving the hotel in San Carlos—and approached the bed.

Olivia asked haltingly if the woman spoke English, and the answer was a regretful shake of the head.

"Maria," the woman said, indicating herself by placing curled fingers against her bosom. Then she gestured toward her guest in question.

"Olivia," said the captive.

Maria smiled and poured a glassful of water from the carafe, then held it gently to Olivia's lips.

Olivia drank gratefully, her nausea subsiding. She settled gingerly back against the pristine pillows, staring up at the ceiling. There were so many things she wanted to ask about, but chattering away at the well-meaning Maria would merely tax her sore throat and strain her already taut nerves.

She must have slept, for when she opened her eyes

again, the sunlight pouring through the terrace doors was thinner, and it met the stone floor at a different angle. There was a rap at the door, and Olivia, expecting the gentle Maria, was not as alarmed as she might have been.

Until the visitor entered the room, that is.

He was the most beautifully built man Olivia had ever seen, standing just over medium height. His hair was rich and dark and slightly too long, and the sides were brushed back sleekly, like the wings of a bird. His skin was like fine sandalwood, and his teeth were improbably white, but it was the color of his eyes that really caught Olivia's attention. They were not brown or black, like those of most Mexican people; they were a deep, arresting shade of violet.

Olivia had every reason to believe the white slaver had arrived at last, and despite her raw throat, she opened her mouth and gave a croaky cry.

He paused and looked back, as though expecting to see a monster following him, smiled, then closed the door.

Olivia let out another hoarse yelp, scrambled to her knees, groped for the fruit bowl beside the bed and sent a pomegranate hurling across the room. It missed his head and split against the door. "Stay back, you pimp!" she screamed.

He laughed, resting his gloved hands on his lean hips. He was wearing cotton pants with shiny silver buttons lining the outside seams, high black boots and a cream-colored shirt open halfway down his chest. In fact, he looked for all the world like one of Uncle Errol's legendary heroes come to life.

"I'm glad to see that I have bought myself a woman with spirit," he said.

Chapter Two

Esteban Ramirez braced himself for a barrage of fruit, since the bowl beside the bed was still full of apples, bananas, pomegranates and oranges, but nothing happened. His lovely, if parboiled, guest just knelt there in the middle of the bed, staring at him in proud, defiant horror.

He felt a peculiar tightening sensation in a hidden region of his heart and knew he'd turned a corner of some kind, that his life would never be quite the same again.

Esteban brought himself up short. Now he was getting sentimental.

He took pity on the woman, though he suspected pity was the last thing she'd want even under the circumstances, and raised both hands, palms out, in a conciliatory gesture. He sincerely believed he was communicating friendliness and safety.

"What is your name?" he asked in polite, precise English. It was possible, of course, that the combination of her terrifying experience and the relentless Mexican sun had done some damage to her mind, permanent or otherwise.

"What do you care about my name?" she retorted after a moment of blustery hesitation. Her arms were folded across her well-shaped breasts, her chin set at an obstinate angle. Even with blisters and bruises covering her sunburned flesh, she was beautiful in an elemental sort of way, like the varying landscapes of Mexico.

Esteban swallowed hard. He had never encountered such a saucy woman before, even on his frequent trips to the United States, and he was both charmed and infuriated by her audacity.

"I demand that you let me go," she rushed on. "If you don't, I promise you I will find a way to summon the police!"

Esteban laughed, delighted by her fighting spirit and more than a little relieved. The mind behind those pewter eyes was as sharply cognizant as his own. "This is a very remote part of Mexico," he said, giving the last word its native pronunciation. "Believe me, you're better off dealing with me than with the *federales*." He folded his arms. "I ask you again, *señorita*. What is your name?"

"What is yours?" she countered, testy as a cornered scorpion.

He should have been reassuring the woman, he knew that—Maria would have him horsewhipped if she found out he hadn't laid the visitor's fears to rest right at the outset—but he was enjoying the game too much. Just being near this woman was like drinking cold well water after a savage thirst. "Esteban Ramirez,'' he conceded, lifting one side of his mouth in a smile.

She raised an eyebrow and pushed a lock of beautiful tarnished-copper hair back from her face. ''Esteban. That's a version of Steven, isn't it?'' She looked him over after his nod, as though deciding whether or not the name suited him. If she decided it didn't, he thought, she just might change it to something she thought fitting. ''You're certainly not the kind of guy people would call 'Steve,''' she observed.

Esteban held back a chuckle, but he supposed his amusement showed in his eyes, the dark blue eyes bequeathed to him by his American grandmother. ''No,'' he agreed. ''I don't think 'Steve' would suit me very well.'' He stopped, waiting. Although he was certain he was doing a good job of hiding the fact, she'd shaken him, this fierce invader with hair the color of a tiger's coat.

''Olivia,'' she finally threw out, but grudgingly. ''Olivia Stillwell, though I don't see that it matters. A slave doesn't really need a name.''

''You are not a slave, Miss Stillwell—it is 'Miss,' isn't it?'' Esteban asked the question in an offhand tone, with a slight and very Latin shrug, but it suddenly seemed as if the *rancho,* his grandfather's silver mines, everything he owned and had ever dreamed of, everything he *was,* depended on her answer.

Remarkable, he thought. I need to get out more.

"Would you let me go if I were married? Because if you expect a virgin, you've got the wrong woman."

Esteban's heartbeat was irregular. He shouldn't have cared whether Olivia Stillwell had ever been with a man or not, but he did. He hoped she had, and at the same time hoped she hadn't. "As I said before, you are not a prisoner. When you are well, you are free to go wherever you wish."

She narrowed her marvelous gray eyes in obvious distrust. "I was kidnapped, Señor Ramirez, brought here against my will. And you said yourself that you bought me!"

"Yes, I bought you. I thought that would be kinder than letting you be passed on to the next prospect, who might not have been so—" he shrugged again "—enlightened."

"I want to go home."

"And you shall. When you have had time to recover from your ordeal."

"No. I have to leave right now. If you'll just let me call my uncle in Connecticut, I'm sure he'll arrange for special transportation."

She didn't have a husband or a lover, Esteban concluded. If she had, she wouldn't have suggested calling an uncle. The realization filled him with a strange joy, but in the wake of that emotion came a quavering despair at the thought of her leaving.

This conflict, well hidden, he hoped, made Esteban furious with himself. He had his choice of women all over the world, far more sophisticated and beautiful ones than she. He did not need this inconsequential redheaded snippet covered in freckles and sunburn and bravado.

Much.

"It is one hundred and fifty miles to the nearest telephone," he said, attempting to speak reasonably. He had already assured Miss Stillwell at least twice that she wasn't a prisoner, but apparently she still wasn't convinced.

It seemed impossible, but Olivia's face actually got redder. "But my uncle will be worried!"

"Things move slowly in Mexico," Esteban said.

She was persistent, which wasn't surprising, really. She had survived an experience that would have devastated most anyone else. "You must have a short-wave radio in case of emergencies. You could relay a message that way."

Esteban sighed. "No," he said. "Here we live much as our grandparents did." He saw her glance at the kerosene lamp on the bedside table, then at the ceiling where a light fixture would have been in another, more modern house. Clearly, she registered the significance of that. "There is a generator to power the hot-water heater and the appliances in the kitchen," he finished.

She shook her head in obvious annoyance. "No radio?" she asked like a skeptical tourist. "No telephone, no TV, no fax machine?"

He chuckled, wanting to go to the side of the bed and take Olivia gently into his arms, but unwilling to frighten her. "Sorry. Things are pretty low-tech around here. Maria has a small television set that runs on batteries. Somehow, though, I do not think you would enjoy Spanish-dubbed reruns of 'Gilligan's Island.'"

She scooted backward, her lower lip jutting out slightly, and hid everything but her head under the lightweight covers. "You haven't been a whole lot of help, Señor Ramirez," she pointed out.

He smiled, reaching back for the doorknob. He was through trying to make his case with the woman, for the time being at least. She didn't believe a word he said, and that irritated him sorely, since the trait Esteban most cherished was his integrity. "Haven't I? If it weren't for me, Miss Stillwell, you would probably be wishing you were dead right about now."

Her eyes went wide at the reminder of what could have happened, but then they flashed with silver fire again. "You'll pardon me if I don't thank you for holding me prisoner in this house," she said stiffly.

Esteban sighed and opened the door to leave, even though her slender figure seemed to be giving off some kind of electromagnetic charge from beneath the loosely woven covers. His whole being, flesh and spirit, strained toward her, and it took all his strength to resist. "I would never expect gratitude from a spoiled American schoolgirl with no better sense than to go wandering in the desert by herself,'' he replied. The words were sharp, uttered out of self-defense.

A second piece of fruit struck the door just as he closed it behind him. He grinned as he walked down the hall.

The *rancho,* as much as he loved it, could be a lonely place. For the next few days, at least, the energetic Miss Stillwell would lend some pizzazz to his normally quiet life.

Maria brought lunch soon after Esteban's departure, a wonderful gazpacho, and her friendly concern made Olivia ashamed of the fruit pieces scattered over the floor. While she sheepishly consumed her soup, the housekeeper cleaned up the mess, her expressive mouth drawn up in a soft, speculative smile.

''I wish you spoke English,'' Olivia said when she'd finished eating and Maria was lifting the tray from her lap. ''Then we could talk. I could tell you about my Uncle Errol and the prizes I've won for my pottery, and you could tell me about your boss. He's plainly a bastard—Señor Ramirez, not my uncle—but I suppose you probably like him.''

Maria was listening politely, even though she clearly didn't understand more than a few scattered words. When Olivia wound down, the other woman smiled again and said something gentle.

After Maria left the room, Olivia got out of bed, her legs still incredibly shaky beneath her, and made her way into the adjoining bathroom. At least the place had indoor plumbing; that was some consolation.

Back in bed, she tried to come up with a plan of escape, dramatic or otherwise, but her thoughts were still too muddled—not surprising, after the way the sun had sautéed her brain the day before. She closed her eyes and slept, awaking hours later to find Maria lighting the lamp on her bedside stand. There was a simple meal laid out on the white wicker table in the corner of the room.

"Buenas noches," Maria greeted her.

The lamplight gave the room a cozy ambience, and Olivia could almost forget that she was virtually a captive in this house. Dinner consisted of rice and a not-too-spicy but very colorful mixture of sliced chicken breast, red and green peppers, carrots and onions.

She made a point of saying *gracias* when Maria returned to carry away the empty dishes and the silverware, and the housekeeper beamed.

For a few minutes, Olivia had been able to forget that she was in a strange and dangerous situation, for all the attendant luxuries. After Maria had left again, however, Olivia felt bereft. She enjoyed the housekeeper's company, even with the language barrier between them, and was grateful for the other woman's help.

It had been Maria, Olivia knew, who had bathed

her when she'd first come to the *rancho*—she remembered it vaguely, like a scene from a fevered dream—Maria who had treated her abrasions with antiseptic and her sunburn with cooling lotion. She owed her silent friend a tremendous debt.

Restless, Olivia decided to venture out onto the terrace. Maybe there was a trellis or something, and in a few days, when she was stronger, she could climb down and run away. Maybe she would even discover that the room was on the ground floor of the house, though she doubted that.

She unlatched the French doors and stepped out onto the terrace. A shock of tropical beauty made her suck in her breath almost as though someone had struck her.

This was not the sand-spider-and-cacti Mexico she remembered from before the kidnapping. No, here there were palm trees swaying against a star-spangled sky, and silvery moonlight wavered on water so blue that its color was discernible even in the relative darkness.

Directly below the terrace was a courtyard of brick and marble, complete with an enormous fountain, tropical flowers in Garden-of-Eden pinks and blues and yellows, and white wrought-iron benches. It was all lit by the moon and stars and by chunky candles glimmering inside glass bowls.

Enchanted, Olivia moved along the railing, looking for a way down. There were no trellises or trees; indeed, the only way would be to take a twelve-foot drop into the hot tub, and she didn't feel quite that adventurous.

As she watched, the emerald-colored water in the tub began to bubble and churn. She was completely unprepared for Esteban's sudden appearance; he crossed the tiled deck, magnificently naked, except for the odd shadow, and lowered himself in.

Olivia was mesmerized for a long moment, though she knew she should retreat. Her face ached with color when he looked up, his teeth as white as the snowy orchids that grew in glorious tangles along the edge of the courtyard.

"Would you like to join me?" he inquired.

Mortified at being caught watching a naked man, Olivia took the offensive in an effort to hide her vulnerability. "You bought me. I suppose you could command it."

Esteban laughed, and the sound reached up through the warm darkness like a caress, making Olivia's breasts feel full and heavy and producing a sharp ache in her most feminine parts. "If I commanded you to come down here, would you obey?"

"Of course not."

He spread his hands, still looking up. "There you have it," he said with a sigh of resignation. "It is almost impossible to find a good love slave these days."

Olivia bit her lower lip, glad she hadn't tried taking

a dive from the terrace railing. Judging the depth of the water by the fact that it reached just to Esteban's waist, she realized she would have compressed her skull into her tailbone. "I thought you said there was no electricity here," she challenged, desperate to change the subject, because all of the sudden she didn't find the idea of being Esteban's captive all that unappealing.

"This?" He indicated the hot tub. "I told you— we have a portable generator. Several, in fact."

Olivia folded her arms. "I think you're holding out on me, Señor Ramirez. I demand that you release me immediately."

"Be my guest," Esteban said, gesturing toward the great world beyond the edge of the courtyard. "I would advise you to head north, carry as much water as you can and avoid being kidnapped again. You were very lucky the first time."

He was right, and damn, Olivia hated that. The least he could do was be wrong once in a while.

"Yes," she said stiffly. "Well, thank you."

Esteban settled comfortably in the hot tub, resting his muscular arms along the sides. Olivia couldn't tell for certain, but she was pretty sure he'd closed those beautiful, sensual eyes of his, giving himself up to the heat and motion of the water.

"You're welcome, Olivia," he said presently, sounding relaxed and resigned. "Anytime you're staggering through the desert, please feel free to have your abductors bring you here. I will be happy to buy you, though I don't think you would command such a high price the second time.''

Olivia knew Esteban was teasing her, and she wasn't amused. "Naturally, I will repay you as soon as I can reach my bank—''

She knew he had opened his eyes, felt his gaze even through the stone railing of the terrace and the thin nightgown she was wearing. "You will indeed,'' he replied formally, "but I have all the money I need. You'll have to think of some other way to settle the debt, Miss Stillwell.''

Chapter Three

Olivia told herself Esteban was only teasing—surely, even in this backward place, he didn't expect her to repay her ransom with her body—but there was enough uncertainty to unnerve her completely. She fled into her room and pushed the terrace doors shut behind her.

Her cheeks were throbbing with a heat far greater than a Mexican sun could have produced, and she stood there in the dim, romantic light of the kerosene lamps, her hands pressed to her face. Although she wanted desperately to disavow her feelings and the images unfolding in her mind, they would not be denied.

Except for a single, highly forgettable love affair in college, Olivia had no real sexual experience. In fact, the one man she'd been with had left her convinced that the whole experience was wildly overrated.

Now, having met Esteban Ramirez, Olivia was beginning to doubt her convictions, not just mentally, but physically. Even being in the same room with him seemed to send a super-charge through her whole body, and it apparently didn't matter whether the conversation was worthwhile or totally banal. In fact, she wasn't sure it mattered if there *was* a conversation.

She climbed back into bed, but she couldn't stop the torrent of imaginings sparked by the sight of Esteban striding naked across the courtyard below, as dangerously graceful as some fierce jungle cat.

She considered the things men and women did together in Uncle Errol's books—they were certainly nothing like the timid encounters Olivia had had with her idealistic poet back at Northwestern—and was shaken by a hot shiver. It was only too easy to imagine doing those things with Esteban, to picture—and God help her, *feel*—his hard, commanding body settling over hers, claiming hers.

Olivia closed her eyes, trying to steady herself against the tide of desire thundering through her. She sank her teeth into her lower lip and attempted to make her mind a blank, but the scenes kept unfurling. Maybe, she thought, it *wasn't* just fiction, the stuff of books and movies, as she'd always believed. She reached out an arm and clung to the bedpost as though fearing she'd be swept away by some invisible flood. Maybe there really were uncharted parts of her nature, places in her being where only a man like Esteban could take her—

"Stop it!" she hissed, now truly desperate to derail her train of thought. Señor Ramirez claimed he'd bought her only to protect her, but he might be lying. He could be a white slaver himself, a link in a chain of criminals, planning to feed and care for her only until she was in a more marketable condition. Why else would he have refused to help her get in touch with her uncle?

Olivia forced herself to relax, but because she'd done so much sleeping during the day, she wasn't the least bit tired. She lay staring up at the ceiling, once again considering her ridiculous plight.

One scenario, being sold to some filthy man as a plaything, or even forced into prostitution, left her chilled with fear. The alternative vision, lying with Esteban in that very bed, doing some of the things she'd read about, made her break into a sweat.

She figured she'd have pneumonia by morning, what with all these abrupt changes in body temperature, if she didn't figure out a way to get a grip.

Somewhere toward dawn, Olivia drifted off, and her dreams were full of whirling colors and churning emotions. When she awakened in the morning, she felt as though she'd spent the night driving railroad spikes into rocky ground.

Seeing her own blouse and slacks lying across the back of a chair raised her spirits considerably. The garments were mended in places, but they'd been washed and pressed, and her underwear was there, too. The prospect of dressing made Olivia feel less like a prisoner.

She took a quick shower, smoothed on the special aloe-vera lotion Maria had been treating her with and put on her clothes. After brushing her hair and teeth and making up the bed, Olivia ventured over the threshold of her room for the first time since her arrival.

The house had a sort of mezzanine with railings on all sides, and below was an indoor courtyard. There were lush green plants in beautiful pots, along with a fountain encircled by a stone bench. Somewhere out of sight, birds sang a muted concert.

Olivia made her way down stone steps, her mind rolling like a wheel spinning downhill. Descriptions of the house would make for authentic detail in her uncle's current book; she wanted to remember everything until she could find paper and pen to write it all down.

Growing bolder with every passing moment, Olivia began to explore, making all kinds of mental notes as she went. There was a big formal dining room, so Esteban probably entertained, despite the isolation of his house. The study walls were lined with books not only in English and Spanish, but French, as well, which meant, to her, that her host was well educated; the substantial, ornately carved desk said he appreciated fine things.

Olivia progressed to a smaller room, outfitted with all sorts of workout equipment, and smiled to herself. That explained, at least partly, why Esteban was so sleekly muscular. He was into pumping iron.

At the front of the house, facing the shining sea,

was a magnificent room with floor-to-ceiling windows. The basic color scheme was a clean, soothing beige, accented by splashes of turquoise and pale peach, and the overall effect was one of the room and the ocean being somehow linked in mystical harmony.

Just being there, mentally getting into step with the silent music of the place, gave Olivia a sensation of being touched, healed. She yearned to capture the sumptuous colors and textures, indeed the soul of Mexico itself, in pottery.

"Good morning."

She jumped, startled by the unexpected voice, and turned to see Esteban standing just inside the doorway, at the top of the three stone steps leading down into the living room. "Good morning," she made herself say, speaking in what she hoped was a calm tone. She didn't want him to know how he frightened her, how he haunted her thoughts and the secret places in her soul that she herself had never visited before.

He was wearing dusty riding pants, black, with the same flashy silver buttons along the outside seams, an equally dusty white shirt opened far enough to reveal a sweaty, well-muscled chest, and a short leather vest.

On anybody else, Olivia reflected, the outfit would have looked silly. On him, well, it inspired dangerous fantasies.

Esteban looked down at his splendidly disheveled frame. "Is something wrong?"

Olivia's face heated; it wasn't the dusty grime that had made her stare and he knew it as well as she did. "I guess it's messy work, running a place like this." She paused. "What kind of place *is* this, anyway?"

He smiled, and the effect was blinding. "I thought you knew," he said, leaning against the doorjamb. "This is a *rancho*. We raise horses and cattle here." He stopped to lift one shoulder. "And there are a couple of silver mines."

It could all be a lie, Olivia reminded herself. A cover for white slavery, or maybe drug-running. She retreated a step at the thought, unable to keep her eyes from going wide.

Esteban looked puzzled for a moment, then assaulted her with another of his lethal smiles. "Relax, Miss Stillwell," he said. "If I were going to drag you off to my bed and use you without mercy, do you really think I would have restrained myself this long?"

Olivia was at once injured and relieved. Naturally she didn't want to be dragged off and used without mercy, as he put it, but she had some very primitive fantasies where this man was concerned, and it hurt to realize he would probably find them amusing.

Since she didn't know how to answer his question gracefully, she simply turned away, pretending to be absorbed in the view. As breathtaking as it was, though, Olivia could think of nothing but the man behind her.

When he laid his hands to her shoulders, she flinched, for she hadn't sensed his approach.

Esteban's touch was incredibly gentle and tender; he might have been a poet, instead of a *bandido* with the heart of a dangerous jungle creature. He turned Olivia, studied her face with mingled bewilderment and defiance in his wonderful violet eyes, and then he kissed her.

Olivia stiffened; nothing in her experience, or even in the night of erotic dreams just past, had prepared her for this. It was like embracing lightning; the power jolted her, making her sway so that Esteban's grip on her shoulders tightened.

He tasted her lips as though they were coated with honey, then persuaded her mouth to open for him. The invasion of his tongue was gentle, but it was compelling, too; for Olivia it was like being conquered, right there in the middle of that sunny living room. Excitement twisted into a tight spiral within her.

When he finally withdrew, her breasts were still pressing against his hard chest, the nipples taut. She was stunned by the incomprehensible force of her desire.

He lifted his hand and caressed her cheek, then moved the pad of his thumb over her lower lip.

"I'm sorry," he said. "You are a guest here, and I should not have taken advantage of you."

Olivia didn't respond; she was too afraid she would burst into tears if she tried to speak. She was still overwhelmed by the force of his kiss, and by the new and frightening awareness that she had crossed a significant personal threshold. In some unaccountable way, Esteban Ramirez had changed her forever. She felt stronger, vibrantly alive, more truly herself than ever before.

He looked at her for a moment, as though studying a stranger he knew he should recognize but didn't, then turned and walked out of the room, pulling on his leather riding gloves as he went.

Olivia stood for a long time, as immobile as the statue in the middle of the fountain in the outer courtyard, simultaneously willing him to return and thanking God that he didn't. The fires he'd started inside her were still smoldering, and the yearning he'd created was so strong that she feared a violent eruption even then. Just walking across the room would have been a risk.

Finally, however, Olivia recovered most of her composure, if not all, and continued her explorations. She encountered Maria in the kitchen, a large and airy place full of light and color, and was forced to eat a breakfast of fresh cornbread, fruit and something that might have been either pudding or yogurt.

After that, Olivia tried to wash her dishes, but Maria shooed her out, waving her white apron and uttering a flurry of Spanish words. Finding a large straw hat lying on a bench on the portico out back, Olivia donned that as protection from the sun and set out for a look at the surrounding terrain.

Esteban and his men were busy over by the corrals, raising dust and shouting. Still sensitive to the glaring sun, Olivia returned to the house. More explorations brought her to the study, where she began thumbing idly through a series of leather-bound albums. The pages were covered with clippings from newspapers and magazines, both in Spanish and English, touting the exploits of *el leopardo*. The Leopard.

Olivia felt a shiver. The scrapbooks were obviously Maria's work, and she soon divined that *el leopardo* was none other than Esteban Ramirez himself. Shaken, she only skimmed a few of the articles that were printed in English, and she made little sense of their contents. All she'd really grasped was that Esteban had another identity.

Discomfited, Olivia left the house again and started toward the white beach. The Leopard. If she didn't know better, Olivia could have sworn she'd stumbled into one of her uncle's stories. It would have been pretty amusing if it hadn't been so scary, and if she hadn't been so attracted to Esteban.

The nickname certainly fit Esteban, she had to admit that. He had the sleek prowess and deadly strength of a leopard. And he might well share other traits. He might be vicious; he might, like the animal, stalk his prey, run it to the ground, tear out its throat.

Olivia made her way along a path lined with thick tropical foliage and onto the beach, her thoughts in even more turmoil than before.

The Leopard. Perhaps Esteban really was a white slaver or a drug lord, as she'd first thought. Or maybe he was simply a *bandido*. He had been quick to assure Olivia that she could go back home as soon as she had "recovered" and, although he'd teased her unmercifully, he had not brought her to his bed. None of which meant that the men who'd kidnapped her hadn't been working for him in the first place.

Olivia had been in some bewildering situations in her life, but this one set a real precedent.

Coming to an inlet sheltered by palm trees and foliage, Olivia sat down on the ground, removed her hat, kicked off her sandals. The sand was so white and fine, she thought, sifting some through her fingers, that she could have stirred it into her tea like sugar.

There was something calming about the little hidden pool, and Olivia's troubled mind began to quiet down. Despite her misgivings, she had a sense of returning to Paradise.

Presently, when she could no longer resist, she took off her trusty blouse and khaki slacks and waded in. The waist-deep water reflected the heart-wrenching royal blue of the sky, and it was so clean and clear that Olivia could see the fine white pebbles on the bottom. The coolness was like balm to her skin, so she slipped under the surface to wet her hair, too.

When she came up, lashes beaded with water, just beginning to absorb the delicious peace of the place, Esteban was standing on the bank, staring at her.

El leopardo, she thought, in that dazed moment before alarm overtook her. He certainly moved with the same stealth as a leopard.

Chapter Four

Belatedly, Olivia folded her arms across her breasts. It was no comfort that Esteban was obviously just as shocked to find her in the pool as she was to see him standing at its edge; the situation was no less perilous for his surprise.

"What are you doing here?" he finally demanded, resting his hands on his hips. He was covered in dust from his magnificent head to the soles of his expensive leather boots.

Olivia's mouth dropped open. She'd been about to ask *him* that question. "I beg your pardon?" she croaked after another few moments of hesitation.

"This is my private place," Esteban said, and once again, Olivia had a sensation of returning to the Lost Garden. She might have been Eve, and the man standing on the shore, Adam.

She bristled. "I'm sorry."

Incredibly, he grinned. "You don't look sorry."

Olivia was still flustered. "I didn't think I had to ask for permission to swim in the ocean, that's all."

He began stripping off his clothes, his motions practiced and uncalculated. "This is not the ocean," he said implacably. "It's a spring-fed pool." He paused, inclining his head as he studied her. "I hope you will not be so foolish as to swim in the sea, Miss Stillwell. The currents are dangerous, and there are sharks.''

Sharks and currents were the least of her problems. "Perhaps you could just come back later," Olivia suggested cheerfully, growing more nervous as he shrugged off his shirt and reached for his belt buckle.

Esteban shook his head, sat down in the sand and wrenched off one of his boots. "*You* can come back later," he countered, removing the other boot and tossing it aside to lie akimbo with its mate. He looked mildly irritated. "*Madre de Dios,* you American women are petty tyrants, for all your talk about independence and personal liberty."

Olivia narrowed her eyes, crouching in the water and trying to cover herself with her arms, painfully conscious that the pool was as transparent as crystal. "That was uncalled for. I didn't attack your masculinity, for heaven's sake. I just suggested that you might want to leave your bath for another time. Besides, I can't very well get out with you sitting there gawking at me, now can I?" She took a breath. "Furthermore, I'll thank you not to insult every woman in my country just because you don't like me!"

Esteban stood again and began removing his pants. He flashed her a dazzling grin before she looked away. "I'm hot and dirty and tired, Miss Stillwell," he said. "I've been looking forward to taking a cool bath in this pool all day. Therefore, if you don't wish to share it with me, you'd better get out." Having made his decree, *el patrón* speaking to the *peón,* Esteban splashed into the water.

Try though she did to keep her eyes averted, Olivia's gaze went right to him like a magnet.

Good heavens, even Michelangelo had never sculpted such a man. Only God could have achieved that kind of grace and perfection.

Soon, Esteban stood only a few feet from Olivia, in the liquid crystal of the pool. It was almost as though time had stopped, and the universe had gone still around them.

"You are very lovely." He said the words like an offhand statement of fact, as though he were admiring a piece of art in a museum.

"Stop looking at me," Olivia snapped, but her response didn't carry the strength of conviction it should have. She was busy struggling to assimilate all the new feelings this man engendered in her.

His laughter was a joyous shout. "Not a chance," he said when his amusement had abated, giving another of his south-of-the-border shrugs.

Olivia edged toward the spot where she'd left her clothes. Then she scrambled out of the pool, grabbed them and delved into the dense foliage, where she began pulling them on over tender, wet skin. It was a frustrating task.

"This is a fine way to treat company," she muttered. "I mean, you'd think, after all I've been through, that I could take a bath in peace, but *no*—"

Esteban laughed again. Olivia couldn't help looking at him, seeing the sun catch in the beads of water in his hair and eyelashes, on his brown chest. "Don't go," he pleaded good-naturedly. "Your virtue is safe with me, I promise."

"Oh, right," Olivia snapped. Her disappointment at being driven from the pond was all out of proportion to good sense. "You're a regular Zorro!"

"Please," he said with a gentle authority. "Stay."

Olivia had fully intended to leave, and in high dudgeon, too, but instead she sank to a sitting position in the warm sand. She wasn't anxious to get back to the real world or, in point of fact, to leave the company of this disturbingly charming and irritating man. Besides, she felt shaky from all that activity.

"I'm not staying because you told me to," she said, lifting her chin. Her clothes clung to her damp skin. "I just want to be here, that's all." The lower half of Esteban's body seemed to waver under the water, like a distorted image in a mirror.

"Of course," he replied, as cordial as Ricardo Montalban greeting a new arrival on Fantasy Island. "Would you mind tossing me the soap?"

It was a simple request, and the bar he'd brought with him was within reach. Olivia complied, but when Esteban began washing his hair, there was something so intimate in the act that she felt they would always be linked by it.

Her blood heated, and her thoughts alone were enough to ensure damnation.

She let her forehead rest on her updrawn knees, willing her heartbeat to slow down and her breathing to be even again. The trouble was, she kept having these images of herself lying with Esteban, not there on the sand, but in a cool, shadowy room between smooth linen sheets. She should just go back to the house right now, she told herself sternly, but she remained as she was, somehow detached from her normally strong will.

Olivia was not prepared for feeling Esteban settle in the sand next to her, his skin cool and wet from the pool. Out of the corner of her eye, she saw that he was wearing a towel around his midsection, but nothing else.

"Oh, God," she said.

He cupped her chin in his hand, gently turned her face, and kissed her. When his tongue entered her mouth, and one of his hands curved lightly around her breast, the thumb chafing her nipple to attention, Olivia figured the inner tumult he caused her would register at least 9.9 on the Richter scale.

She trembled as he eased her backward into the sand and stretched out beside her. Although she spread her fingers across the roughness of his damp chest, she could not, would not, push him away. The attraction was simply too ferocious, but even so, Olivia knew she was *choosing* to make this tentative surrender.

He moved over her, let her feel the hardness and the power of his body without crushing her under its weight, but the towel and her clothes remained between them.

Finally, mercifully, he released her mouth, and Olivia gasped with relief, only to give a whispered gasp as he began nibbling at her neck. When he opened her bodice and bared a waiting breast to his lips and tongue, she wove her fingers into his hair and held him close, unable to protest. The feeling of his mouth on her nipple was fiery and sweet, and she wanted it to go on and on.

When Olivia was writhing in the sand beneath him, Esteban turned gracefully onto his back and drew her along, so that she lay with her breast above his mouth like ripe fruit on a vine. He wedged his thigh between her legs and gently gripped her hips, moving her tantalizingly against the steely muscle. All the while, he suckled hungrily at her nipple.

Olivia was utterly and completely lost.

Something was happening inside her, something Olivia had only read about before. Something on a level with the formation of a new universe.

After an eternity of moments, she reached the pinnacle she'd been straining toward with both body and soul. Her body arched in a shattering explosion of pleasure, and she thrust her head back and shouted hoarsely to the sky. Esteban drank from her until the sweet spasms had finally passed and she'd fallen, exhausted, to the sand beside him.

"El leopardo," she whispered, still too dazed to think coherently.

But Esteban gripped her shoulders hard, and wrenched her into an upright position. "What did you say?"

Olivia stared at him for a moment, still drunk on the release, her breasts still bared to his gaze. "I called you *el leopardo,"* she finally said, confused.

"Tell me why," he rasped, giving her a slight shake.

Olivia was bewildered, and she hesitated to mention the scrapbooks she'd seen in the study. She sensed that they were private, and maybe he didn't want her to know about his exploits.

Whatever those exploits had been.

"I came across a reference to the Leopard, that's all," she replied, her body still thrumming from his skillful attentions. "It wasn't hard to guess it was you."

He released his hold on her shoulders, and she was almost sorry that the contact was broken. It had not been painful, after all, but there had been a certain command in his hold that strong women sometimes go a lifetime without finding.

"You didn't hear anyone refer to me by this

name?'' he asked after a long time, looking not at Olivia but at the dancing blue-topaz surface of the pool. "You did not see men who looked out of place among the others?"

Olivia touched his shoulder with one hand and distractedly closed her bodice with the other. A tentative smile twitched on her lips. "I don't think so—I don't even know any of your men by name," she pointed out quietly. "What's the matter, Esteban? Why does this upset you so much?"

He thrust himself to his feet, snatched up his pants and let the towel drop to the sand, leaving the choice of watching or looking away to Olivia.

She looked away.

"I cannot explain it now," he answered as he dressed. "You must go back to the house, Olivia, and stay there until I tell you it is safe to move about the *rancho.*"

Olivia couldn't help noticing how much more formal Esteban's English became when he was troubled. She felt a very primitive urge to comfort him, and yet something inside her balked instantly at this new threat to her already limited freedom.

"I won't do any such thing," she said evenly. "I'm not a mole—I need light and sunshine and fresh air. And you keep saying I'm not a prisoner."

Esteban's glare was as fierce as the Mexican sun. "I have said it, and it is so," he told her. "I do not tell lies."

Olivia rose to her feet and faced him, her hands on her hips. "You're not exactly Mr. Communication, either," she retorted. "You want to keep me here—for the time being, at least—but you refuse to tell me why. Now you're intimating that I might be in real danger, but again, you won't explain. Is that fair?"

"It is expedient," he replied, as though that settled everything. And then he started up the path leading to his magnificent house, his shoulders taut with tension. Olivia followed, not because of any desire to obey his dictates, but because the pool and its lush surroundings no longer seemed like Eden.

Esteban could not shake his uneasiness over Olivia's reminder of his days as the Leopard. The hair on his nape was still standing, and he knew now that there had been a feeling of imminent peril in the air since Olivia's arrival on the *rancho*. All his old instincts, still finely honed even though it had been years since he'd led the raids that had earned him a small but lethal army of enemies, had warned that something wasn't right. In his fascination with the American woman, he had simply chosen to ignore the alarm bells in the pit of his stomach and the deeper chambers of his mind.

This was unlike him.

He looked back at Olivia, who was trudging sullenly along the path behind him, and faced the most difficult possibility he could think of. She might be one of them, sent to the *rancho* specifically to take revenge.

Now you're being paranoid, he told himself, turning his attention back to the path ahead. Still, Esteban had not lived to look back on his days as the Leopard by being naive or by underestimating his foes. He would find out exactly what was going on, face it and deal with it.

In the meantime, he would make sure Olivia Stillwell brought no harm to herself or others.

Chapter Five

When Olivia stormed into her room a few minutes later, she found that Maria had been there before her. A simple midday meal of fruit, salad and small delicate sandwiches waited on the glass top of the wicker table, and on the bed was a long, gauzy, emerald-green dress with flowing sleeves and a ruffled, off-the-shoulder neckline.

Olivia's temper cooled slightly as she thought of the housekeeper's quiet kindness, and she took a closer look at the gown. It probably belonged to Maria, but she had taken in the seams, using tiny, perfect stitches, so that Señor Ramirez's American guest would have something to wear besides her own slacks and blouse.

She went into the adjoining bathroom, leaving the pretty gown where she'd found it, and splashed her face with cool water. She was careful not to look at her reflection, however, fearing her eyes would be suspiciously bright and her skin flushed with an achy backwash of passion.

Olivia returned to her table, with as much dignity as if she were about to dine at the White House with her famous uncle as an escort instead of dining alone in what amounted to a luxurious jail cell. She ate the miniature sandwiches daintily, finished with the fruit salad, and then moved the dress to the empty closet, kicked off her sandals and stretched out on the bed.

She was still bruised and sunburned from her ordeal with the kidnappers, and Esteban's kisses and caresses next to the pond had left her so languid that another burst of anger would have been more than she could manage.

Olivia yawned, closed her eyes and drifted off to sleep.

Sometime later, sounds—shuffles and bumps and whispers—began to intrude on her rest. Slowly, they drew her upward, out of the sheltering depths of the dream state, and she sat up, frightened. For a few moments she remembered only the kidnapping, and nothing about Maria's kindness or Esteban's pleasuring beside the turquoise pool, thinking she was still in the hands of her abductors.

Then, when her eyes had finally focused and she'd taken several deep breaths, she recalled where she was. Thus far, despite her doubts and suspicions, she'd been safe in this place, and well treated.

Still, for all the reassurances Olivia offered herself, something new was going on. There were people in the hall.

She went curiously to the door and, after tugging at her blouse and smoothing her hopelessly tousled hair, she clasped the doorknob and turned it.

There were two men in the hallway, dressed like

members of Pancho Villa's band, and they both had rifles. Olivia gasped, raising one hand to her chest.

"Where is Señor Ramirez?" she demanded tersely, after gathering her courage.

The guards both spoke at once, babbling in Spanish so quick that the words flew past her like a flock of excited birds. All Olivia knew was that the men had been assigned either to keep her inside the room or someone else out. Neither possibility was very comforting.

"Never mind," she said, drawing on all her bravado. "I'll find him myself." With that, Olivia started through the doorway, only to have the men cross their all-too-real rifles in front of her to make a barricade.

That answered one question. She was being kept in.

Olivia would not let herself panic. She made a stabbing gesture at the floor with her right index finger, hoping it conveyed a certain amount of authority. "Bring Señor Ramirez here!" she ordered loudly, enunciating each word as though that would somehow translate them for her listeners.

The taller of the two men put a grubby hand on Olivia's shoulder and gently pressed her back from the door. Then, in an apparent afterthought, he took a folded piece of paper from the pocket of his vest and held it out.

"These men are here to protect you. Kindly do not drive them insane," Esteban had written in a strong

hand that somehow conveyed a smile. "If you are too
frightened, you may come and sleep with me. E.R."

"This situation gets more like one of my uncle's
books with every passing moment!" Olivia com-
plained, blushing because Esteban had invited her to
his bed and because she wanted so much to go. Then
she crumpled up the note and tossed it into the hallway, past the mustachioed faces of the guards.

One of them politely pulled the door closed, and a
moment after that, a key turned in the lock.

Olivia was overwhelmed by a barrage of emotions—frustration, anger, confusion, fear. She
couldn't think about Esteban, because that stirred un-
wanted sensations in the innermost depths of her person, so she turned her thoughts to her uncle.

Here she was, a captive in Mexico, with God only
knew what kind of fate awaiting her, all because Errol
McCauley had decided to write a book about a so-
cialite, a matador and a black-market operation. *He*
was safely ensconced in his circa-1750 house in Connecticut, or his condo in Vail, or his beach place on
the Georgia coast, no doubt sipping white wine and
chatting with his longtime companion. In fact, Olivia
would have bet her best pair of Italian shoes that neither of them even knew she'd been abducted along a
dusty back road and sold to a man people called the
Leopard.

Olivia paced furiously, her arms folded. Even
worse, when and if she finally managed to get back

to the United States and recount the experience, dear Uncle Errol would almost certainly rub his palms together and ask for an accounting of every detail of every moment. Such things were grist for his mill, and instead of sympathy, he would probably just give his niece a fat bonus and an airplane ticket to someplace where she could get herself shanghaied all over again.

She stopped in the middle of the room. Maybe her uncle was eccentric, maybe he'd always been different, but she loved him and missed him enormously. Fifteen years before, when she'd been a very unhappy eleven-year-old tucked neatly out of sight at a rigid boarding school in New England, both Olivia's parents had been killed in a car crash in France. Uncle Errol had immediately come to collect the numb, confused child, and he'd put her straight into a public school in Connecticut, where she wore regular clothes and went home to a regular house every day when classes ended.

Olivia sighed, reflecting. Sure, her life with Uncle Errol had been unconventional—it couldn't have been otherwise, with him and his friend James sitting side by side in the audience at her piano recitals and school programs—but he'd been more of a parent to her than either her father or mother. She'd felt safe with him, and loved, and the town had been remarkably tolerant because there were so many local artists and everyone knew *they* were different.

She sat down on the edge of her bed, brow puckering into a frown. Olivia had always felt a little guilty for loving Uncle Errol so much, for being so glad to go and live with him. It seemed like a betrayal not to miss her parents more, not to grieve for them, but the truth was that Olivia hadn't really known Jack and Susan Stillwell. They'd put her in boarding school the day she turned six, and afterward neglected to call, write or visit. During those vacations when Uncle Errol didn't come to fetch her, she either stayed at school or was shipped off to some mansion belonging to family "friends," where she was ignored by the adults and usually tormented unmercifully by the children.

So it seemed to Olivia that her childhood, which she thought of as a happy one, remarkably enough, had begun at the age of eleven, when her mother's brother had claimed her and made a place for her in his extraordinary life.

Tears brimmed in Olivia's eyes. Uncle Errol had been there for her when she was eleven, and many times since, but she was a big girl now, and she would have to get out of this one on her own.

The question was, how?

Esteban stood before the wall of windows in the living room, watching the tropical sunset breed fire on the restless sea. He had showered after returning from the pool—the cold spray hadn't reached the blazes raging in his groin—but he had worse problems now than the need to bury himself deep in Olivia's softness.

The past he'd thought he'd buried was back.

A decade before, when Esteban had long since completed his studies in England and progressed to the continent, where he gave a new meaning to the term "prodigal son," his grandfather had summoned him home.

There had been no question of disobeying; Abuelito—Grandfather—wielded a much more profound authority than simply being *el patrón* on a remote, if lucrative, Mexican *rancho*. Esteban's father had been the spoiled second son of a neighboring family and had run away without marrying his rebellious young mother. After she was killed in a riding accident, it had been Esteban's grandfather who had looked after him, with a lot of help from Maria.

Esteban's destiny had always been to become *el patrón,* no matter how he might have tried to persuade himself to the contrary. After he'd seen that his grandfather's health was failing and had a few shouting matches with the regal old man in the bargain, Esteban had, as the Americans said, gotten his act together.

He'd learned everything he needed to know, and much more, about raising purebred cattle and fine horses and the management of his silver mines. The latter produced little now, were all but shut down in fact, but the proceeds had been invested wisely almost from the day Abuelito had discovered the ore, and the profits had grown into vast sums, gathering interest in American and Swiss banks.

The isolation of the *rancho* had been a problem for Esteban, however, especially after his grandfather's death. Even though he loved his work, he would occasionally become so restless that he couldn't eat or sleep.

It was during one of those times, when he'd gone to Mexico City for a little R and R, that Esteban had met the American. He always thought of him by his nationality instead of his name, because even though the man had sworn he was called Tom Castleberry, Esteban had never believed him.

Over the coming months, Esteban had encountered the American virtually everywhere he went. Finally, the older man told him a long and intriguing story about a dangerous foreign government setting up a strategic base of operation in the wilds of Mexico. He produced impressive identification and documented proof, and the long and short of it was that Esteban and a few trusted men were recruited for counterespionage purposes.

Esteban smiled bitterly, standing at his window all these years later, remembering. It had been just the kind of offer that would appeal to a hotheaded young man who longed for excitement and adventure.

God knew, he'd gotten those things and more. Af-

ter the bad guys had started moving in their equipment, and even small missiles, Esteban had led raids
on their camp. They'd fought back, all right—he had
the scars to prove it—but after a while they'd given
up and retreated into Central America.

All this without formally involving either the
American or Mexican governments.

Esteban's code name had been *el leopardo,* and he
had not heard the phrase since the last time he'd seen
the American in the small *cantina* in Mexico City
where they'd agreed to meet. The agent's final words
to Esteban had been, "Watch your back. Maybe we
won this one, but there are plenty of people around
here who would have profited from that little missile
project, and some of them know who you are. You've
made some dangerous enemies."

The words echoed in Esteban's mind as he turned
away from the dying sun. It didn't bother him so
much that he had endangered himself—he thrived on
trouble, because it gave him an edge and kept his wits
sharp—but he had inadvertently involved Olivia, and
the thought of anything happening to her filled him
with a raging terror.

After a moment, he focused on Maria, who had
probably been standing there for some time. She
smiled, handed him the snifter of brandy he was just
realizing he wanted, and spoke to him in Spanish.

"The pretty Olivia was not happy to discover that

she is a prisoner in her room. She's been demanding to see you.''

Esteban took a grateful and pensive sip of his liquor. When he'd returned to the house, a messenger had been waiting with a message from the United States. Tom Castleberry, the American agent who had dubbed Esteban ''the Leopard'' in the first place, had been found dead in a cheap motel room. The circumstances had been mysterious enough that the State Department had felt compelled to notify others who might be a target.

He was not afraid for himself, but when Esteban thought of what those vengeful bastards might do to Olivia, especially if they guessed that he cared for her, he had immediately posted two of his most trusted men outside her door.

He handed the empty glass to Maria, with a nod meant to convey his thanks. ''Miss Stillwell,'' he replied, in the soft, musical language of his birth, ''may demand all she wishes. I am still *el patrón* and I do not take orders from a woman.''

Maria arched one eyebrow. ''I think *this* woman is different,'' she ventured. ''She belongs to this place, and to you, the way the lyrics of a love song belong with the music.''

Esteban kissed Maria's forehead; she had been his nurse as a child, and now she was his friend. ''You've been watching those American soap operas again,'' he teased, but secretly he was beginning to imagine

Olivia in his bed, at his table, beside him as he rode over the land he cherished. He saw her blossoming with his child, and the longing to feel her beneath him was so intense it was painful.

His spurs made a clinking sound as he crossed the central courtyard toward the front door, purposely resisting the urge to lift his eyes to the balcony as he passed beneath. Even when he'd handled this current difficulty with his old enemies, he thought sadly, there would be no hope of a future with Olivia. She saw him as a captor, and besides, they came from two very different cultures. Two different centuries.

The whole thing was impossible, he decided, and the sooner he put Olivia Stillwell out of his life for good, the better off he'd be.

Chapter Six

Olivia was left to stew in her frustration and helpless anger for several tumultuous hours. Then Maria arrived, bearing a stack of richly bound volumes and a small velvet box.

With graceful charadelike movements, the housekeeper managed to convey that Olivia was to rest quietly for a few hours, then dress for dinner. The box contained a beautiful set of antique silver combs, and the books, expensive classics printed in English, were apparently meant to offer much-needed distraction.

Having little choice and feeling enormously grateful for the books, Olivia agreed to Maria's kindly decree with a nod, and settled down to reread *Jane Eyre*. Mercifully, the beloved story kept her mind off her precarious situation for a long, therapeutic interval.

Later, Olivia donned the loose and ultrafeminine green gown Maria had altered for her, pinned up her rich auburn hair and arranged the lovely old combs for accent. Although the cut of the dress was definitely south-of-the-border, the silver ornaments and Olivia's old-fashioned hairstyle gave her a startling Gibson-girl look.

This woman staring back at her from the bathroom mirror was a stranger, a person she had never encountered until that moment. She was sophisticated and sensual, aware of her power as a woman. Able to accomplish anything she set out to do.

It was alarmingly plain that this fresh facet of Olivia's personality wasn't just visiting; she'd come to stay, bringing along a whole steamer trunk full of bright, shiny new dreams, hopes, goals and wishes.

Olivia smiled and, of course, the image smiled back. "I've been waiting for you for a long time," she said softly.

But there was still the matter of her captivity.

Esteban came to collect her himself, and his glorious violet eyes seemed to melt when he saw her. He muttered something in Spanish, and Olivia felt the words like a caress, even though she didn't understand them. She straightened her back.

"I will not be held captive, Esteban," she said in a firm but slightly tremulous voice. "If you don't trust me, then please don't pretend to be my friend."

He looked spectacular, wearing dark trousers, a flowing shirt and a black leather vest decorated with gleaming silver studs. On any other man, no matter how handsome, the outfit would have looked theatrical; on Esteban it was as natural as skin. "I trust you," he said thoughtfully, "though I'll admit I'm not sure why." With that, he held out his arm. "You look very lovely tonight," he said, escorting her past the guards, who stood on either side of the door, their expressions solemn and vaguely disapproving.

Olivia felt a sweet shiver go through her, but she couldn't let her doubts be dismissed so easily. She needed assurances that things were going to be different. "You will send them away?"

Esteban glanced back over one shoulder and spoke quietly to the men, who immediately abandoned their posts.

"There," he said. "They are gone." He did not lead her down the side stairs, but through a pair of arched double doors farther along the hallway.

The suite, obviously Esteban's private domain, was dimly lit with candles, and even though Olivia couldn't see much, she knew the place was huge and filled with substantial masculine furniture. On the far side, another pair of doors opened onto a large terrace; the piece of sky visible through the opening was studded with stars.

Out of the corner of her eye, Olivia made out the shape of Esteban's bed, which was large, with thick posts and a canopy of some sort. She swallowed, filled with a sense of delicious foreboding.

She wanted to stay here, this dangerous new Olivia, and give herself to Esteban in the rich Mexican darkness. She wanted to nurture his seed in her body and bear a child as arrogantly beautiful as his father. She wanted to set up a potter's wheel and a kiln, and capture the raw, stunning beauty of the land around her in clay.

On the terrace, where candles flickered and flowers

filled the warm air with their lush scents, Maria had prepared a table. There was a bottle of wine in a silver cooler, and various dishes under engraved covers. Two places were set with Limoges china—Olivia had developed an eye for such things because Uncle Errol was a collector—and heirloom sterling.

Olivia let Esteban draw back her chair in the old-world way, feeling like a completely different person. She'd read her fair share of sensational psychology and wondered if all the trauma of recent days had caused her to develop a new personality.

Desperate to break the spell of Esteban and the moonlight and the dark chamber behind them, she said, "You agree, then, that you won't keep me locked up in my room anymore. It's a barbaric thing to do, you know."

Esteban sampled the wine in that ritualistic way of a true expert, then poured a glassful for Olivia. "The word 'barbaric' doesn't begin to cover the fates that can befall a woman wandering around certain parts of Mexico by herself. And this is one of those parts."

Olivia sighed. She no longer wanted to leave this man and his spectacular land, and yet she had very grave doubts that anything real and lasting could develop between them. After all, they came from different cultures, different backgrounds, different *centuries* for all practical intents and purposes. "I'm not sure any of us are safe anywhere," she mused.

Esteban, to his credit, did not pretend to misunderstand. He, too, cherished his freedom; he loved the *rancho,* among other reasons, because he could range from one far-flung border to another, with no more constraints than a nineteenth-century bandit. *"Sí,"* he agreed. "And perhaps it is not a good thing to be safe all the time."

Olivia took a sip of her wine. It was a delicious vintage; Uncle Errol would have raved, then ordered cases sent to all his friends. "Do you live here all year round?" she asked, feeling more relaxed.

"No," Esteban replied, handling his knife and fork with an élan Olivia had rarely seen in men his age. "I have a place in Santa Fe, and I enjoy traveling."

Olivia thought of all the countries she'd visited, all the cities, and sighed again. "I do, too," she said, "but now I feel like stopping somewhere, putting everything I've seen and heard and felt into my art."

"Art?" Esteban looked genuinely intrigued. They were developing a bristly friendship, they'd nearly made love, and yet he didn't know about her passion for pottery.

She told him, in glowing terms, forgetting for a few minutes the unsettling nature of their relationship, all about her prizes and small successes. "Of course I probably won't earn a lot of money, at least not for a while, but that isn't really a problem. I make a good salary and I've saved quite a sum because I haven't had many living expenses."

He smiled. "Tell me about your childhood," he

said. "I'll bet you had freckles, and pigtails, and were constantly skinning your knees."

Olivia laughed. "You're right on two counts, at least. I did have freckles and pigtails, but I wasn't allowed to skin my knees until after Uncle Errol came and rescued me from boarding school." She went on to give a condensed but truthful version of her life, and felt a little foolish when she'd finished. Usually, she didn't divulge a lot of personal details to others, because it was difficult for her to open up.

Esteban reciprocated by telling her about his grandfather, and growing up on the *rancho*. He, too, had been sent away to school, mostly in Europe, but the effect had been very different for him. He had, in essence, learned to balance the old world and the new with an easy grace that Olivia frankly envied.

His words were as smooth and elegant as the wine, blending with her blood in much the same way, and it was too late to steel herself against them. Even though she was ravenously hungry, a sure sign that she was recovering from the rigors of her recent experiences, she might have left Esteban's table for his bed, had he suggested it. That scared her more than anything.

He sat back in his chair when the meal was over, looking troubled all of the sudden, distracted. "You must be very careful, Olivia. There are men..."

Olivia's heart beat a little faster as she remembered

the clippings in Maria's scrapbooks. How she wished she'd read every word of them. "What men?"

Esteban hesitated for a long time. "Men who are my enemies," he said. "If they've noticed you—and it would be wishful thinking to believe they haven't— they will see you as a perfect means of revenge. They've been waiting a long time for such an opportunity."

Although she felt a chill move down her spine, Olivia felt compelled to argue. "Surely no one could get into the house," she insisted. "The guards would never let them pass."

Esteban thought for a long moment, then conceded, "It is true that I trust my men."

Olivia chewed industriously, eager to reply. "You could always send me back to the States," she said, and it was crazy, how much she hoped he would refuse.

He studied her for a long moment before answering. "Something is unfolding between us. I want to see what it is."

She looked up at the magnificent array of stars, bright as the fancy buttons on the vests Esteban wore in the daytime, and sighed with pleasant resignation. The moon spilled a wash of silver light over the sea, the tropical foliage, the rugged mountains in the distance. "So do I," she whispered at last.

His hand moved to enclose hers, and the dry strength of his touch made Olivia's blood shout in her veins. His thumb, callused and deft, moved over the delicate flesh on the inside of her wrist. "You will be allowed to move freely about the house," he said, his tone hoarse, as if he was making the offer unwillingly. "But you must not so much as step out onto the terrace without an escort."

Olivia cherished this small victory, but something inside wouldn't allow her to be content with it. She raised one eyebrow, took a sip of her wine and asked, "Aren't we on a terrace now?"

Esteban's magnificent shoulders stiffened. "Obviously, I am with you. Manolito and Luis are in the courtyard below. You would not be safe here if this were not so."

Olivia had no idea how to respond, and her emotions were churning. She honestly didn't know which eventuality terrified her more: being abducted by these mysterious enemies of Esteban's, or falling so deeply in love with the Leopard that she was willing to throw off her life in the twentieth century like a thrift-shop dress. Living here, with Esteban, would be like stepping into the pages of a novel...

...where one or more of the major characters could end up dead. The thought dampened Olivia's romantic thoughts, but her body was still seething with volcanic heat. Every gesture Esteban made, however innocent, stirred things up even more.

In the end, to Olivia's great disappointment and relief, he did not carry her to his bed. He simply escorted her, wine-dazed and warm, back to her own room.

She slept only intermittently that night; her hungry body, taught to want satisfaction and then denied it, was restless. In the morning, Olivia made a drastic decision.

All her pretty dreams were just that—pretty dreams. She had to get out of this backward country and home to the world she knew but didn't love before she was as addicted to Esteban's lovemaking as others were to cocaine or opium. Her longing for him was already a deep, primordial need that clawed at her insides, and her only hope was to get away.

Forget.

She washed and dressed in her battered slacks and blouse. Since there was no breakfast waiting on the wicker table like before, she concluded that Esteban had not changed his mind about dismissing the guards. She crossed the room to try the heavy door.

It was unlocked, and there was still no sign of the seedy ranch hands who had been posted in the hallway the day before.

Olivia flew down the stairs. She slipped into the study to see if the scrapbooks containing the clippings about Esteban were still there, but they'd disappeared. She chided herself for not reading the English accounts of the Leopard's exploits when she'd had the chance.

Maybe, a cooler part of her mind retorted, she

hadn't *wanted* to know the whole truth in the first place.

Olivia went on to the kitchen.

Maria was there, stirring batter in a bowl, and she smiled and gestured toward a table near a sunny window. Seated on the threshold of the open door was one of the men who worked for Esteban. He had a rifle lying across his knees, and he yawned copiously while Olivia sat down to eat her breakfast.

Even after finishing and washing and putting away her plate and silverware, Olivia lingered. Pretending an interest in the Spanish radio show Maria was listening to while she ironed a pile of cotton shirts that were surely Esteban's, Olivia kept an eye on the guard sitting in the doorway.

Perhaps he had pulled night duty, or maybe he was just plain lazy. In either case, the man kept yawning loudly, and presently he sagged against the jamb. Olivia forced herself to stay calm, knowing Maria was perceptive, not wanting the housekeeper to sense what she was planning.

After a seeming eternity, Maria left the kitchen with the crisply pressed shirts, humming pleasantly. Olivia waited until she'd been gone for at least a minute, lest the woman return for something she'd forgotten, then bolted for the door.

It was easy to slip past the guard, who was now snoring.

Maybe it was feminine intuition that drew her toward the outbuildings—she'd been wanting to explore them. Then again, maybe it was just luck. God knew, she was overdue for some of that.

In any case, when Olivia wrested open the door of the largest shed, she saw an intriguing and very familiar shape under a dusty tarp. Lifting the edge of the canvas, she felt, at one and the same time, a leap of hope and a twinge of very real despair.

Contrary to the impression he gave, Esteban had not totally divorced himself from the modern world. The hidden object was a red Blazer with four-wheel drive and all the options.

Holding her breath, Olivia tried the door on the driver's side, and it opened. To her amazement, the keys were hidden under the floor mat near the gas pedal. She crept back to the door, which she'd left slightly ajar in order to let in dusty rays of sunlight, and peered carefully in every direction.

Then she went back, climbed behind the wheel and, squeezing her eyes shut, turned the key in the ignition.

The Blazer started.

Stunned at her continuing good fortune, Olivia opened her eyes and studied the gas gauge. So much for the benevolence of the gods; the needle rode just a hair above the empty mark.

She shut off the engine and let her forehead rest against the steering wheel while she dealt with her frustration and a vague, nagging sense of joy. She'd found transportation, a vehicle equipped for the rugged Mexican terrain, and the tank was empty.

"Hell and hallelujah," she muttered, for it took both words to cover the broad range of her feelings.

Chapter Seven

If there was a Blazer, not to mention several generators to serve parts of the *casa,* Olivia reasoned, carefully replacing the tarp that hid the vehicle, there must also be a gas pump hidden away somewhere. Unfortunately, she couldn't take the time to search for it, since she was bound to be discovered at any moment.

She looked around carefully before stepping out of the shed. The door was wide enough for a car to pass through, and it opened from side to side. Olivia closed it, drew a deep breath and started back toward the house.

The guard—she'd heard Maria call him Pepito— was still asleep, his big, dusty sombrero scrunched against the doorjamb, but his exuberant snores were turning to snuffles. He was probably waking up.

Olivia slipped past him and took a can of soda from the big generator-powered refrigerator, passing Pepito an innocent smile when he snorted awake, laboriously turned in her direction and gave her a suspicious glance.

She saluted him with the cold drink. ''Here's to Los Estados Unidos,'' she said.

Pepito made a sound that sounded like the Latin equivalent of a harrumph. Obviously, he was no great fan of Mexico's neighbor to the north, and he probably thought baby-sitting a woman was beneath his dignity.

Olivia smiled winningly, turned on her heel and left the room. Unable to face returning to her room, even though it was a pleasant place, she went to the living room and stared out the windows, drinking in the gold-washed turquoise of the sea, the impossibly deep green of the trees, the violent colors of the tropical flowers. She yearned to lie in the white sand beside the pool again, with Esteban's hand on her body, his mouth greedy at her nipple…

She turned, drunk on the view and on her own thoughts, actually uncertain whether she could remain standing or not, and he was there.

"No wonder they call you the Leopard," Olivia said. She'd tried to make the observation sound like a joke, but she knew she'd failed. She had been too weakened by the realization of his presence; her voice was too small and too meek.

Esteban was covered from head to foot in dust, but he was no less regal for the fact. Here was a man who knew who and what he was, and believed in his identity. He looked at Olivia in a way that raised her temperature.

It was humiliating. She'd made herself available, and her wanting was about as subtle as a neon sign in front of a Las Vegas casino. For all of that, Esteban seemed to find her eminently resistible.

"Maria found these things for you and laundered them," he said, tossing a bundle of denim and cotton clothing into her arms. She hadn't noticed that he was holding anything. "Change and meet me in the dining room. We'll have the midday meal and then, after *siesta,* we'll ride out."

Olivia's heart leapt joyously, but at the same time her throat constricted with grief. "Are you saying that you're going to take me back to the United Sates?"

Esteban regarded her for a long moment, his patrician face unreadable, and then shook his head. "No. A band of my finest horses has strayed, to the south we think. I must go after them."

She took a step toward him, then stopped, unsure of her feelings. They were in such a contradictory tangle that she couldn't make sense of them. "And you're taking me along? Why?"

"Because I cannot leave you here."

Olivia swallowed. If only Esteban would do that, she'd have a chance to find the gas pump, fill up the Blazer and make a run for it. "You said yourself I would only be safe within these walls, with guards outside."

He shoved a hand through panther-black hair coated, like the rest of him, with dust. "I would not be able to concentrate on finding the horses if I had to worry about you the whole time I was away. Please. Just do as I have told you."

Ever since Olivia had met this man, it seemed to

her, she'd been of two minds. She wanted to escape, mostly to spite the arrogant *leopardo,* she had to admit, and yet the idea of riding with him and his men was like the fruition of a fantasy.

"I'm not a very good rider," she confessed when Esteban was halfway across the room.

He didn't turn around. "I am," he countered and then, as though that settled the entire matter, he strode out.

Olivia went upstairs and untied the string that held the clothes Esteban had provided. There were two worn cotton shirts, long-sleeved, and two pairs of ancient jeans.

She took off her own blouse and slacks and changed into garments that had probably been left behind by some ranch hand who had moved on. He'd been a small man, and though his shirts fit Olivia perfectly, the pants were tight across her hips and the waistband stood out a little in front.

Even so, when Olivia appeared in the dining room ten minutes later as ordered, the expression in Esteban's eyes said he liked what he saw. He rose from his chair, seated her, then sat again.

He'd visited the pool, for the dust was gone from his hair and skin, and his clothes were fresh. Olivia felt envious for several reasons—Esteban had so much freedom, he'd enjoyed the cool privacy of the pond while she'd been sweltering, and she remembered only too well the primitive pleasure of surrendering in the soft white sand.

Maria served a luncheon of sliced fruit, cold cuts and her own newly baked bread, and left the dining room wearing a secretive smile, as though she knew something Esteban and Olivia had yet to even guess at.

"What about Maria?" Olivia asked. "Will she be safe here alone?"

"She won't be alone," Esteban replied, settling back in his heavy, beautifully carved chair to study Olivia with shameless leisure. "I'm leaving two men to keep watch. Besides, Maria is not a target."

After the meal, during which Esteban said remarkably little and yet devoured Olivia with his eyes, Maria came to clear the table. Esteban stood, drew back Olivia's chair and pressed one hand lightly but firmly to the small of her back.

"What...?"

He propelled her through the inner courtyard to the stairs. "It is time for *siesta*," he said. "In Mexico, we rest during the hottest part of the day."

Olivia's heart had stuffed itself into her windpipe. Even the weight of Esteban's hand at the base of her spine had aroused her, as had the sleepy, sensual images the word *siesta* had brought to mind. "I'm not tired," she faltered, testing the waters.

If the brightness of Esteban's grin could have been hooked up to solar reflectors, it would have provided enough power for three states. "You will be," he promised.

He escorted her past her door and through his own, closing and latching the graceful arch of carved wood behind them.

Olivia's cheeks were bright red, and this time she couldn't blame the sunburn. "I'm not your play-thing," she whispered, angry because she would be practically anything he wanted and he knew it.

Esteban pulled her plaid cotton shirt from her jeans. "You are like ripe fruit—a sweet, juicy peach, I think. It was all I could do not to lay you out on the dining room table and enjoy you right then and there."

Olivia yearned to defy him, but some elemental part of her nature had taken over and she couldn't. She gave a soft gasp when Esteban gripped both sides of the shirt and pulled, so that the mother-of-pearl snaps gave way. He pushed the fabric back.

Away.

Because of the sunburn and the fierce Mexican heat, Olivia wasn't wearing a bra. Her plump breasts were bare under Esteban's gaze, their pink tips hard-ening, reaching.

"*Madre de Dios,*" Esteban rasped, sounding stunned, as if a woman's body were a new invention. Then, his hands tight on the curve of her waist, he bent and, using his tongue, teased each morsel until Olivia was leaning back in his embrace, groaning.

Just when she was nearly insane with need, he began to suck, gently at first and then with greed.

Presently, he set her on the edge of the bed, removed her sandals and jeans. When she tried to rise, afraid of the force of the passion she knew he could make her feel, he stilled her, placing his hands on her hips. She whimpered and flung both arms back over her head as he nuzzled her, kissed the quivering insides of her thighs, then boldly conquered her greatest secret with his lips and tongue.

Olivia's hands clawed at the bedclothes, and she tossed her head from side to side, wild in her surrender. "Esteban," she choked out. "Oh...*Esteban!*"

He slid his palms beneath her bottom, lifted her slightly, and continued to enjoy her just as he might have enjoyed the ripe, sweet, juicy peach he'd spoken of earlier. Olivia raised her feet to his shoulders, but not in an effort to push him away. She needed to anchor herself to him, to be touching something other than his tongue and his hands.

He slid her closer, then reached up to grip her ankles hard. Olivia shouted with pleasure as her climax first lifted her body high off the bed, then twisted her from side to side. If Esteban was worried that someone would hear, he gave no sign of it. He stayed with Olivia until the last vestige of ecstasy had been extracted, until she lay wilted and half-conscious on the mattress, eyes unfocused, her breathing fast and shallow.

She was vaguely aware of being moved, of Esteban removing his clothes, stretching out on the bed beside her. His hand moved in soothing circles on her stomach, and his nakedness teased her ultra sensitive flesh like the brush of a feather.

"Please," she murmured moments later. That one word was all she had strength for; Esteban had taken everything else.

Still, he knew what she wanted, and he denied her; she felt the shake of his head rather than saw it. "No, *dulce*. Rest now." His voice was gruff, hypnotic. "Rest."

Olivia's lashes fluttered as she fought to keep her eyes open, and even the dangerous realization whispering in the back of her mind could not bring her to consciousness again. She slept, but the cruel knowledge was there, like a burr in the tender folds of her spirit.

To Esteban, this was all a game. He liked to make her respond to him sexually, but he consistently refused to make a surrender of his own. She was a diversion.

She drifted into a fitful sleep, and in her dreams she wept with disappointment and grief.

Olivia awoke at twilight, a sea breeze blowing over her body and her eyelashes wet with tears. Esteban's side of the bed was empty, but the sheets still bore his singular scent and the air was tinged with the scent of his cologne.

Sitting up, her arms wrapped around her legs, Olivia let her forehead rest on her knees and sobbed. It was bad enough that she loved the Leopard and had to leave him, but to realize he'd only been playing with her body and emotions was shattering.

He came in as if summoned by her thoughts, and approached the bed silently. She looked at him with red, puffy, defiant eyes.

"Don't touch me, damn you," she hissed, trying to slide away. "You've had your fun!"

He was quick, like the animal whose name he bore, and before she reached the far side of the bed he'd tangled her in the top sheet and dragged her back.

"What is it?" he demanded. "What are you talking about?"

Olivia tried to fling herself at him—in a passion of fury—but she was still tightly bound in the sheet; it was as restrictive as a straitjacket. "You think it's funny, don't you? Making me want you so much, making me cry out because the pleasure is more than I can bear, then walking away without actually making love to me!"

Esteban might have been an actor instead of a rancher. His face drained of all color and he looked stunned for a moment, then coldly angry. "Did I not please you?"

"Please me?" Olivia was positively livid with rage and hurt, but he still had her trussed up like a chicken in a burlap sack. "You weren't trying to make me happy, you were *road testing* me, like a car you might decide to lease for a while!''

Esteban's jaw clamped tight for a long interval; it was plain he was struggling for self-control. ''So,'' he finally whispered, ''it troubles you that I have tried to respect your honor. You do not like being treated like a lady.'' He gripped the sheet with one hand and began unbuttoning his shirt with the other. ''Well, my lovely little captive, have it your own way.''

Chapter Eight

Deftly, Esteban flipped the sheet that had enclosed her like a cocoon, in the same way a magician might wrench away a tablecloth without disturbing the china and silverware on top. Unlike the wizard's dishes, Olivia was definitely displaced; she did a complete revolution in the air above Esteban's feather mattress and plopped on her back into its softness, naked as truth.

She swallowed, watching with wide eyes as her captor-host removed his clothes again. Honor demanded that she oppose him, even though, on the deepest level of her awareness, she knew she wanted to lose.

"Don't you even *think* it," she whispered.

His eyes flashed. "By the time I have you," he said, "you'll be begging." He stretched out beside her, cupped the back of her head in one strong hand and kissed her. She tried to keep her mouth shut, but his tongue was too persuasive, too expert at pleasuring her. Finally, with a whimper, she opened to him.

"You are a pompous SOB!" she gasped the moment he freed her.

"*Sí,*" Esteban replied. He seemed to know her protests were hollow, and he smiled at the game. "You are not a virgin, yes?'' He inquired practically, when he had kissed and caressed her into a state of near hysteria.

''No,'' Olivia admitted, moaning the word.

''Then you will be able to take me inside you without pain, and there will be only pleasure,'' Esteban replied, his voice sleepy and low. He rolled onto his back in a graceful motion and set Olivia on top of him, her legs parted over his hips.

She felt the size and power of him pressed against her belly, and closed her eyes, overwhelmed.

Esteban lifted her slightly, and she felt his manhood move into place like a rocket rolling onto a launch pad.

''Oh, my,'' she cried in a hoarse whisper, as she felt him glide slowly, powerfully into her.

''Open your eyes and look at me,'' Esteban ordered, though not unkindly.

Olivia blinked, wonderstruck, and her expression must have been a dazed one. The last thing she wanted to do then was have a meaningful conversation.

Esteban gripped her hips, raising her along his length with merciless leisure, then bringing her down again. When she'd traveled him once, twice, three times, he finally went on. ''What am I doing to you, Olivia?'' he asked reasonably.

She trembled as a shock of yearning went through

her, bit her lip for a moment, and then answered him in two very intimate words.

He let her just sit, filled with his manhood, while he teased her nipples with expert fingers. "Would it be so good between us if I were only using you?"

Olivia didn't trust herself to speak.

Until Esteban held her hips again and gave her three long, mercilessly thorough strokes.

"No!" she sobbed, the word bursting from her in an explosion of desperation and surrender.

"Why not?" He was rubbing her stomach now, making her wait. Mastering her.

Olivia was wild with the kind of primitive need that had probably enabled mankind to survive through so many millennia. "Oh—Esteban—I don't know—I swear I don't know!"

Esteban raised himself to enjoy one of her pulsing nipples for a long, sweetly torturous interval. "I have taken you. From today forward, you will be my woman."

"Yes," Olivia moaned. There was a wealth of meaning in that common word: surrender, joy, defiance, fury.

He twisted, never breaking his bond with Olivia, thrusting her beneath him, and kissed her again, savagely. When he raised his head, he searched her face with unreadable eyes and then gave himself to her, full force, with nothing held back.

Olivia's fingernails dug into the supple flesh of his

back—that was something she'd only read about until this glorious, tragic day in the Leopard's bed. The hard, slamming motions of his hips, the rhythmic invasion of his manhood, all of it conspired to drive her wild.

When it finally happened, when satisfaction overtook her, her body buckled repeatedly while, at the same time, her spirit soared. It was as though she'd just jumped from an airplane and found that her parachute wouldn't open, except there was no fear. She tumbled through the sky, end over end, knowing that when she struck the ground there would be another cataclysmic release, then nothing.

It was happening, she was about to collide hard with the earth. Olivia tensed violently in Esteban's arms, gave the keening cry of a wild thing mourning in the dark, and for several seconds she didn't exist because she'd given everything she had and everything she was to the man she loved.

When she returned to herself, Esteban was just crossing the threshold. His head was flung back, his teeth bared, and the muscles in his chest and upper arms stood out as he balanced himself on his hands and lunged deep.

A string of soft Spanish words escaped him as he emptied himself into her, and Olivia couldn't resist caressing him, murmuring tender words as he confronted an elation that was obviously excruciating.

When at last his lean and unabashedly muscular

body had relaxed, Esteban collapsed beside Olivia with a despairing moan and dragged her close to him. His embrace was perfect, firm and protective but somehow not restrictive.

Olivia smiled, even though if anything she was in more danger instead of less, and closed her eyes. The velvety breeze sneaked between the woven drapes covering the terrace doors and flowed over her bare skin like lotion.

He was a fool, Esteban thought, lying propped on one elbow, watching Olivia sleep. He'd made up his mind not to have this American temptress—in his opinion, she needed a spanking more than the sweet, fevered exercise he could provide—but in pleasuring her he had created an undeniable need within himself.

Her nipples were peaked, like inviting confections, offering themselves to him. Esteban swallowed, admiring the rest of her small, succulent body. Her hips were wide enough for childbearing and for receiving him, but not broad. Her thighs were like firm cushions, absorbing the impact of his fervor when he mounted her, and her stomach was flat and smooth.

He couldn't help imagining her swelling, ripening, as his child grew within her.

The idea made him hard—hard enough that he wouldn't be able to ride at sunset when they would leave for the southern part of the *rancho,* seeking the lost horses.

He put the animals out of his mind for the moment, valuable as they were, and traced the outline of Olivia's soft, kiss-swollen lips with his index finger. Her lashes fluttered and she looked at him with those marvelous pewter-colored eyes of hers, and she smiled.

Something bitter and rigid melted deep inside Esteban. He tasted her mouth. "I need you," he said in a throaty voice. He hoped the extraordinary truth of the statement didn't show.

"Come to me, then," she replied. "Let me comfort you." With a small, seductive sigh, she wriggled against the sheets, as inviting as the pool on a brutally hot day.

Esteban felt everything inside him tighten and then vibrate at her words, like a guitar string drawn so taut that another twist would either snap that string or break the instrument. With a groan, he gathered her close to him, settled on top of her, devoured her mouth with his own.

She was ready for him, her eyes dreamy, her womanly place moist and warm. With a soft croon of welcome, she arched her back and received him, and Esteban had a sense of returning home after years of wandering.

When her thoughts were finally coherent again, which was a long time later, Olivia was more certain than ever that she had to escape Mexico the first chance she got. Esteban's power over her was fright-

ening in its scope, and if she stayed until he'd made
her pregnant, his hold would be even greater. Plus,
Señor Ramirez led a very dangerous life. To stay
would be to share that peril and maybe force a child
to share it, too.

She watched as Esteban and his men saddled their
horses in the twilight. Olivia supposed she could have
dealt with all the other stuff—women were coping
with worse things all over the world—but the fact that
made her dreams impossible was something else. Esteban would never marry her; she would be the Leopard's woman, but never his wife. Men like Esteban
only wed women of their own social status and relig-
ion; everyone else would be classified as a mistress.

Olivia had had a fairly broad education; her uncle
was an adventurous soul and had taken her on safari
in Africa, to see the pyramids in Egypt, mountain-
climbing in Tibet. She'd had a number of exciting
times on her own, of course, doing research for Uncle
Errol's books. For all of that, however, Olivia had
never learned to ride.

There must have been a lot of trepidation in her
face when Pepito rode over on his overworked horse,
leading an energetic little chestnut mare behind him.
He spat something in Spanish and tossed the reins to
her.

Resigned, Olivia gripped the saddlehorn, as she'd
seen the others do, put one foot in the nearest stirrup

and hoisted herself up. In the process, she dropped the reins.

The mare danced and sidestepped so much that Olivia was really afraid the creature meant to buck her off, so she took a new, white-knuckled grip on the saddlehorn. Esteban rode over and, with a grin, bent to collect the dangling reins and hand them to Olivia. He ran the tip of his tongue over his upper lip, briefly reminding her, and Olivia felt her cheeks burn.

She saved her pride by turning her thoughts from the wholehearted, lusty way she'd responded in Esteban's bed to the prospect of escape. She had a horse now; maybe she would get an opportunity to ride back to the ranch house, find the gasoline pump, fill up the Blazer and head for home at top speed.

One question gave her pause. What, exactly, was she going to do with the rest of her life?

She was pondering that earth-shattering question when Esteban shouted an order. He gripped the mare's bridle to bring her apace with his own fierce stallion, and Olivia shifted uncomfortably on the hard saddle as she drew certain parallels. Soon they were riding across the sand, Esteban and Olivia in the lead, fourteen armed and mounted men close behind.

Olivia bounced painfully for some time, until she got the hang of slipping into rhythm with the horse. She knew she was going to be sore the next day.

Out of the corner of her eye, she watched Esteban, waiting for him to tire, but the night wore on and he showed no sign of fatigue. Finally, when the moon was high and coyotes could be heard howling their mournful concertos, the band stopped at a rustic cabin that backed onto a bluff. There were a few scrubby trees around, along with some grass, and there was a horse trough that would logically be filled from the rusty-handled pump standing at one end.

Esteban said something to the men, who were eager to water their horses and, Olivia suspected, themselves. Then he swung one leg over and slid to the ground; probably, he had been riding as long as he'd been walking, so comfortable was he in the presence of these snorting, head-tossing, temperamental animals.

Raising his hands to her waist, Esteban lifted Olivia down from the saddle, letting her body slide along the length of his before her feet finally touched the ground. His palms lingered against her sides, and for a moment, he looked as though he meant to kiss her. Olivia wasn't surprised when he didn't; that would have been a violation of the macho creed, showing such tenderness in front of the others.

He gestured toward the cabin, which leaned wearily into the side of the bluff like a traveler who could venture no farther. "Go inside," he said. "There is a lantern and a box of matches on the table to your left."

It all seemed pretty high-handed to Olivia, his assuming she'd obey him like a trained puppy. "What if there are spiders and rats in there?'' she whispered, folding her arms.

"I'll protect you," Esteban whispered back, his eyes laughing in the bright moonlight.

"So far," Olivia retorted tartly, arms still folded, "you've been a regular Robin Hood." Then she stomped toward the cabin, hoping the sarcasm in her words would distract Esteban from the fact that she was obeying his command.

Chapter Nine

Inside the cabin, the darkness was thick and the air smelled of dust, mice and long neglect. Olivia yearned to bolt back through the rickety doorway and cling to Esteban like gum on the sole of a shoe, but she could not shame herself that way.

After squaring her shoulders and taking a deep breath, she groped for the matches Esteban had mentioned, found them, struck one against the rough timber of the doorjamb. Weak light flared, along with the scent of sulfur, showing the promised lamp, a table with a candle at its center, two flimsy chairs and a bed with a rope frame but no mattress or box spring.

Muttering, Olivia worked the filthy glass chimney from the lamp base and moved to light the wick, only to have the match burn her fingers and then go out. She swore, hearing skittering sounds behind her in the darkness of the cabin, and the raucous, irreverent laughter of Esteban's men.

How much did she really know about this man? she asked herself, as she felt for another match and finally managed to get the lamp burning. Suppose she had misjudged Esteban Ramirez entirely? Suppose there was a drunken party and he turned her over to his men?

She turned to look at the pitiful room, hugging herself, taking particular note of the impossible bed. Surely he didn't expect her to sleep there, but if not, where?

Without a squeak of the ancient floorboards or so much as a clink of his fancy spurs, Esteban entered the cabin. Olivia knew when he was there; she felt his presence prickling against her skin like heat from a fire.

He closed the door quietly. "As a boy," he said in a low voice full of remembrance, "this was one of my favorite places. I used to hide here when I was angry or hurt about something, and for a time my grandfather would let me think he didn't know where I was."

Olivia turned, catching a fleeting glimpse of the boy before he took refuge once again in some hidden chamber of his soul. "We're not staying here, are we?" she demanded, to hide a rush of tenderness. It wouldn't do to care too much, not when she would be leaving soon and never coming back.

Esteban sighed, though Olivia wasn't entirely sure he hadn't seen through her ruse. He removed his gloves and the round-brimmed hat that hung down his back from a string when he wasn't wearing it. "Yes," he answered gravely and at length. "For tonight, we are staying here. Be grateful—tomorrow night the mosquitoes will have a much easier time getting to us."

Olivia shuddered, and that elicited another smile from Esteban. He adjusted the smoking kerosene lamp to his liking, then went outside again. He returned minutes later, carrying two rolled blankets, a canteen and a pair of saddlebags.

Even though she was afraid, and certain she'd finally stumbled upon her last great adventure, Olivia was glad to see him.

He went to the rope-bed, gave it a shake to dislodge the worst of the dust, then spread one of the blankets over the top. The other he folded at the foot.

"You're actually going to sleep on that thing?" Olivia inquired, hands on her hips. She wasn't feeling obnoxious, exactly, just tired and testy and scared.

Esteban answered with a nod and, "Yes, *dulce*. And so are you—unless you'd rather curl up with the rats."

Olivia raised an eloquent eyebrow and said nothing, and Esteban laughed. He pulled back one of the filthy chairs at the table and thumped it against the floor instead of dusting the seat.

"Here," he said. "Sit down and I will give you some supper."

Olivia wondered what kind of supper she could possibly get in a place like this. Roast prairie dog? But she sat. She was about to topple over from exhaustion and she was very hungry.

Esteban brought fruit from one of his saddlebags, along with two slightly dented American candy bars,

a plastic bag containing several of Maria's fluffy biscuits and some canned sandwich meat.

"What about the men?" Olivia asked, feeling
guilty about her greed. After all, there were more than
a dozen riders outside, and they might have been
questionable types, but they were human, with stom-
achs that needed filling.

Esteban bent to kiss her forehead lightly. "They
have provisions of their own, *dulce*," he said.

Reassured, Olivia ate with gusto. There was no telling what tomorrow would be like, and she needed her
strength.

In the meantime, Esteban, evidently feeling no
need to eat, went outside. When he returned, he found
Olivia finished with her dinner and pacing the small
expanse of the cabin.

She gave him a pained look when he entered, and
he interpreted it correctly, chuckled and held out his
hand to her. The men had laid their bedrolls out
around a small bonfire, and the horses nickered inside
an improvised corral.

Well away from the cabin, Esteban indicated a
cluster of bushes. "There," he said.

He waited with his arms folded while Olivia
slipped out of sight and did her business. When they
returned to the cabin, Esteban immediately disappeared again.

Olivia felt deserted, thinking he would probably
play cards with the men all night, but instead he came

back carrying an old basin brimming with hot water. He dragged one of the chairs over beside the rope-bed, then set the basin on its seat.

Following that, he crossed the room to blow out the lamp.

The cabin was in sudden, primordial darkness— surely a cloud had crossed the moon—and Olivia, who had been standing near the table, floundered inwardly. It was like being dropped into the utter void at the bottom of the deepest ocean, a place where the fish have no need of eyes.

Then she felt Esteban's arm around her waist. He evidently had the vision of a jungle cat, as well as the nickname, for he took her easily to the bed and gently undressed her.

When she was naked, he began to wash her with warm water and a piece of cloth that was probably a bandanna. He cleansed her face and hands first, but then the bath became more intimate.

Olivia shivered.

"Cold?" Esteban asked, his voice seeming independent of his body in that black room.

Olivia shook her head. "No. You're going to make love to me, aren't you?" she asked worriedly.

"Yes, *dulce,*" he answered. "Very thoroughly."

"But..." Olivia began in a wailing whisper, "I'll yell—I won't be able to stop myself—and all those men out there will hear me!"

Esteban chuckled, and continued to wash her.

"They already know what is happening in here to-night," he said. "As for your yelling, well, you were doing that on the beach, and then again today during *siesta*. It is no secret that you enjoy your pleasures, little one."

Olivia's cheeks were on fire.

He eased her down onto the rope-bed, which felt like a hammock and swayed in a comforting way, and covered her with the second quilt. She heard quiet splashing while he washed, but still couldn't make out even the outline of his body.

"Why did you bring me here?" she asked when she was no longer strangling on her pride.

"I told you," Esteban replied smoothly, joining her. Instead of stretching out beside her, however, he knelt and straddled her, turned her onto her stomach, then lifted her onto her hands and knees. "I wanted to protect you from my enemies."

Olivia felt the tip of his manhood tease her femininity, sucked in an excited breath and squeezed her eyes shut for a moment. "Who will protect me from you, Leopard?" she asked.

He teased her with an inch or so, giving, then withholding, then giving again. "No one," he replied. He eased in farther, and his hands reached beneath to cup her full breasts.

She made a whimpery sound, a sound of frustration and yearning.

"What do you want, *dulce?*" Esteban prompted, knowing very well what the answer was.

"All of it," Olivia burst out hoarsely. "All of you."

Esteban toyed with her nipples while he rewarded her for her surrender, moving deep inside her, deeper than she'd ever dreamed a man could reach.

She gave a small, strangled sob, but it was pure pleasure and Esteban obviously knew that. He withdrew, then gave her even more than he had before. "I'm going to yell," she fretted frantically, seeking him, bucking under him like a mare under her stallion. "Oh, please, Esteban, I'm not going to be able to help it, I'm going to *yell.*"

"Good," he said. "Let the whole world know that my woman is happy in my bed."

Olivia feared she'd go right through the rope-bed and land on the dusty floor, so hard were Esteban's thrusts and so vigorous was her own bounding and leaping beneath him, but somehow the net held.

Finally, Olivia's journey was complete. In those last moments of thunder-and-lightning bliss, her skin was moist with perspiration and musk. She threw herself back against Esteban in a spasm of passion, delighting in his muffled gasp and the subsequent stiffening of his powerful body, and she was still responding moments later while he held her breasts and kissed the damp ridges of her spine.

"I yelled," she said dismally a long time later, when she could speak.

"I'm afraid so," Esteban replied, holding her close against his side. He didn't sound the least bit regretful.

Olivia used what little energy she had left to kick him in the side of the leg. "Macho creep," she said.

He laughed, wrapped his arms around her and dragged her on top of him. "Be careful, or I will make you do it again. Perhaps at a higher octave."

Having no doubt that he could, and would, Olivia forced her ready temper to subside. She made no effort to move off of him, but entangled one finger in the hair on his chest and let her chin rest on his collarbone. "Do you think we'll find the horses tomorrow?" she asked.

Esteban smoothed her perspiration-damp hair back from her face. "Maybe tomorrow, maybe the day after that. We'll find them."

Olivia sighed and scooted up so she could rest her head on his shoulder, wondering what Esteban would say if she told him she thought she'd fallen in love with him.

It would probably be a great joke.

"Sleep," he said, as though sensing her turmoil. Olivia closed her eyes, and when she opened them again, the first light of dawn had invaded the cabin and Esteban was still lying beneath her.

He smiled. "Convenient," he said.

Olivia stared at him and started to wriggle away, but he caught her hips in his hands and held her. He had her again, with finesse, and she buried her face in his neck to muffle the moans the resultant climaxes wrung from her.

After another basin bath, another trip to the bushes, and a largely unhealthy breakfast, Olivia mounted her horse and rode out with Esteban and the others. She was very grateful for the straw hat Maria had given her before they left, because it not only protected her from the sun but hid her face from the gazes of all those curious ranch hands.

When she dared to risk a glance at Pepito, he smiled, and Olivia was mortified all over again. Her reputation was ruined, if she'd ever had one in the first place. She began to think more and more of escaping.

At midday, when the sun was at its zenith, they stopped at a charming old mission house with a bell and white adobe walls. While the horses drank at the trough and the men rested on the brick floor of the shady courtyard, Esteban and Olivia talked with the priest in his chapel. At least, Esteban did. Olivia couldn't make out much of the conversation, so she just sat at the trestle table, drinking deliciously cold water from a plain cup.

"Did the *padre* know anything about the lost horses?" Olivia asked as they left. The old priest had used only one word she recognized—*siesta*—and she suspected she and Esteban would rest until the glare of the sun relented a little.

"I didn't ask him about the horses," Esteban replied, opening a door that led to a plain room decorated only with a crucifix and furnished with two inhospitable cots.

"Then what was all that talk about?" Olivia asked, selecting a cot and sitting down to pull off her shoes.

Esteban gripped the waistband of her jeans and pulled her playfully back to her feet, then not so playfully against him. "He thinks we should be married."

Chapter Ten

The stone floor of the small room, worn smooth by the traffic of many years, seemed to sway a little under the soles of Olivia's feet. At the same time, her traitorous body was fully occupied in reacting to such close contact with Esteban's commanding frame.

"Married?" she croaked, as though she had never heard the word before. She certainly had not expected Esteban to raise the subject, even after their lovemaking.

He touched her nose. "The *padre* says we will surely burn in hell for all eternity, if we don't correct the oversight right away," he told her.

"Now there's an appealing prospect," Olivia answered, trying to keep her voice light.

Esteban smiled and rested his hands on her shoulders. His thumbs made caressing motions in the hollows of her collarbone. "It was probably not as poetic as some proposals," he admitted.

Olivia swallowed hard. "That was a proposal?"

"Yes," Esteban said with a sigh, as though surprised by his own actions. "Marry me, Olivia. Stay with me. Laugh with me, sleep with me, capture the beauty of the land in your art."

She swayed, swallowed again. Sometimes it was

such a dangerous thing, hoping. "Esteban, there are so many problems—"

"We will solve them all," he said, his lips warm and insistent and so very close to hers. "Where is it written that all problems, real or potential, must be worked out before the wedding?" He paused, and his sigh moved against her mouth, sending a fever racing through her blood. "What has begun between us will not be stopped, *dulce*. I cannot keep myself from touching you, and yet I was raised to believe that one woman in a man's life must be cherished, honored above all others."

Olivia felt tears of happiness sting her eyes, but she was afraid, too. She reveled in the gentle kiss that followed.

Esteban cradled her face in his hands, wiped a tear from her cheekbone with one callused thumb. "I believe you are that woman," he told her.

She was struck by an attack of practicality. "But we haven't taken blood tests, or gotten a license—"

Esteban's white teeth showed in a cocky grin, and his eyes danced as he scolded her. "How many times must I remind you, my stubborn little desert flower? This is the heart of Mexico—*old* Mexico. Things happen here that could never take place in any other part of the country, let alone north of the border."

Olivia's heart was hammering. She thought of Uncle Errol and the delight he would take in this outlandish situation, and of how he'd always urged her to be bold and take chances, to grasp at life with both hands. She decided to reach out for what she wanted. She loved Esteban desperately, and she yearned to be his wife, as well as his woman.

"All right," she said. "But I'm scared."

Esteban bent his head, nibbled at the fragile flesh beneath her right ear, then confided, "So am I."

They returned to the *padre* and were married in the shady courtyard under a carefully nurtured, leafy tree, and while Olivia didn't understand most of the words, she felt their meaning in her soul. The only thing that kept the ceremony from being perfect was the fact that Esteban had never told her he loved her.

Olivia knew from long experience that nothing in life was perfect, and Esteban *had* said she was "that one woman" in his life, the one to be cherished and honored. She had sensed centuries of tradition behind his words.

"W-would this marriage be recognized in the United States?" she asked, when they were alone once again in the little room with the stone floor.

Esteban folded his arms and cocked his head to one side, looking smug. "It is recognized in heaven. If you returned to your own country and married another man, you would be a bigamist."

Olivia felt herself go pale. She wasn't particularly religious, but she did believe in God and in the sanctity of wedding vows.

He gave another of his Latin sighs and sat down

on one of the merciless-looking cots to pull off his boots. That done, he stretched out, apparently to rest. He shifted and sighed while he made himself comfortable, causing Olivia an embarrassing barrage of sensation, then yawned, laid his hat over his face and, without another word, went to sleep.

Olivia could have killed him.

Presently, she lay down on the other cot, her mind spinning, trying to absorb the fact that she was married.

Some honeymoon this was, she thought. Her groom was already asleep, and their marriage bed would be a monk's pallet.

For all of that, she was happy, too happy to sleep. She rose, crept out of the room and went to the low adobe wall of the mission to look out at the desert. She saw a pink flower blooming on a cactus some distance away, and suddenly had to see it up close, touch it, find out if it had a scent. She wanted to bring that particular shade of pink home in her mind and blend a glaze to match it exactly.

She looked around and saw that the mission was deserted—like the Leopard, his men were indulging in their *siestas*. Olivia decided to climb over the wall and check out the cactus flower. She would be back before anyone even knew she was gone, though fear of Esteban's displeasure was not her reason for hurrying—she knew what the relentless Mexican sun could do to her if she stayed out too long.

The desert blossom was so delicately lovely that Olivia's throat constricted at the sight of it, and her eyes brimmed with fresh tears. She was about to go back to the mission, only about a hundred yards away, when she saw a rock formation farther out. It suggested an interesting new shape, one she wanted to copy in clay, and she wandered toward it.

After that, it was the layers of pastel colors against the distant horizon. Olivia was hypnotized, her brain whirling with wonderful ideas, and she kept walking. It was only when she took refuge from the sun under the teetering roof of an old shed with no walls, that Olivia realized the mission was no longer in sight.

She bit her lower lip, studying the rugged and unforgiving, yet beautiful, terrain around her. All she had to do was walk back that way...

Or was it *that* way?

Esteban stretched luxuriously when he awakened from his *siesta*. In the cool of the approaching evening, he and Olivia and the others could push on in pursuit of the stray horses. He glanced at the opposite cot, expecting to see her curled up there, perhaps delectably naked because of the heat, but the bed was empty.

A cold feeling zigzagged through the pit of Esteban's stomach, but he immediately stemmed the panic rising inside him. Olivia had merely awakened before he had and gone off to find the amenities, such as they were in this isolated place. Or she might be sitting quietly in the garden where the *padre* liked to hide away while pondering great mysteries of the spirit.

Someone had set a bucket of cool well water outside the door, complete with a chipped enamel dipper. Esteban brought the *agua* in, drank thirstily, doused the back of his neck. Then he set out to find Olivia.

Esteban was pleasantly waylaid by the *padre,* who wanted to talk about building dormitories and classrooms at the mission so that children could come to live there and be educated. He had spoken with representatives of an organization up north, in Los Estados Unidos, that would be willing to provide books, supplies and a couple of teachers, but money was needed for the buildings. A great deal of money.

Esteban listened, though the whole time one part of his mind wandered the grounds of the mission, seeking Olivia. He nodded at suitable intervals.

"We could house forty to fifty children here," the father concluded in Spanish. "The lost, abandoned ones who would otherwise be alone on the streets of our troubled cities, living by their wits."

Esteban was feeling a strange pulling sensation, as though someone had tied a string around his soul and was now trying to lead him somewhere. *"Sí,"* he answered. "You know I will help. Have you seen Olivia?"

"Your wife?" Padre Tejada teased. "I assumed she was with you, my son."

Esteban could no longer contain his concern—or his rising anger. She had left him, after promising to share his life. It had all been a lie to her, a way to humor the man she regarded as her captor.

Worse, she had deliberately endangered herself. The fierce desert harbored so many evils, so many unexpected pitfalls, and it was so easy to get lost. She could stumble right into the hands of his enemies, or meet up with those characters who had kidnapped her in the first place.

Esteban pushed his hat back off his head so that it dangled between his shoulder blades and stepped into the shadowy quiet of the chapel. He hadn't set foot in a church since his grandfather had died, but the rituals came back to him easily enough.

He dipped his fingers into the holy water in the font at the back of the small sanctuary, crossed himself, genuflected. There were no statues at the altar— those were for more prosperous parishes—but the crude wooden cross on the wall spoke to him as it never had before.

Esteban knelt at the railing beneath the cross and offered the first earnest prayer of his adult life. *Protect her.* His head was bowed, his hands clasped. *I beg You to protect her.*

Nightfall came and Olivia still had no idea which way to go. She remained where she was, thirsty and scared, knowing she would only make her situation worse by wandering. The desert air, so mercilessly hot by day, was cooling off rapidly, and she knew the night would be very cold.

Her mind strayed back to the one before, when she'd tossed and moaned on that rope bed while Esteban taught her one delicious new pleasure after another. She ached to feel his arms around her again.

By now, she reflected, bringing herself back to the gloomy present, her husband had certainly discovered that she was gone. He would assume she had purposely abandoned him, and he might be so angry that he would simply wash his hands of her and not even make the effort to ride out looking for her.

"Esteban," Olivia whispered, but her soul shouted the name.

It grew darker, and she tried to sleep, hugging herself, shivering against the desert chill. The stars overhead seemed enormous, but counting them, a game that had gotten her through some difficult times in the past, was of no comfort.

She dozed, awoke shivering, and dozed again. And then she dreamed she heard a horse nicker and the jingling of a bridle. Something long and steely hard nudged her chest, and that was only too real.

Her eyes flew open. She looked up in horror to find the barrel of a rifle, clearly illuminated in the bright light of the moon and stars, pressing her breastbone.

The stock and trigger were in the hand of a man Olivia had never seen before.

He smiled, but made no effort to withdraw the gun. "Ah," he said. "The Leopard's woman." His English was heavily accented but only too clear. He looked around, somewhat theatrically. "Ramirez is not here," he said with emphasis, even though it was obviously a fact he'd long since decided upon. The stranger sighed. "His horses stray, his woman strays. It is too bad. Could it be that the Leopard is not such a man as we have always believed?" With that, the man threw back his head and laughed raucously.

Olivia's first instinct was to panic, but she wouldn't allow herself the indulgence. The rifle still pressed to her chest, she scooted upright, slowly, an inch at a time. If there were other *bandidos,* they were well hidden, for she could see no one but this one man.

"Who are you?" she demanded, as if there were some way she could force him to tell.

"Pancho," he replied, reaching down to clasp her shirt with his free hand. He wrenched her to her feet with an easy, wiry strength. "Are we going to be friends?"

Olivia glared at him to let him know she wouldn't welcome his attentions. "Yes," she replied evenly. "We can be 'friends.' All you have to do is get back on your horse, ride out of here and leave me alone."

Pancho laughed, shook his head. "Too valuable. There is a man who would pay *mucho dinero* for the woman the Leopard loves." His dark eyes glinted, and he stroked the underside of her chin with the edge of his thumb. "It would please him to have you, and to send word to Ramirez that you are enjoyable."

Olivia's stomach roiled, and for a second she thought she would throw up all over Pancho's boots. In that same instant, it seemed that her personal universe had been wrenched into perspective; the mysteries were solved, she knew what was important.

Love. Esteban. The child she secretly hoped she was already carrying.

"The Leopard loves many women," Olivia finally threw out, falling back on bravado. "He will not miss one."

Pancho shook his head and made a deprecatory sound deep in his throat. "No. Esteban Ramirez cares for just one woman, and that is you. We know. We have been watching. Come, we leave now." He tied Olivia's hands behind her back and hoisted her up onto his horse. They set off through the night toward God only knew where.

Olivia was in shock by that time, sick with fear. Something told her that this new man, to whom she was being taken like so much pirate booty, was nothing like Esteban.

At sunrise, they rode over a rocky rise and then down a verdant hillside to where a relatively small but stately brick house stood. From her perspective,

Olivia could see a swimming pool and a tennis court and a corral full of sleek horses.

The ones missing from Esteban's herd, some sixth sense told her.

A tall blond man with startlingly blue eyes approached, looked her over as though she weren't human, as though she couldn't understand what his scrutiny meant.

"This is the Leopard's woman," Pancho announced proudly.

The azure eyes lit up. "I see," he said, and although his English was more cultivated than Pancho's, it was still marked by a thick Spanish accent. He ran a hand over Olivia's leg, clenched his fingers around her ankle in a bruising hold when she would have twisted away. "Very good," he said. "We have only to wait. The Leopard will surely appear."

Chapter Eleven

Olivia was doing her level best to keep her composure, but under the circumstances it wasn't an easy task. "What are you?" she asked her new captor, who had dragged her unceremoniously into his house without bothering to unbind her hands. "A drug dealer? A white slaver?"

The Mexican was standing at a beautifully carved sideboard in his airy parlor, pouring brandy into a crystal snifter. He chuckled and raised the glass in a mocking toast. "Nothing so dramatic. I make my living selling weapons and cooperating with certain governments."

Olivia was scarcely relieved by this announcement. After all, she was in the hands of a man who would sell out whole countries if the price was right, not just individuals. "What is your quarrel with Esteban Ramirez?" she asked, partly to stall and partly because of a sincere desire to know.

The mystery man smiled. He was really very handsome, but his looks were spoiled by the essential vileness of his nature, which pervaded the room like a bad smell. "He interfered with a project that would have netted millions of American dollars. I was nearly ruined, and it has taken me several years to regain my financial footing. My design is quite simple, and it is twofold—I will repay Ramirez for the sufferings he caused me, and make certain he cannot repeat his transgressions.''

Olivia felt the color drain from her face. This man meant to *kill* Esteban. The knowledge made her reel inwardly, but on the outside she was deceptively calm. ''He will laugh at you,'' she said, falling into step with her captor's formal, carefully paced English. ''I am nothing to him.''

The monster ran his eyes over her with mingled contempt and interest. ''Even better. You would lie to save the Leopard. My instincts tell me that he will go still further to save you, *señorita.* I believe he might well be willing to lay down his life for you.''

Olivia closed her eyes tightly, fighting for control. She wanted to fall apart, to give way to utter panic, but too much depended on her ability to keep her thought processes clear. Esteban's life, for example, and most likely her own, as well. ''You are wrong.''

''We shall see,'' he responded. ''In the meantime we must make certain that you retain your appeal.'' He set the snifter aside, empty, and clapped his hands loudly, causing Olivia to start. ''Juana!'' he shouted.

A slender Mexican girl appeared almost immediately. ''*Sí,* Señor Leonesio?'' she said.

Olivia could see, even in her state of quiet terror, that Leonesio didn't appreciate the fact that his name had been revealed. Probably, he hadn't planned on introducing himself.

The master of the house blurted an order in rapid, furious Spanish, and Juana winced. Olivia reflected that the girl was probably as much a captive as she was, and felt sorry for her.

When Leonesio had finished his diatribe, Juana turned to Olivia, who was sitting on a small couch, and uttered a single word that was clearly a summons. Her enormous dark eyes implored the prisoner to obey.

Figuring anything was better than staying in Leonesio's presence, Olivia rose, every muscle shrieking with soreness, and followed Juana out of the room and up an elegantly rustic staircase.

"You must not try to run away," Juana whispered in labored English when the two women were alone in an upstairs bathroom. She was cutting the bonds from Olivia's wrists. "The wind brings Leonesio news of everything that happens."

Olivia stared into Juana's eyes, rubbing one aching wrist. "You speak English," she marveled.

Juana shrugged and began filling the big tile-lined tub with tepid water. "Not much. I listen. I say words to my person until I know them like rosary."

Olivia was touched. "Are you... Do you love Leonesio?"

Juana made a bitter sound. "He says I will be his

woman when I am older. I will be trained to make pleasure.''

A shiver went through Olivia. She closed her eyes. "Who is his woman now?''

"He has many.'' Juana looked at Olivia pityingly. "I think you will share his bed for a time.''

Olivia shook her head. "I'll die first.''

"He will have you whipped if you say refusing,'' Juana said in her convoluted English.

The image made Olivia sway. "Dear God.''

Juana added jasmine-scented salts to the bath and gestured for Olivia to get in. Although she wanted to rebel in any and every way she could, she was covered with dirt and dried sweat and fear, and being clean might do something to restore her reason.

Olivia took off her shoes, her jeans, her shirt, her underwear, and climbed into the bath. Juana hovered nearby, dark eyes averted, while Olivia shampooed her hair and washed her aching body. After she was finished, a huge, soft, thirsty towel was provided, along with a long, gauzy, white gown, a very expensive lace teddy with the price tag still attached, and a pair of sandals.

Juana led Olivia into a luxuriously furnished bedroom, urged her to be seated at a vanity table and began brushing her hair dry. When she'd done that, she said, "I bring food. Make strong.''

The last thing Olivia wanted to do was eat, but she saw the sense in Juana's words. She would need physical strength, and it was crucial that she keep herself from giving in to threatening hysteria. Her own life, and maybe Esteban's, could depend on those things.

She meant to make the most of every advantage and every opportunity, however small. When Juana left the room, turning the key in the lock after she'd stepped into the hallway, Olivia rushed to the French doors that led onto the terrace.

There was nothing below except a big brick patio that extended to the pool. The drop was at least two stories, and if she jumped, Olivia reasoned, biting into her lower lip, she would be veined with cracks from head to foot like an old piece of china.

She went back into the bedroom and paced—thinking, planning, plotting. Coming up with absolutely nothing. Olivia didn't like to admit it, being a take-charge sort of person, but unless Esteban rescued her, she was in for it.

"Leonesio," Esteban said, when at twilight, he and Pepito found the place where Olivia had been taken. In times of crisis, he operated on Murphy's Law: If anything can go wrong, it will. Leonesio de Luca Santana was the most devoted, the most ferociously vengeful of his enemies, and one of Leonesio's men stumbling across the fleeing Olivia would have been the absolute worst thing that could have happened. "The rumors are true, Pepito. He's back."

"*Sí,*" was all Pepito said in response. At Esteban's

insistence, they rarely spoke of the old days and the people they had thwarted.

"Go back to the mission for the others," Esteban ordered quietly. "You know where Leonesio lives when he is in Mexico."

Pepito nodded. *"Sí,* the St. Thomas estate." He paused. "There will be a fight," he finished, with a certain relish.

Esteban thought of a battle, imagined Olivia caught in the crossfire and closed his eyes. "Not if we can avoid it," he replied hoarsely. "All I want is my wife, alive and unharmed."

"Sí," Pepito agreed automatically, but he looked skeptical. Men like Leonesio thrived on conflict, and they both knew it.

Esteban gestured for his *amigo* to ride out, then swung back into the saddle and set off toward the luxurious hideaway that had belonged to several owners over the years. When Esteban was a child, the place had been the home of Enrique St. Thomas, his friend. Rico had had a fiery Mexican mother and an equally temperamental French father, and when Esteban and his grandfather had visited, it had seemed that the whole house was charged with the St. Thomases' passion for each other.

Tragically, the explosive couple had perished in an epidemic of influenza about a decade before. As he rode steadily toward Olivia—she was the focal point of his whole existence, the magnet he could not resist—he wondered where Enrique was now. It would be good to see his old friend again.

The darkness was thick by the time Esteban reached his destination. He tethered his horse well back from the inner edge of the lush palm trees and tropical plants that surrounded the familiar house.

There were guards, of course, but if Leonesio's small army was around, there was no evidence of it. Just three sentinels, one leaning against a gatepost, smoking, two pacing the outer grounds.

It was a trap, of course. Leonesio wanted revenge for plans that had been thwarted a long time ago, and he knew Esteban would come for Olivia. He was waiting.

Esteban sighed. He had vowed never to play this game again, but that had been before that redheaded American woman had turned his life upside down. Having no choice, Esteban Ramirez put off his regular identity and became, once again, the Leopard.

Overcoming the guards proved so easy he was almost disappointed.

Dinner was served on the patio at an umbrella-covered table next to the pool, and Olivia was ordered to appear.

She joined Leonesio with cool dignity, her manner even and quiet, but she was aware of every cricket and bird sound in the foliage that edged the low stone wall encircling the grounds. Maybe it was just wishful thinking, but she could have sworn Esteban was somewhere nearby—it was as if she could feel his heartbeat thumping in unison with her own.

"You will share my bed tonight," Leonesio announced, after taking a sip of his claret.

"In your dreams," Olivia replied bluntly. "I'd rather sleep with a lizard."

Leonesio threw back his head and laughed. "So much fire. No wonder the Leopard is obsessed with you."

Olivia forced herself to sip her wine calmly and even to nibble at a few bites of the sumptuous food. "You're building yourself up for a big disappointment. Señor Ramirez has already grown tired of me. By now, he's bought himself another plaything."

"He bought you?" Leonesio set his wineglass down and leaned forward, pleased.

"That idea *would* intrigue you," Olivia remarked. "I'll bet your parents spend a lot of time wondering where they went wrong."

Again Leonesio laughed. "I am exactly what they raised me to be," he responded presently, "but we were discussing your statement that Ramirez bought you."

"Two men kidnapped me off the road when my rental car broke down," she answered, as though such things happened every day. "They sold me to Señor Ramirez, and I escaped him as soon as I could. Only to be captured by you, of course." She paused, sighed philosophically, hoping the enemy would believe her lie about escaping.

Then, suddenly, Esteban was there, vaulting silently over the fence behind Leonesio, and she prayed the knowledge didn't show in her face. "The life of a white slave is not easy, Mr. Leonesio. Or is that your first name? Do you have a nickname?"

The distraction kept Leonesio occupied long enough for Esteban to lock one arm around his enemy's throat and wrench him to his feet.

"*Sí,*" Esteban growled, tightening his hold. "This is *el pollo*—the chicken."

Leonesio made a strangling sound and flailed.

Esteban's gaze moved to Olivia, took in her flowing white dress, narrowed. "We will discuss your part in this little adventure later," he said. "For the moment, you will return to the house and remain there until I come for you. Is that clear?"

Olivia wasn't entirely sure that being rescued was going to represent a significant improvement in her circumstances. Esteban was obviously furious, and she could just imagine the blistering lecture he would deliver once Leonesio and his men had been dealt with. She nodded, disappointed that he hadn't embraced her, hadn't even said he was happy she was safe, and went into the house without a word.

She and Juana sat together on the leather sofa in Leonesio's study, waiting. When a gunshot sounded, both women jumped, and Olivia bolted for the door, certain Esteban had been shot, that, for all of it, she'd lost him, after all.

She collided with him in the doorway.

Probably, the shot had only been a signal to his men.

"You do not follow orders very well, *dulce,*" he said, his voice gruff.

Olivia hurled herself into his arms, buried her face in his neck. "I'll probably never be very good at it," she said, her voice muffled by his flesh. "But I love you, Esteban Ramirez. And whether you believe me or not, I never want to be away from you again!"

He held her apart from him, searched her tear-glazed eyes somberly. "You will stay? But you ran away—"

"I didn't run away, you idiot. I was looking at cactus flowers and things and I got lost," Olivia blubbered. She drew a deep, shuddering breath. "Before I came to this crazy country and met you, I was living my Uncle Errol's life, not my own. Now, for the first time ever, I'm really *me,* and I don't want to give that up!"

Esteban's smile said he understood. So did his kiss.

One month later...

Uncle Errol was wearing a white Armani suit, perfect for the tropics, and looked as pleased as any mother of the bride.

He'd shipped down Olivia's kiln and potting wheel

as soon as she called him from Mexico City and announced that, even though she and Esteban were already married, they intended to have a formal ceremony at the *rancho*.

Olivia smiled, watching him from the terrace outside her room. The whole courtyard was decked out in flowers and ribbons, and long tables groaned under platters of Maria's world-class food. Guests from every corner of the globe mingled, sipping champagne in the late-afternoon sunshine.

Esteban stepped up behind Olivia, slipped his arms around her, kissed the place where her neck and shoulder met. She was wearing a long white dress with an off-the-shoulder neckline, so there was plenty of skin to tempt him.

"Happy?" he asked.

Olivia let the back of her head rest against his shoulder.

"Oh, yes," she answered. "I'm happy."

He turned her in his embrace, gave her a lingering kiss that promised many splendors for the night to come. She was still a little dazed when he linked her arm with his and led her inside so that they could descend the stairs and exchange vows for the second time.

"Just don't expect me to promise to obey," Olivia said.

Esteban chuckled. "I would not believe you for a

second, even if you did,'' he answered. "I love you, Señora Ramirez.''

Olivia smiled up at him, with her eyes and her heart, as well as her mouth. "And I love you, my Leopard.''

LONESOME RIDER
Heather Graham Pozzessere

Chapter One

Indian Territory, 1867

He had only been standing at the bar at the stage-coach stop a few minutes when she first arrived.

And from the moment she arrived, he should have known there was bound to be trouble.

Even with the war long over now, and hordes of Easterners and, in particular, displaced Southerners traveling west by wagon loads now, such women were rare.

In fact, he didn't think he'd ever seen a more beautiful woman—white, black or Indian.

Something drew his eyes to her the moment she walked through the door. He'd heard the stage arriving, of course, and that was surely why he, ever wary, had allowed his gaze to slide toward the door. And then he had seen her.

The setting sun was behind her and she stood silhouetted for a moment in the door frame, trying to pierce the misty environs of the inn, he imagined. But while her eyes adjusted, his were free to drink her in.

She had chosen her clothing well for her westward

journey: a simple cotton gingham day dress with a
bodice that buttoned all the way to the neck. She
couldn't possibly be wearing more than one petticoat.
Yet the very simplicity of her dress seemed to en-
hance all that was so very elegant about the woman.
She was tall and slim, but beautifully, gracefully
curved at the right places. Her throat was long and
white and regal. Her face belonged on a statue—one
of those ancient Greek ones—it was so exquisitely
shaped and molded with fine cheekbones, a straight
nose, perfect lips, wide-set eyes and femininely
arched brows. Her hair, drawn into a net, knot at her
nape, shone beautifully despite its severe restriction
there. It was a fascinating color, not red, not gold.
Soft tendrils escaped the knot to wisp gently over her
forehead and delicately frame the edges of her perfect
face.

She stepped farther into the room, her expression
giving nothing away. It was an all right place, such
as stage stops went, Blade reckoned. Neat enough,
with a number of wrought wood tables strewn here
and there, a big cast-iron stove squarely in the center
and a long bar stretching the length of the room.
There were rooms upstairs for overnight guests, intended for the more gentle types of clientele traveling
west these days. There were no handsome carpets
about as might grace the floors of many such an es-
tablishment back East, and there were certainly no
pretty paintings to decorate the walls. But Jeeter and

Molly Dickinson, the sprightly old couple who ran the place, kept it up, kept it nice, kept it clean. Poker games went on some evenings, and some evenings, Molly was as likely as not to sit back in her old rocker and grace all her guests with a little Bible reading.

There was no reason that the woman with the beautiful face and fiery hair shouldn't have come here, Blade decided.

But from the moment she approached the bar and old Jeeter assured her she could have a lemonade, Blade felt certain that there might be trouble.

Since he stood at the end of the bar, it was natural that her eyes should fall his way when Jeeter went off to call Molly from the kitchen for the lemonade. She studied him with a certain fascination, then seemed to realize that she was staring. She blushed to a rosy hue and quickly turned away from him, focusing her eyes on the bottles on the shelves behind the bar.

What had she seen? he wondered. Anything more than a tall man with nape-length ebony-dark hair, black eyes and hard features? Anything more than a half-breed?

The stagecoach driver had come in now, a graybeard with a full face of whiskers and a little jerk to his walk. His guard, the man riding in front with him, followed behind him.

His beard was grayer, but he was skinnier, smaller and had a more pronounced limp. Maybe he was exceptionally good with the rifle he carried. Blade hoped so. Blade picked up his whiskey and left the bar area free to them, striding across the room to a table in the rear. He sat with his back to the wall— he never exposed it, never.

He was barely seated before it began. The door burst open again and another group came in, surveying the place from the door. Men. Three of them.

All three were dressed in long, dirty dusters as if they'd been out on the trail some time, sleeping in their coats and wearing them through whatever. They wore old slouch hats pulled low over their brows. They had a look about them that indicated they were brothers. All were of the same medium to tall height, had the same sandy colored hair, and the same rough and craggy features.

The tallest of the three—perhaps the oldest or the leader—strode straight toward the bar. Jeeter had just come back with the lemonade. "Whiskey, a bottle of it, and good stuff, not watered-down slop," the man said to Jeeter. Jeeter looked uncomfortable right off, glancing toward the stagecoach driver as if he might find some assistance there.

Jeeter turned to the bar, found a bottle and set it on the bar. "Glasses," the man growled. "What do we look like, a herd of animals?" He started to laugh and turned to one of the men behind him. "A herd of animals, eh, Petey? Is that what he thinks we look like?"

Blade could have answered that question quickly and easily, but for the moment, he was determined to hold his peace. He didn't want trouble himself. Not here, not today. There was still too much that he just had to get done.

After that nothing much would matter.

"It's the best whiskey in the house," Jeeter said.

But the man wasn't listening anymore. He had turned his attention to the woman standing at the bar and he exhaled in a long, slow breath, then finished the sound with the touch of a whistle. "She's the best in the bar, I dare say!" he exclaimed, ignoring the whiskey bottle and walking toward the woman. "Hello there!" he said.

She turned to him, refusing to slink away. Her eyes slid over him in a scathing fashion. "Hello," she said in reply, the sound of her voice as cold as ice. In all of his life, Blade didn't think he'd ever heard anyone say a single word with such ice-cold distaste.

The man at the bar tried to ignore the sound of it, but the tick at his throat and the blotchy color that came to his face belied the look of calm he tried to give her. "What are you doing in these parts? Traveling by stage, eh? I'll get you wherever you want to go much faster, honey. And I'll make the trip a hell of a lot more interesting."

From his rear table, Blade could see her eyes now as she stared at the man. They were green. Sharp,

sparkling, bright, beautiful green. They held a startling sizzle of cool anger.

"No, thank you," she said, once again her words
unerringly polite, and yet her tone...

Enough to freeze the flames in hell, Blade thought.

"Now, wait a minute," the man murmured, inch-
ing closer still.

The old stage guard stepped forward. "Now you
wait a minute there, sonny—" he began.

The man spun around. "Petey! Jed!"

Petey snatched the rifle from the guard's hand.
Then Jed spun him around so that he started to go
flying against the wall.

"See here!" Jeeter spat in outrage, but Jed had
leapt over the bar by then, and before Jeeter could
pluck up his old dusty Colt—one that had seen some
good service in the Mexican War—Jed had seized the
weapon and pointed it at old Jeeter.

Now the fellow at the bar touched her, reaching out
dirty fingers to stroke one of those tendrils of her
gold- and fire-colored hair. "My name's Matt, lady,
and I like to hear it. I like to hear it screamed out real
good and it don't matter none whether the scream
comes from pain or pleasure."

It didn't seem that there was any way to avoid trouble. Blade was deftly, silently on his feet. But the
woman wasn't going down without a fight, either.
Even as Blade approached the pair, her hand was connecting with the fellow's face, nails clawing it appar-

ently, because Matt-who-liked-to-hear-his-name was crying out himself.

"Bitch!" he swore, and, grasping her, started to slam her down on one of the rough wood tables.

That was Blade's opening. He gripped Matt by the shoulders, wrenching him up. He spun him around to face him, and when he made sure that Matt saw him he gave him a sound punch to the jaw.

Matt went down, clutching his chin, eyes on fire, furious.

"Shoot the breed!" he roared.

Blade spun, the knife from his calf flying. He caught Jed in the hand before the man could begin to fire Jeeter's old Colt.

Petey was aiming the guard's rifle at him. Blade drew his own Colt, leveling it right at Petey's eyes.

Petey dropped the rifle.

Blade stepped over Matt, reaching a hand down to the woman. She accepted it, meeting his eyes, and leapt up from the table. Then she cried out a warning.

He swung around. Matt was up, reaching for his gun. Blade swung out with his fist again, determined he wasn't going to leave any dead men lying around for the law to find, not if he didn't have to.

He caught Matt, and saw that Jed was leaping across the bar, coming for him. He started to turn, then saw that the woman was both quick and opportunistic. She had grabbed the whiskey bottle and cracked it over Jed's head. Glass cracked, whiskey sprayed, and Jed went down. That left Petey, who was rocketing toward Blade again.

Petey was wild—all brawn, no brain. Blade stepped aside, let Petey shoot by, then brought both hands clubbing down upon his back.

Petey fell to the floor with a soft sigh.

Blade met her eyes again. Over Petey's prone body. She was studying him anew. Carefully, with no apology. And no blush now.

What was she seeing?

A half-breed still. Maybe she was glad that he was a half-breed, thinking his speed and skill must have come from the years he had spent killing and scalping the white men who had first come to tame this land.

Maybe she was even wondering if he spoke her language.

"Good going, young fellow!"

It was the stage driver, hurrying to him, reaching out to shake his hand. "I can tell you, son, the company will have a fine commendation for you!"

Blade shook his head. "No, no commendations. Thanks. I just think you should get on your way."

"There could be a reward!" the stage driver said. "A monetary reward! You can't just let—"

"No commendation!" Blade repeated, unaware that his voice was every bit as cold as hers had been earlier. "You need to get under way here, before another group like this shows up."

The driver seemed to have sized him up quickly

and was ready to obey. "Mrs. Dylan, he's right. Seems our best move now is to get going on, before more riffraff shows up." He spat on Matt's downed body and stepped over it.

But Mrs. Dylan didn't seem to be in any kind of hurry. Her green eyes were set on Blade. A rush of heat swept through him suddenly. She wasn't just the most beautiful woman he had ever seen, she was the most desirable. She brought tension and hunger to his loins, and a raw, savage pain to his heart.

He'd been alone for years now. He'd known whores and ladies in that time. This was different, because she was different, and he didn't want to feel this. He was suddenly furious. She had caused this, surely. With her cool voice, her emerald eyes and her lithe, so elegantly curved figure.

"Lady, you need to get going! You should be high-tailing your pretty rear right back East—"

"I'm not going back East!" she snapped coolly.

"Then you need to get going!"

"Will you excuse me just a moment, gentlemen," she said to the driver and the guard. "I'd like to speak to this man."

"Watch out for the ones on the floor, Mrs. Dylan!"

"I will," she promised.

The two left the bar. Jeeter was busy mopping up behind it. Blade surveyed the woman, his eyes narrowing as they swept over her.

"What?" he demanded.

"I'd like to employ you."

"What?"

She spoke quickly and earnestly. Her voice, as cool as it could be, was wonderful and melodic to him. "I might have been in serious trouble here if you hadn't come along. I realize that this is a dangerous and raw place. You seem to be at loose ends—perhaps in danger of having your face flattened yourself," she said, indicating the unconscious men at their feet. "I can pay you very well. Very well indeed."

"I'm not for hire."

"But I really need you—"

"You really need to go home!"

"I can pay you well."

He was startled when he suddenly grasped her arms, drawing her against him. "You can pay me well? Well enough? Well, let me tell you how I'd want to be paid. You. I'd want you, Mrs. Dylan, just the same way old Matt here wanted you."

She jerked away from him, her emerald eyes liquid as she stared at him. She should be sufficiently outraged, furious, he thought. And she'd walk away, thinking about her beautiful, marble flesh being mauled by a…half-breed.

"And what if I were willing to pay?" she whispered.

"What?"

"What if I were willing to pay?" she demanded defiantly.

"We're not talking about a one-shot deal here, lady!" he said roughly. "We're talking about whenever and wherever I choose. Think about it—I may not be worth my price!"

Her eyes, emerald ice, surveyed him once again. "It's damned sure you're not worth that price," she assured him. She started for the door at last. She swung around to face him. "You're good, but not that good!" she told him, that same ice in her eyes, the challenge more than he could resist.

"Oh, lady," he said softly, "you just don't know how good."

He felt the green fire of her eyes warming him, awakening him, and—damn her—exciting him.

No, he wouldn't fall for this kind of woman, not now. There was still a raw, gaping, bleeding hole inside of him where his heart should have been. There were things he had to do, and he could not—would not—get involved....

"Good day, sir!" Mrs. Dylan said, then turned and left as regally as she had come.

The dying sun touched her hair. And she seemed to leave in a blaze of fire, Blade thought, resisting the urge to smile.

Chapter Two

There were two reasons Blade determined to follow the stagecoach. He'd set the trash brothers—Matt, Jed and Petey—on their horses and promised them dire consequences if they were ever to meet up with him again, but there was still the possibility that the men would go after the stage, for revenge if nothing else. He'd had to get them out of the saloon, though, since he couldn't rightly leave them for old Jeeter.

But even if the outlaws didn't follow the stagecoach, it was heading right through a corner of Apache territory. Mescalero Apaches were a people fed up with the land already taken from them and determined to give little quarter to the white populace, which had often dealt mercilessly with them. If the whites called them savage, so much the better to the Mescaleros.

He stayed behind, though, at a good distance. And for the first few hours, he began to wonder what he was doing. The stagecoach was going to go through the wilderness just fine. The brothers from the inn wouldn't have been patient enough to follow prey this long. His only fear now was the Mescaleros, and so far, it seemed, they were being quiet. With the war over, forts were popping up all over the place, and all the trails were being heavily traveled by the military, sometimes hundreds of men in U.S. cavalry blue. Perhaps the Mescaleros were keeping their distance because of the increasing number of reinforcements. At any time now, the military bugle could be heard, calling fighting men into action.

He was being a fool. He should turn around and head back. One look at this woman was enough to know that she was pulling him along by nether parts of his body, and, in truth, he wanted no part of it.

Yet he kept riding.... At least, Blade justified, she was going in the same direction he wanted to go.

By nightfall, they would be coming up on Jackson Prairie, one of the small towns that had sprung up in the past ten years. It was thriving nicely enough. It had come under Indian attack once in that time, but a cavalry fort was only a twenty minute ride away, which had given the residents courage to hold their own. They had repelled the Indians before the bugler and the cavalry had arrived, tenaciously shooting their rifles from their bedroom windows. Jackson Prairie, it seemed, was new and wild and reckless, but here to stay. There were good wells, which tapped into a fine water supply, and against the dry dust bowl of much of the land around it, it was a welcome haven. Even before the war, the land around Jackson Prairie had begun going for fair prices. It was good, wide open space, perfect for cattle grazing.

Once the stagecoach reached Jackson Prairie, there

wouldn't be any need for him to follow. Jackson Prairie wouldn't be a bad place to spend the night, Blade thought. A little whiskey, a good bath at the boardinghouse and a game of cards. And women to be had for the asking.

Strange, but the thought suddenly didn't seem to do too much for Blade, unless the woman was a tall, slim, elegantly dressed Easterner....

Mrs. Dylan had already offered herself, more or less, he recalled. But somehow, with her, that just made him angry. It wasn't her vocation, and she hadn't suddenly been smitten with him.... So what would make her so determined to make it in the West that she would so quickly make such an offer to him?

The answer eluded Blade. And even as he sought it, he realized that he had ceased to pay attention to the stage, now just a speck on the horizon.

There were buttes surrounding the valley. And looking up, to his right and left, Blade could see horsemen on those buttes.

Apaches. Mescaleros. Five riders to the south, another three to the north. His only hope was that their weapons might be old and outdated, that what rifles they had weren't repeating ones. He spurred his horse, leaning now, pulling out his Colt. If he could reach the stage before the Indians could...

But he couldn't. The driver saw the threat coming and set his whip to his team. The stage began to race wildly, careening down the rutted trail through the wilderness. The guard was up on one knee from his position on the box, firing at the Indians, who were converging on the stage.

The Indians were nearly naked. Some were in leather leggings and vests, their bronze arms gleaming, ink black hair waving, bare flesh covered with paint. Some wore only breechclouts, and more of their muscled, gleaming flesh was apparent.

As Blade raced in behind the war party, one Apache fell from his horse, caught by a shot from the stage guard's rifle. Blade fired with his Colt, bringing down a lagging rider. Then, as he spurred his bay gelding to greater speed, he saw another rifle appear, from the window of the stage.

She was firing. The very elegant and beautiful Mrs. Dylan was firing from the stage window. She hit one of the Apaches in the shoulder and the man shrieked out in pain and fury, flying from his mount onto the dirt of the trail. Within seconds, Blade's fine bay was leaping over the fallen man.

He could hear the stage driver shouting to the horses. "Get up, get up!" The whip cracked in the air. The remaining five Apaches were closing in, Blade close on their heels. He aimed and fired again. Missed. Fired, and took one of the men from the rear.

He felt a bullet whiz by his ear and he ducked lower against the bay.

Suddenly, Blade heard a grinding sound. He was just taking aim again when he realized that the treach-

erous trail and reckless speed were causing the stagecoach to capsize. The vehicle was wavering, rock-
ing...crashing down hard upon its side. The horses,
jerked back in the fall, screamed and whinnied, trip-
ping over the harness and themselves. The driver flew
wide, the guard flew farther. The Apaches, four now,
ignored them, converging on the compartment.

On the woman.

No fire rang out from the compartment. Was she
dead? Blade wondered, and his heart seemed to slam
hard against his chest. Damn her, she should never
have been here!

Another bullet seemed to chip at the flesh on
Blade's cheek, it came so close. He instantly returned
the fire. An Apache made a clean fall into the dust.
His three companions hurried on, one wrenching at
the door to the passenger compartment, the other
pausing upon the downed structure to aim his rifle at
Blade.

Blade leapt from his horse, diving into the dirt just
in time to miss the shot. The Apache stalked, his knife
gleaming. The muscled warrior slammed against him
like a living wall of brick, and they tumbled in the
dirt. Blade found himself on his back, the Apache
straddled over him, hatred in his black eyes, cold fury
constricting his hard features. The Apache's knife
glittered right over his eyes, coming closer and closer.

Blade gripped the Apache's wrist, knowing that he
fought for his life, that the Mescalero would offer him

no mercy. Their eyes met. For aeons, it seemed, they were suspended in time and space, neither able to best the other. From the corner of Blade's eye, he could see that the other survivor of the attacking war party had wrenched open the door.

And found the woman. The one the driver had called Mrs. Dylan.

She was unconscious, and that was why she had stopped fighting. Unconscious, or dead.

Her hair had come free from the knot at her nape. It hung down from her lolling head like a waving sheet of pure golden fire. The Apache was about to take her with him.

And she would disappear forever....

He gritted his teeth, straining harder against his enemy. Black eyes met black eyes. Then, with a tremendous burst of energy, Blade shoved against the man, flipping him. Their positions were changed, but the Apache still held the knife, wickedly long, sharp silver, flashing in the afternoon sunlight. Blade stared at it, tightening his grip upon the Apache's wrist. The warrior suddenly cried out. The knife fell.

Blade used his fist then, hard against the Apache's chin. His enemy went limp. Blade leapt up, catching the last Indian just as he was about to mount his horse.

Mrs. Dylan came to just then. Immense emerald eyes opening to see the painted man carrying her away. She let out a wild shriek, her arms flying, nails raking. The Apache threw her down as she drew his blood, then the flat of his hand connected hard with her cheek. She cried out and started to rise again, true alarm blazing in her eyes.

But Blade caught the man's shoulder just then, swinging him around.

The Apache was good. He caught Blade in the jaw before Blade could duck. For a moment, Blade saw stars. Then he saw that the Apache meant to take the advantage, and he quickly countered with a fierce blow to the Apache's gut. The man started to double. Blade joined his fists together and brought them down on the Apache's nape. The Indian fell with a whish of air and a grunt. Blade rubbed his knuckle for a minute, looking at the fallen brave. Then he stared over to where she lay, arms pushing up against the dirt. Breathing hard, she stared at him.

What was she thinking? One bronzed savage for another? he wondered. She was the one who had propositioned *him.*

He reached out a hand to her. She accepted it, rising gracefully. "I told you to go home," he said.

Her chin was high. "And if you had accepted my offer, you could have been making some gain for what you just did for free."

"Go home."

"I'm trying to go home."

"Go back East."

"I have nothing back East."

"Well, what do you have here? You nearly had yourself a whole tribe of Mescalero Apaches! What good would that have done you?"

Her emerald eyes surveyed him with a level cool. "But it didn't happen. You came back."

"Yes, that's right. And you've already agreed that you might be a fitting payment for me, so maybe it wouldn't make much difference to you if a dozen or so Apaches were to demand their own payment."

Her hand lashed out to strike him. But he was quick, ready for anything she might do, and his fingers were winding around her wrist before she could touch his flesh. He wanted to shake her. Shake her until she understood what an idiot she was; she was a rose on a barren landscape, a delicate flower trying to root in stone.

He wanted her to know just what she was willing to offer. No, he wanted her, period. Right then and there, on the dust of the plain, hard and fast. He would show her how raw and wild the world could be. How savage. How damned cruel, and savage....

"Thank the Lord above us!" The dry cackle sounded before Blade could say or do a thing. It was the stage driver, picking his way over the shivering, frightened horses and harness to reach him and Mrs. Dylan. "It's you again. I'm telling you, young fellow, you deserve some kind of commendation! Gold, my man, gold! Something to set you up fine in the West. The investors in this company will surely be willing to pay something, I'm right damned sure of it—oh, pardon for the language, Mrs. Dylan, I do beg your pardon.''

"Oh, I imagine Mrs. Dylan can deal with a little rough language, old-timer,'' Blade said dryly. "She seems to deal well enough with just about everything else.''

Her emerald eyes were locked with Blade's black ones. She didn't say a word for the longest time, just stared at him. Then she turned to the driver. "Shorty, what will we do now? Can the stage be righted? What about the horses?''

"We'll have to get them up and see how they fared,'' Shorty said.

The guard, his broken rifle dangling uselessly from his hands, was standing by the lead horses. He threw his rifle aside with disgust and reached down, running his hands over the haunches of the first horse. "This fellow seems to be in one piece. We just need to get them up carefully. They're sure to be all bruised up and frightened. Can't let them panic again or they'll strangle us and themselves in the harness. You've done us fair and fine so far, sir,'' he said, tipping his hat to Blade, "if you wouldn't mind giving us a few more minutes of your time…''

Shorty snorted. "What about these fellows?'' He indicated the Apaches. "Some of them just might come to—madder than a hive of bees!''

"You deal with them, Shorty. Tie 'em up if'n you

don't want to shoot them. I need this young buck—''
The guard broke off, wincing at the term he had used
for Blade. Buck. Indian. Like the Apaches on the
ground.

Blade smiled, walking toward the guard and the
horses. "Sioux," he said briefly. "My mother is
Oglala. She's gone now, but I still miss the family. I
go back whenever I can. There's nothing like a good
scalping raid to get the juices flowing, you know?''

He stepped past the man, placed one hand on the
lead horse's nose and one on the harness. He whispered softly to the horse. "Easy...."

With a simple pull, the animal was up. The other
horses followed suit, one screaming with pain. Blade
walked around to the animal, running his hand over
the sweating flank.

"Broken," he told the guard. "You're going to
have to put this one down, and reharness the others.''

By that time, Shorty—with the elite Mrs. Dylan's
help—had tied up the Apaches. Blade was surprised
they hadn't just shot the Indians. The white men
seemed to find the Apaches and Comanches the most
savage of the Plains Indians—well, along with Pai-
utes, maybe, since they believed in human sacrifice,
with or without white men around. Many white people didn't think that they were shooting people, they
just acted as though they were putting down animals—just the way they were going to have to put
down the horse.

But Shorty didn't seem to be that kind. He was still grinning. Blade might have given the stage guard a turn with his talk about scalping parties, but he could see that Shorty knew it had just been talk. Shorty seemed to know that whether or not Blade was dressed like a white man, he had no intention of ever pretending to be anything but what he was—a half-breed, one damned proud of the breed part of the term. Blade admired his mother's people, loved his grandfather and loved their way of life—the hunting, the fishing, the warmth in the tepee in the cold of the night....

But he couldn't go back right now. He had lived in the white man's world with his father, and had seen too much. He had seen his father killed, along with the others. His Sioux grandfather would understand, as other men might not, that there were things he had to do. Or he could *never* go back.

"It's going to take some time to get this harness back in shape," Shorty said, scratching his head. He looked at Blade. "Think you could take Mrs. Dylan on in for us, sir?"

Blade smiled, lowering his head, conscious of the fact that Shorty was an all right old fellow. "I—"

"I don't mind waiting," Mrs. Dylan said flatly, chin high. She was oblivious to the trail dust on her cheeks and gown and unaware of the elegant mantle her hair created, streaming down her back. "There's a rock over there—"

"And every Indian in the territory might be out in two minutes, once they see the gleam of your hair," Blade warned her coolly. "They're enterprising fellows. Even if they're not interested themselves, they do a lot of trading with the Comancheros. White slavery. It's a booming business."

She gritted her teeth and flashed him a heated gaze. "I've come this far—"

"Mrs. Dylan, ma'am, it would be a fine favor to both Sam and myself if you would be so good as to ride on into town with this gentleman," Shorty said.

"This gentleman?" she inquired sweetly, staring at Blade.

Blade grinned, staring in turn. "Renegade, half-breed. Do them the favor, Mrs. Dylan. You're dangerous. You're going to get these nice old men killed."

She inhaled, blinking briefly, then she turned to Shorty. "I'll ride on in with—" she broke off, arching a brow at Blade. "With—?"

"McKenna, Mrs. Dylan," Blade chimed in. "My name is McKenna."

Her brow remained arched, as if she wasn't convinced he could really have a name like McKenna. "I'll ride in with Mr. McKenna," she told Shorty.

"We'll have your things in just as soon as can be, Mrs. Dylan," Shorty assured her. "Just go on into the Jackson Prairie boardinghouse. Mrs. Peabody will see to your needs. And we'll be there mighty soon, I swear it.''

"Thank you, gentlemen," she said. She turned to Blade. He strode over to his bay and waited for her to join him. She hesitated at the horse. He wondered if she wouldn't leap right up, but if she was going to do so, she was certainly taking her time. Without further ado, he set his hands on her waist and hiked her up on his bay.

It felt good to hold her so, Blade thought. Good to feel her beneath his touch. She was elegantly slim, but he could feel the curves of her hips and the heat that burned through her.... He leapt up behind her, arms encircling her as he took the reins.

Her back went very stiff against his chest. She could feel him, too. He was damned sure of it. She was so very much aware of him behind her, touching her.

"Is this a long ride, McKenna?" she demanded.

"You want it to be a short one, is that it, Mrs. Dylan?"

"Well, it seems that the sooner we are out of one another's company—"

"What happened to 'thank you'?"

"What?"

"What happened to 'thank you'?" Blade repeated. "I did just save your life. Or, at the very least, your freedom and virtue. The last doesn't seem to mean a great deal to you, but surely the first of those does!"

She twisted in the saddle. For a moment he saw the green fire in her eyes. She was itching to slap him. Hard. Gouge into his eyes, probably.

"Don't even think about it," he warned her softly, and leaned very close to her earlobe, breathing in the sweet scent of her, feeling again the miraculous warmth of her. "You want a fast ride, Mrs. Dylan? You've got one!"

And he spurred his bay.

The fine, faithful horse took off in a staggering leap, and the three of them began to race against the plain, against the dying day, for Jackson Prairie.

Chapter Three

Blade's horse barely slowed its gait as they came into Jackson Prairie, racing through the roads on the outskirts, slowing to a trot only when they reached the one big street that slashed through the town—Main Street by name. Most everything was right there. There was a bank—the First Savings and Loan of Jackson Prairie—and there were numerous shops, including Harvey's Barber and Mercantile Shop, and Mrs. Havover's Domestications. There was a dentist's shop, Dr. Weatherly Dayton, M.D., a tailor, a cooper, and more. There were two blacksmiths, and there was plenty of trade for both of them, and their shops were in either direction off Main Street, one being on South Street, and one being on North Street.

Mrs. Peabody's boardinghouse was dead center on Main Street, directly across from the Jackson Prairie Bar and Saloon. Blade reined in on Mallory, his big bay, right in front of the boardinghouse, slipping off the horse's back quickly and reaching up for Mrs. Dylan.

Her hair was exquisitely windblown, completely freed from its dignified knot, a wild mane of fire and gold all around her. Her eyes seemed brighter still against it, furious with the recklessness of his wild

ride, he imagined, and yet meeting his eyes with that
challenge that never faltered. He had his hands around
her waist so there was little she could do but set hers
upon his shoulders as he lifted her down. She was
close, so close, sliding against the length of his body.
His jaw locked and then his whole damned body
seemed to lock. And since she wasn't wearing more
than one thin petticoat, she must have felt the rock
hardness of his body, just as he felt each sweet curve
and nuance of hers. He suddenly wanted to throw her
from him—simply because he was so very loath to
let her go.

She opened her mouth as if she were about to say
something to him, but just then the door to the estab-
lishment, which was up two steps to the wooden sidewalk, suddenly opened, and they swung around
together.

Mrs. Peabody stood there, surely having heard
them ride up. She was a portly lady with very round
blue eyes and silver hair and a quick, easy smile.
"Good evening," she told them pleasantly, looking
them both up and down. "Why, it's Mr. McKenna,"
she murmured, smiling.

Blade didn't come into many towns, and he didn't
give his name out often. But if there was any place
he'd managed to feel that he belonged in the last few
harsh years, it had been here. It was the closest thing
he'd known to home—since his own had been burned
to the ground. There were few people he really liked,

fewer still he really trusted. Mrs. Peabody was one of the even fewer still that he liked *and* trusted.

"Evening, ma'am," he told her, then realized that he was still holding the golden-haired Mrs. Dylan by the waist.

And Mrs. Dylan was still holding him by the shoulders.

Her hands snatched suddenly free from him.

"Is this Mrs. McKenna, sir?" Mrs. Peabody asked. "Will there be one room needed for the night, or two?"

"Two!" Mrs. Dylan said swiftly, smoothing down her crumpled blouse, then the wild mane of her hair. She took two steps away from Blade, meeting Mrs. Peabody's kindly gaze. "I'm Jessica Dylan, Mrs. Peabody. I'll be staying a few days, if you've got room."

"Why of course, Miss Dylan—"

"Mrs. Dylan," Blade corrected politely. He decided to enlighten Mrs. Peabody. "There was some trouble with Mrs. Dylan's stage."

"Apaches!" Mrs. Peabody exclaimed, holding her heart.

"Yes, but it turned out all right."

"Mr. McKenna is very resourceful," Jessica Dylan said, and it sounded as though she were trying to speak while grating her teeth all the while.

"Mrs. Dylan isn't bad herself—with her fists or a rifle," Blade said pleasantly.

"Well, that's wonderful, young woman, just won-

derful!'' Mrs. Peabody applauded. ''You come right
on up here, Mrs. Dylan, and we'll get you squared
away. I'll put you in the blue room and have a tub of
hot water brought in right away so that you can bathe
off the prairie dust and tension!'' She came down the
steps and slipped a matronly arm around the younger
woman's shoulders, sniffing over her shoulder to
Blade as if he was somehow responsible for the things
that men did in general. He lowered his head, grinning, and followed as Mrs. Peabody led Jessica Dylan
up the steps and into the foyer.

They entered a narrow hallway with a set of stairs
that led to the second floor. The sitting room and dining room were to the left, both furnished with richly
upholstered chairs and handsome settees, with pretty
lamps and frill work. The men's rooms were to the
right, including a library with leather armchairs and
sofas and brass spittoons. Blade had spent many an
evening in the library. Tapestried carpets covered the
polished wooden floors, and the curtains were just
right for all the windows in each room—the ladies'
rooms having frilly adornments, the men's rooms
having draperies of a plainer style.

They didn't pause downstairs, but hurried up the
long stairway, Mrs. Peabody calling out as they did
so. ''Jane! Jane, get the boys moving if you will. We
need the tub and lots of water up here! Quickly
now!''

''Yes, Mrs. Peabody!'' the maid called from below.

Then the maid was yelling to someone else to get a move on.

There was a small landing at the top of the stairs, then there were hallways stretching out in both directions. Blade followed the women until they stopped before a door. Mrs. Peabody pressed it open, a firm hand on Mrs. Dylan's back pushing her on through.

She turned her stout body about like a barrier, facing Blade. "You'll have the green room, right next door, Mr. McKenna. And you just go on down and help yourself to a brandy in the library and relax a spell. I know you'll be wanting a bath before dinner, but you'll just have to wait a bit. I've got more tubs, but I haven't got more help to fill them up. If you don't mind now, the lady goes first!"

Blade smiled. "Why, that's just fine, Mrs. Peabody. I don't mind waiting in the least. And the green room is here, next door, right?"

"Right as rain."

The door closed on Blade. He grinned, then stepped out of the way as he saw two of Mrs. Peabody's boys, one a black lad of about sixteen, his blond-haired companion a year or so younger, both strong and with clean-scrubbed faces that attested to Mrs. Peabody's insistence on cleanliness in her house.

Someone had told him once over at the saloon—some old geezer who looked as if he might have been allergic to water, both drinking it and bathing in it—that Mrs. Peabody was so insistent on danged blasted bathing that she had one tub for lady guests, one for gentlemen, and one for her hired help, and that all three had to be replaced just about once a year.

Blade nodded to the boys with their heavy load, then hurried down the stairs and outside. He slipped his saddlebags from his bay's shoulders and walked the horse around to the stables where a slim Chinese lad was brushing down one of Mrs. Peabody's carriage horses. He left Mallory with the boy and went into the house, leaving his saddlebags with his clean clothing, shaving equipment and all on the hardwood dresser with the wavery mirror in the green room, so called, of course, as it had been painted green.

He noted that there was a door against the wall near the dresser. One that must lead into the blue room.

Mrs. Peabody was an interesting lady, he mused.

And then he wondered if he was glad or dismayed about the door. Irritated, he told himself that the damned thing didn't matter either way. He'd stay tonight, and he'd spend his evening at the saloon. Maybe he'd even spend a few hours with one of the perfumed ladies there.

No. One of the whores, not ladies. It was the "lady" part he didn't like about Jessica Dylan. That and more—much, much more. The way she fascinated him. The way she was just so damned beautiful and beguiling. The way she made him forget too damned much.

He left his room, hurrying down the stairs again,

to pour a brandy and sit back in one of the handsome leather chairs in the library. He closed his eyes, savoring the fine brandy as it rolled over his tongue then burned slowly down his throat.

The whiskey over at the saloon wasn't nearly as fine as Mrs. Peabody's. But nothing about the saloon was as fine as anything at Mrs. Peabody's—even though Mrs. Peabody and Henry Larkin, the saloon's owner, were very good friends. Blade had a feeling that although the two of them were running very different establishments, they both had similar, shrewd heads for business. The saloon offered everything that Mrs. Peabody's didn't, and vice versa. Mrs. Peabody's was elegant and refined—the saloon was far from it. But then, there were some damned good poker games to join over at the saloon, while there sure as hell—heck—were no poker games to join at Mrs. Peabody's.

Both Henry Larkin and Mrs. Peabody were making very good money. Stagecoaches were a miserable way to ride west. They were small, cramped and crowded. Most stops were poor indeed, with mudchink guesthouses in which the mud sometimes fell on guests as they slept at night, especially during the dry season. There were other miserable places, establishments run by men who wiped the dinner plates clean instead of washing them for the next set of travelers. In such a world, both the saloon and Mrs. Peabody's place were just a small step from heaven.

He sipped more brandy and leaned his head back. He'd seen a hell of a lot of the West in the last few years.

Ever since the war had ended. Looking. Always looking. Because he couldn't stop now, not until he found the men who had destroyed everything and everyone he had ever loved.

Not until they were avenged.

He leaned back in his chair relishing the warm burn of the brandy in his throat. He closed his eyes. Sometimes, because of the memories, he hated to do so. Sometimes, he would see a spring day, with a few white clouds drifting across the sky. Then he would see Mara waving from the well, and his father standing on the porch, smiling at him and Mara, so damned proud that he was about to become a grandfather. Then Mara would be running toward him. He would wave at her to stop, because she shouldn't be running then, it was too close to her time.

Then...

The men. Three of them would be on their horses, clad in red leggings. They would be coming out of Kansas, onto the Missouri side. Coming because John McKenna had damned John Brown for being a heinous murderer and not God's instrument against the inhumanities of man....

He could hear it still. Dear God, he could hear it still. The first blast of the shotgun. He could see it all, again and again, as if the world had slowed, as if he watched it all take place again in the black recesses of his mind and heart.

He could see the first bullet hit his father right in the chest. He could see the handsome old man fly back, snapped against the logs of the farmhouse. He could see the crimson stain spill across his white cotton shirt.... He could hear his own scream. His cry, his warning, and he knew exactly where he was—again.

He had started to run, and felt the agony in his chest, burning his lungs. He never had a chance of reaching Mara. There had been another burst of fire. God, he could hear it explode, too. Then he could see Mara, flying backward, falling, falling to the ground.

And she, too, had been stained in crimson, a massive hole in her chest, and he had been running and screaming. He had seen men—had seen their faces. He had thrown himself upon the first of them, the blue-eyed one, still mounted, and had dragged him down, his bare fingers around his throat, throttling him.

Then there had been the pain. Blinding, searing, like a flash of fire and light before him. Then there had been darkness. Blackness, a terrible void.

Blade didn't want to awaken from it, he didn't want to survive. He was afraid to awaken, he wanted it to be a dream, never the truth, dear God, he didn't want to awaken....

"Mr. McKenna!"

Startled, he jerked his head up. He'd dozed. Resting there on the fine leather chair in Mrs. Peabody's library, he'd done what he hadn't done for a long, long time.

He'd let down his guard.

It was her fault. The woman's. Jessica Dylan's.

But it was Mrs. Peabody standing in the doorway, smiling benignly. "I didn't need to waken you, Mr. McKenna—"

"Blade, Mrs. Peabody. We've been friends some time now."

"Well, then, that's fine, Blade, but you'll have to remember that my Christian name is Rose."

He smiled. "That's fine, Rose."

"I wouldn't have interrupted you—you were really resting so nicely—except that I know how you love a good steaming bath when you come off the trail. It's all ready for you upstairs. I've gotten that nice Mrs. Dylan all taken care of, and now it's your turn! I'll be seeing to my dinner now. I haven't had a guest in a day or two, and now you and Mrs. Dylan in one night. I'm anxious to whip up a fine meal for you both. It's so nice to have the company." She cleared her throat delicately. "I know how you like a game of poker, too, *Blade,* but I do hope you'll be having dinner here before adjourning over to Henry Larkin's place."

He stood, setting down his brandy glass. "Rose, your meals are always the finest in town, and you know that quite well. Of course I'll be having dinner with you."

"And Mrs. Dylan."

"And Mrs. Dylan. And then I will be spending the remainder of the evening over at the saloon."

"Fine," Rose said, her chubby little hands folded before her, her lips set in a sweet smile. "Get on to your bath now, before the water cools."

She left to walk toward the kitchen, which was a separate building reached via an enclosed walkway, because she wasn't about to have her nicely furnished house burned down by a cooking fire. Blade hurried up the stairs.

He paused outside Jessica Dylan's room. He couldn't hear anything. Shorty hadn't come in with the stagecoach yet, and Blade found himself just standing there, wondering what she was wearing after her bath.

He swore at himself and moved on.

The tub in his room was wonderfully inviting, steam rising in great swaths from it. He stripped down quickly, careless of where he cast his boots and pants, shirt and jacket. He started to sink into the water, wincing when the burning heat first touched his flesh, then slowly sinking all the way in. There was a holder with soap and a cloth, and he picked up both, scrubbing his face first, then his arms, then the rest of his body. He ducked his head beneath the water and scrubbed his black hair. Finally, he sat back, rinsed the cloth, and set it over his face. It felt so damned good just to lie there. He could doze easily again.

Damn! He didn't want to doze again, didn't want to dream, didn't want to remember.

He froze suddenly, curling his fingers around the tub, aware of motion and movement in the room. There was a clicking sound.

Her.

She had come through the connecting door. He could follow her movements exactly. He had been living too long in a state of constant awareness— chasing and on the run—not to have his senses keenly attuned to sound and movement.

And smell. Mmm, he could smell her. The clean, fresh scent of her porcelain flesh....

She was standing above him. Hesitating.

He ripped the cloth from his face, staring at her heatedly in return.

"Yes?" he demanded icily.

She stared and jumped back, but then stood her ground.

Her hair was free, all about her shoulders, just washed and fire dried and radiantly beautiful. He ached to reach out and touch it. Gold and copper. It glittered, it beckoned, it beguiled. No more so than her perfect face, her emerald eyes. Her...person.

He no longer had to wonder what she was wearing. Mrs. Peabody had provided her with a dressing gown. It was far too short, and he could plainly see her long, slim bare feet and her slender ankles, hinting of very shapely, long legs. The gown was a pink frilly thing, with a V bodice that didn't quite close well at her throat and breast, being far too large for her. Her flesh was beautiful. Her throat, long and extremely elegant. The hint of the rise of her breasts…

His fingers clenched very tightly around the rim of the wooden tub and he barked at her, "What?"

"Don't scream at me," she said.

"Don't sneak in on me. You do that at the wrong time, and you'll find yourself getting shot."

"I wasn't sneaking—"

"You don't even come in on a man quietly in the West, Mrs. Dylan. You will get shot."

"Only an outlaw would be so wary—"

"And I never did tell you that I wasn't an outlaw, did I now, Mrs. Dylan? I just might be one. The worst kind of an outlaw."

Her chin lifted. "There's only one thing I do know about you, Mr. McKenna," she said flatly.

He arched a brow.

"You are one hell of a rude bastard!"

He grinned, sliding deeper into the water, eyeing her warily. "What?" he said again.

"Dammit, I need you to work for me," she said, aggravated.

"I'm busy. You need to go home."

"Who the hell do you think you are to decide who can and who can't make it in your precious West, Mr.

McKenna?'' she demanded coolly. "I'm not going back East. I've told you. I am home. I have land near here. My husband bought it when he was stationed at the fort. Before—he died. It's mine now. It was important to him, and I'm staying.''

"You might find yourself dead within a week," Blade said coldly. He needed her out of here. He was staring at her pale throat, at the fascinating rise of her breasts, at the way one of the pink frills rose and fell with her every breath. He could feel the heat of her stare on him, warming him, entering him. His flesh was afire, so much hotter than the water.

"Not if I have you—" she began.

He stood, heedless of whether he shocked her or not with the bronze length of his body.

She was, after all, in his room.

"I'm not for hire, Mrs. Dylan. I've got my own way to go, and I need to keep moving.''

"Maybe I'm moving the same way.''

She was trying to keep her eyes level with his. They slipped now and then. Maybe she was heading the same way. He'd heard he might find just who he was looking for at the fort. They were damned near it now.

The beautiful white marble of her throat and face was swiftly turning crimson. He realized he was naked, returning her stare.

"I'm not going away, and I need help, and I can pay you very well—" she began, then broke off.

He had stepped out of the tub. Wet and bronzed from head to toe, he was suddenly against her, heedless of soaking Mrs. Peabody's dressing gown, sweeping her hard against him, into his arms. He couldn't resist. He couldn't resist the urge to touch her, the anguish to hold her. He had to feel her flesh, had to know if it was really as soft as silk, as perfect as it appeared. He had to grind his lips down upon hers, to taste them, to find out if they were as sweet as the promise they seemed to give....

Her heart thundered against his. He formed his mouth to hers, forcing her lips to part. He ravaged her mouth, hungrily kissing her, tasting her.... Oh, God, the taste of her was sweet. Mint and lilac. Her lips were perfect, unwilling, ungiving, and suddenly parting to the onslaught of his as her fingers dug into the muscles of his arms.

Surely she felt him. All of him. The fire and the hardness, the burning and hungry demand. He lifted his lips from hers, afraid of what he'd do if he couldn't get her away. His fingers bit into her upper arms. His eyes blazed hotly into hers.

"I think I've told you my price," he said hoarsely.

She was shaking, her emerald eyes blazing. "If I have to—" she began miserably.

"Oh, you'd have to. And I'd have to have a hell of a lot more than you've just given to find out whether or not you're good enough to meet the price."

Her flushed skin went white. Her hand was about to fly, her fingers just itching to get to his face once again.

"No, Mrs. Dylan, not on your life!" Blade yelled, and swept her up into his arms. She gasped startledly, her arms around him to keep from falling.

He strode across the room, swinging open the adjoining door with his bare foot. He set her down on her bed. "Go home!" he roared. And he slammed the door between them.

He heard a cry. A very soft, quickly stifled cry of pain and dismay. He grated down hard on his teeth, swearing silently. Why did it seem to tear at him that he had hurt her, that he had been so brutal? It was better than what he might have done.... So much better than just taking her. Having her then and there. Sating the hunger, the longing, the anguish....

He swore and turned to his bath. Henry Larkin's Jackson Prairie Bar and Saloon was just across the way. And he was going there just as damned fast as he could.

Chapter Four

There was one thing definite about Jessica Dylan—the woman was tenacious.

It was amazing. Blade had murmured an excuse to Mrs. Peabody after all, and had taken his meal over at the saloon. Soon after, he had found himself in the midst of a pretty good poker game, the stakes rising swiftly, the play running smooth and fast. Roxy Niemes, one of Larkin's girls, resplendent in a short black and crimson affair that left more of her legs bared than covered, was perched right behind him, keeping his whiskey glass filled and occasionally draping long painted fingernails idly upon his shoulders. She was discreet, quietly watching the play, patiently waiting.

He was doing well. Damned well. He already had taken a fair amount of gold from the men at the table, one of them a middle-aged, sandy-haired cattle herder, one a young blond miner and one a tall, dark and lean Easterner in a fancy dress frock with an extravagant red cravat.

A hand of five-card stud had just been dealt. One down, three up, the last down. The miner had two kings showing. Blade had a pair of tens. There was a third beneath his hand. The miner threw in his bet, waiting for Blade to call him or raise him.

And that was when he saw her.

She walked into the saloon with supreme confidence—and arrogance, he determined. Her hair was neatly knotted again at her nape with very soft tendrils escaping to frame her elegant face. She was dressed in a beautiful gown in shades of blue, with rows of black and white lace at the sleeves and hem and bodice, which dipped low upon her breast. She paused just inside the doorway, her emerald eyes sweeping the many tables where men sat about gambling or propositioning the girls or just swilling down their whiskey. She stared at the long bar, the stunned, mustachioed barkeep, the stairway that led to the rooms above, and then to him. He had forgotten to throw his coin down. The miner cleared his throat, and Blade dropped his gold.

Her emerald eyes blazed into his.

She turned to the barkeep. "A whiskey, please."

The bartender coughed softly. "Ma'am, I don't rightly know if you've seen what kind of place this is—"

"Are you refusing to serve me, sir?"

"Why, no, of course not, ma'am. A, er, whiskey, coming right up."

It was Blade's deal. He was moving the cards through his fingers too slowly. It didn't matter, though. The rest of the players had seen Mrs. Jessica Dylan, and they had forgotten the game.

They all stared at her, gaping. Then they regained

their manners and closed their mouths. The Easterner stood first, tipping his hat to her. The cattle herder leapt up next, and then the miner close behind.

Blade gritted his teeth, black eyes locked with hers, and stood. Roxy made some small noise behind him. If Jessica Dylan gave any notice to Roxy at all, she gave no sign.

"Gentlemen," she murmured softly.

"Ma'am!" It came in a chorus from the lot of them, only Blade remaining silent.

"May I join you?"

The cattle herder cleared his throat softly. "Why, ma'am, we aren't playing parlor cards."

"It can be a rough game," the miner added.

She smiled very sweetly. "Nevertheless, gentlemen, I'd love to join you. It is an honest game, I believe."

"Dead honest," Blade promised her. He had sat down at last, and stared into her emerald eyes once more. What was her game?

"Then, if you all don't mind..."

The miner hurried to the next table to draw a chair for her. The cattle herder cleared room for her whiskey. She sat and looked at the table. "Someone has called someone, so it seems."

Blade flipped over his cards, showing three tens. The pot was his. The deal passed to his left.

To Mrs. Dylan.

She picked up the cards and shuffled them like a

professional cardsharp. They flew around the table. "Let's make it five-card draw, gentlemen. Jacks or better to open. Dollar ante." She was swift, and she was all business.

The men at the table were suddenly moving very fast.

Roxy made another of her *tsking* sounds in the background. "Need another, hon?" she whispered huskily to Blade, pointing at his glass.

Another? He needed the whole damned bottle. He nodded. Roxy filled his glass. He gulped down the amber liquid, staring at Jessica Dylan. "How many cards, Mr. McKenna?"

He slid one across the table. "One."

Luck was with Blade. One card completed his straight. She had bet against him and lost.

The next hand, the miner's deal, Mrs. Dylan took with a full house.

The game progressed. Mrs. Dylan proved that she was a good player, never showing her cards when she didn't have to, seeming to know when to fold, when to hold, when to cut her losses, and how to win.

The cattle herder fell out first, the well-dressed man next, then the miner. That left only Blade and Mrs. Dylan.

The hour had grown incredibly late. Even Roxy sighed in a pique and joined the few remaining men in the room at the bar. It didn't matter. Blade hadn't even managed to look at Roxy in hours. He'd barely heard her voice. She had paled away, faded like an old photograph.

Perhaps that would happen to any other woman with Jessica Dylan in the room.

Blade kept his black-eyed stare hard on her.

She kept her emerald gaze equally strongly upon him. She was playing way more than a card game here, and he knew it. She had tried to do a lot of gambling with him already. What was she after with this? Trying to make him lose all his money so that he would be forced to enter her employ? He didn't know. He was suddenly determined to win the game.

She was capable of a good bluff, he had seen that already. He began to call her bluff, time and time again. At first, between the two of them, the wins and losses still seemed about even. But then he managed to get her to keep up with his raises on a pat hand— three aces, two kings. She couldn't beat it, and she didn't. Next hand he was amazed to see his cards fall in every bit as nicely. Draw poker. He held two queens. She opened. And then she dealt him another queen and two aces, and asked for three cards.

"You opened," he reminded her.

"So I did." She shoved her coins on the table. "Fifty dollars."

"A hundred."

"I see your hundred. I raise you a hundred."

"I see your hundred—and I'll raise you two."

She started to push in the coins, then bit her lower lip in irritation. She seemed to be a few short.

"I can write you a promissory note—"

He shook his head. "Whatever we're gambling for needs to be on the table. Right now."

She looked at her cards. They must have been good. As good as his? He didn't know.

But he was a gambler. Was she? he wondered.

"I have my earrings," she said, reaching for them. But her ears were bare. "Oh!" she murmured, lashes sweeping downward. "I left them right across the street in my room. If you'll just—"

"No."

"What kind of a gentleman are you?" she demanded irritably. "I can make good on any of my bets! If you'll—"

"No," he said flatly, leaning forward. "All bets on the table. Here and now."

She stiffened. "And just what is it you want on the table?" she inquired coolly.

He shrugged. "I'll take—you."

Her eyes flashed with anger. "I've offered you myself before, if you recall."

He shook his head again. "Not for any business deal, Mrs. Dylan. Just for the night."

Her eyes burned. Her fingers were itching again, he knew. She'd love to slap him. She'd really love to whack him across the face. She was so determined, and so desperate, it seemed, at times.

"And what do I get in return?" she asked.

"Might I remind you, my money is all on the table."

"It's not enough," she insisted.

He lifted his hands, palms up. "You can fold," he reminded her politely.

Her teeth gnashed together. "I want more!" she insisted.

She was a fighter, he thought, and he was startled by the sudden emotion he felt for her. She didn't quit.

And she hated like hell to lose.

He leaned forward. "All right, let's lay it all on the table. If I win, I get you for the night. No strings attached. If you win, you get me. In your employ. For free. For, let's say...maybe a month. How's that?"

She was breathing very hard, he could see. Her breasts were rising and falling swiftly.

"Is it a deal?"

"Deal," she said very softly. He started to turn his cards. Her fingers fell over the back of his hand. "How do I know you won't renege?"

"You'll have to trust me."

But she stopped him again. "How do you know I won't renege?"

He smiled. "Because I won't let you," he assured her confidently. "I collect on all debts owed me."

His black eyes met her emerald ones. And once again, he began to turn his cards. He started with an ace, another ace, a queen.

"Two pairs!" she exclaimed, her triumph sliding into her voice. She laid down her hand.

It was a good hand. Three jacks, two kings. A damned good hand.

But not good enough.

She started to reach for the pile of coins on the table. He cleared his throat loudly. "Ahem, Mrs. Dylan."

She stopped, freezing with her palms around the coins, staring at him.

He laid out his last two cards. "I've a full house, too, Mrs. Dylan. And mine is queens high."

"Oh!" The sound escaped her. And once again, those elegant, blazing green eyes were on him. His fingers fell upon hers, curling hard when she would have wrenched her hand away. "You're mine, Mrs. Dylan—for the night. And thank the good lord! The night is still young!"

He let her snatch her hand free. She started to rise.

"Reneging, Mrs. Dylan? Don't forget, I collect on all debts owed me."

"No! I'm not reneging!" she snapped back. "I pay all my debts," she assured him. And her voice was suddenly husky, he thought. Feminine. Vulnerable. Enticing him to a new hunger. "Just not here!" she whispered. Her eyes were on his. Unblinking. "I'll be waiting to pay. The—the doors connect," she reminded him.

Then she turned. And, head held high, she fled gracefully from the Jackson Prairie Bar and Saloon.

Chapter Five

Mrs. Peabody's was very quiet when Blade returned. He heard a clock strike. It was one a.m.

He came into his room and leaned against the door. Inhaling, exhaling. What did he think he was doing? Taunting her, trying to torture her into going home? Why the hell did he care what happened to her?

He gritted his teeth. He did care. Maybe it was the first time he'd cared in a long time, and maybe it was damned hard to have to feel again instead of move on, seeking nothing but a vengeance that had now turned ice cold, but all the more determined. Why her?

There were no answers. Hell, maybe there were, he thought again. All he had to do was look at her, watch her, hear her voice. He'd cared when he'd followed her to begin with. He'd cared because he hadn't wanted to see blood running against her marble flesh, because he hadn't wanted to hear her scream.... Because once he had seen her, he hadn't wanted to imagine another man touching her, hurting her, having her.

He pushed away from the door. He wasn't going to demand anything from her. The poker game had been his bluff. She needed to go home, whether she saw it or not. It was his last chance to convince her. He could never really touch her. She would be like a taste of honey, sweet, beguiling. She would make him hungry, again and again.

The door between the rooms was closed. He stared at it for a long moment, then angrily crossed to it. He threw it open, certain that he'd find her still defiant— or gone.

But she was not gone.

She was there. She stood before the window with the curtains in her fingers, drawn back slightly. Her lower lip was caught between her teeth. She was in a silky gown of soft, sheer blue. It molded over her breasts, fluttering against the length of her. Her flesh was just visible beneath the sheer fabric. She had stood there, watching the road, waiting for him. Miserably, from the look in her eyes and the way she chewed on her lip. But determinedly. He had told her that he collected on debts.

She had told him that she paid them.

She spun around, staring at him, her fingers falling uneasily over the fabric of her very sheer gown as if she just realized how translucent the gown was, how very much she had given away.... And longed to cover once again.

He closed the door between the rooms, narrowing the space between them. He leaned against it, crossed his arms over his chest and stared at her, eyeing her slowly, from the tip of her golden head to her bare toes. He tried to still the thunder that suddenly began to beat within him.

"Go home," he told her softly. "Go home."

"I cannot go home," she insisted.

"Go home, and we'll call off this stupid wager."

There was moisture in her eyes. It made them dazzle like gems against a night sky. She seemed very vulnerable then, and he didn't want her hurt. He'd put her on some kind of damned pedestal, and he'd be happy if she'd just go home. East. Where the world wasn't great, he thought, but where the dangers weren't quite so many, quite so fierce, quite so constant, either. Away from warring Comanches, Apaches, Comancheros. Away from bitter halfbreeds, longing for a touch of paradise against the anguish and emptiness....

"Do whatever you want," she told him. "I cannot go home."

With an impatient sound he was across the room. He gripped her soft smooth arms tightly in his hands, shaking her hard. "Don't you understand what you're going to find here? I'm not invincible! I'm flesh and blood. Even if I stayed with you, I'd probably die with a bullet or an arrow in my heart."

Her chin was high, her head back. She hadn't made a sound, not a single protest against the rough way he held her. "You told me you were good," she reminded him. "So damned good."

"But I can still die—and leave you alone, don't

you see? And if you think I can be a bastard, lady, you haven't seen anything yet.''

''I have to stay!''

''Can you really pay the price to do it?'' he lashed out.

''Yes.''

No, damn her! She didn't know what she was saying, what she was offering.

''All right,'' he whispered fiercely. ''All right, have it all your way. And pay up, lady, pay up!''

His fingers moved over the soft, sheer fabric that so barely covered the beauty of her body. With a narrowly controlled burst of violence, he grabbed the fabric, ripping it from throat to floor with a soft hissing sound that seemed as loud as a gunshot in the night. She gasped, her fingers reaching for the split sides.

''No,'' he warned her, shaking his head. ''You want to pay your debts, time to pay them. You want to take chances with savages, well, Mrs. Dylan, fine. Start with me.''

He still never meant to hurt her.... Never meant to touch her.... Not just for her, for himself. Because he dared not take that first sip of honey....

But at the moment, none of it mattered. His hands were upon her, he was drawing her to him, sliding away the last of the silky blue fabric, finding her naked flesh. It was smoother than any touch of silk. Jesus. He crushed her against him, feeling the rise of her breasts, stroking his palms and fingertips down her back, seizing her lips with his own. He felt her trembling beneath him. Her hands fell upon his chest....

Her lips parted beneath his. Sweet. A taste of honey, he thought. He plundered her mouth deeply, ravished it. She clung to him, accepting the onslaught, her heart thundering as his lips came from hers at last, touched upon her throat, her shoulder, down to her naked breast. She was beautiful, perfect, her breasts hard and firm, the nipples an exquisite rose shade, puckered now, and hardening against the harsh lave of his tongue. Her breath caught. Another gasp escaped her. Her fingers curled into his dark hair, into his shoulders. She stood trembling still, damn her, not fighting him yet. He pushed himself against her, touching her flesh, savoring it with his fingertips, with his lips, with his tongue.

His heart hammered. His loins ached, his desire soared, and the hunger, the thunder, the beat within him was unbearable. Fight me, damn you! he longed to cry to her.

But she just stood, trembling, her fingertips on him seemed so erotic, her scent filling him, her incredible ivory-skinned body an aphrodisiac that threatened to engulf him. He saw the darkness of his hands against the pale cream of her body. Fight me, he thought again. Dammit, make me stop this before I find myself damned....

But she didn't fight him. And from that point, it didn't matter. He bent down until his face lay against the warm silk of her belly, his lips touched and tasted, and his hands curled around her buttocks. Then he was rising, sweeping her into his arms and striding across the room. He laid her on the bed, the blue bed, with its clean sheets and soft plump comforter and feather pillows. Her hair spread across the sheets like gold against a blue sky, pure fire and elegant softness. Her eyes had fallen, but they didn't meet his. Still, she didn't move, and the beat of her heart seemed to thunder within her chest, her frantic pulse visible at her throat.

The length of her stretched before him. She didn't reach for the covers, didn't turn, just lay there as his eyes raked over her, her elegantly slim throat, the fine bones of her shoulders and collarbones, her breasts, firm and erect, the slimness of her waist, the curve of her hip, the long, shapely length of her legs, the soft, blazing gold enticement between them....

His boots hit the floor first. His shirt and pants quickly followed. She heard him strip, heard his clothing hit the floor, and still her eyes didn't open. But she knew what she was getting. She had seen him before.

Naked, he came down beside her. He felt the heat of her body with the length of his own. Desire erupted, hard and searing within him. Longing, aching. He straddled her, found her lips, and kissed her with a strength that was far more hunger than force. He found her tongue and filled her mouth. Dropping his head lower, Blade caressed and tasted her breasts once more, stroking her belly with the flat of his palm, threading his fingers into the down of her triangle, lower, touching her, stroking her...

A sound emitted from her. She moved, just shifting, gasps catching in her throat, her body trembling against his touch. She seemed exquisite. He eased himself down the length of her, forcing her thighs apart with the weight of his body. He touched her with the wet heat of his tongue, stroked, delved.

Another sound escaped her, one that caused her to twist violently, burying her face in the pillow lest her cry be heard. She trembled wildly as he held her, stroked her, caressed her.

He rose above her, cooling the fire that swept through him with a soaring need. Her eyes remained closed. She trembled wildly, but when he took her lips they parted swiftly at his touch, answering the hunger within them. He stroked down the length of her body with his thumb, parting her. Then he entered her, taking her with a hard, swift movement.

She uttered a cry that she could not swallow quickly enough, a ragged sound of pain. And, of course, he knew why, even as it was too late to possibly erase it, for he had already torn through the barriers of her innocence. He went dead still, cursing himself, cursing the hunger and drive and anguish that still pulsed through him.

The one cry was all that had left her. She lay silent, unmoving. She was pale, and her eyes were closed. He remained impaled within her. Words, harshly spoken, tore from his lips.

"Open your eyes!"

She did so, their emerald depths glittering, defiant.

"You can't be any Mrs. Dylan."

"I am Mrs. Dylan," she whispered. There was a film of wetness on her eyes. Tears. She wasn't going to let them fall. "I swear to you, I am a Mrs."

"Mr. Dylan was an abstainer?" he asked mockingly. He was still furious with her, furious for what she had allowed him to do, furious with himself for having done it. Furious for wanting her so desperately even now....

"Mr. Dylan died," she said flatly.

"Damn you, Jessica!" he swore at her suddenly. "We could have stopped this at any time. Now the damage is done—"

"There is no damage!" she cried. "I did what I chose—"

"Because you will not go home where you should be?" he asked.

"I—"

"Have it your way, Mrs. Dylan!"

Indeed, the damage was done, and he was as explosive as gunpowder, fevered, in agony. He cupped her chin in his hand and found her lips once again. He kissed her hard, deeply—near savagely—and began to move inside her. What cry she might have emitted was swallowed by his lips. His hands roamed freely over her body, cupping her buttocks, holding her, guiding her, stroking her soft flesh. Her hands fell upon his flesh, nails biting into his shoulders. Her lips soothed his wounds. She seemed to sheathe him with warmth and wetness, her body a sweet glove, her warmth a golden fire. His hunger built, the speed of his thrusts multiplied. No matter that he had tried to take care, and perhaps it mattered no longer. Her gasped breaths were escaping sweetly by his ear, coming faster and faster. She moved beneath him, body held too tightly to his by the force of his hand upon her buttocks, yet melding so sensually to his, naturally finding his rhythm, his hunger. He whispered to her, assured her, led her, lifted her. The fire exploded inside of him and he knifed even more deeply into her, shaking with the force of the climax that had seized him. He eased himself again and again into her and from her, watching her face, but her eyes were closed again. Before he would move from her, take himself from her, he needed to *see* her.

"Look at me."

She did so. Eyes still liquid. Her face still pale. Her lips trembling just slightly.

"Damn you, I never meant to hurt you—"

"You didn't hurt me. Well," she murmured, her eyes falling, "perhaps—a little. But—"

He groaned, falling to her side at last. She was struggling for the covers. He kept the weight of his body hard upon them.

It was too late for her to cover up now. Too late, because he was so damned aggravated, so furious. And more.

He was entrapped. Just as if she had cast some gold-and-fire net around him, a fragile web that, nonetheless, held him powerless. He couldn't leave her.

Blade had touched her, had her, held her. He wanted her again and again. He wanted to teach her that there could be so much more. He wanted to feel the movement, the heat of her kiss upon him, the liquid movement of her limbs. He wanted to know her—what went on in her mind, what gave her reckless courage and raw determination....

"It was my choice!" Jessica said angrily. He could hear the pain in her words, and he winced.

He came up on an elbow, staring at her. "I wouldn't have been in here if I had known!" he nearly roared.

"Shh!" she whispered as wild alarm filled her eyes.

He gritted his teeth. "So you don't mind sleeping with a half-breed, you just don't want the world knowing about it?"

She inhaled sharply between her teeth. Then, she

tried to leap away. He dragged her back, the weight of his body pinning her to the bed when she struggled.

"Damn you—" Blade said again. He could feel her lie still, rigidly still, her emerald eyes staring into his, her face so very beautiful, so very proud.

"How dare you!" she said angrily. "Don't blame me for whatever chips you carry on your shoulders!"

He started. He had never really known that he carried a chip on his shoulder. He'd spent his life being proud of being Sioux. But his father had been a fine man, too, a good man, a strong one, a fair one. And he'd lived in his white father's world for a long time. He'd learned that there were many men and women who considered any Indian a savage, a different breed, untamed, uncivilized. And so he'd spent most of his life making damned sure that everything he did, he did the best it could be done.

Once, his fastidiousness had made him invaluable to Quantrill, and when he walked away from Quantrill's white man's savagery, he had used his running, shooting and fighting abilities to fight with Mosby in the East, in the Shenandoah. He'd known all along that the Union generals were determined to hang Mosby's men when they caught them, and so he had been determined never to get caught. It hadn't mattered. If they'd known him from before, he'd have had a price on his head. He hadn't planned on staying with Quantrill long, it was just that Quantrill had been the one after the Red Legs, the Kansas Jayhawkers.

He had learned early a certain stoicism. That had helped him on the day. His Rebel troops had lain down their arms. Surrendered. Surrender had meant that it was time to go after those men again. The men who had stripped him of his life.

Blade rolled his weight from her once again, stepping to the floor. Naked, he padded to the window in the silence of the night. Jessica went for her sheets, instinctively. He could see her movement from the corner of his eye.

From somewhere near, a wolf howled. He saw Jessica shiver, yet he didn't think it was from the strange cry of the wolf. How could she be such a damned strong-willed woman and yet seem so achingly vulnerable and beautiful, binding slender ribbons inexorably around his soul? She made him want her again. Made feelings beat within him once again, just looking at her there. He knew that if he touched her...

"Damn you!" he said softly, to the night.

"Why!" she cried, a note of passion in her voice. "You can turn now and walk away. You won, I lost, remember? I always pay my debts. You're free. You can leave whenever you want. I've paid—"

He swung on her. "Paid? I think I said for the *night*. It's only half over, the best that I can see!"

Jessica fell silent, a blush staining her cheeks. Blade strode to the bed, newly aroused, and not giving a damn that she would see his hardness. She had nothing against half-breeds and she was willing to sell her soul to stay. She wanted to play the game no matter how rough it became.

He wrenched the sheets from her and straddled her. She clenched her jaw, her eyes flashing, her hands coming up against his chest. But he caught them.

"One month," he told her. "You wanted me, you've got me. One month. So you manage to do whatever it is you have to do out here in that amount of time."

"But—"

"What is it that you're so determined to do?" he demanded.

Emerald eyes locked with his. "Land," she said softly. Her lashes swept over her eyes, then her gaze met his once again. "I want to claim the land. It was my husband's."

She was lying—or at least, she wasn't telling him everything, Blade thought. "One month," he said. "Then you're on your own."

"I'll pay you well—"

"Damned right," he said very softly. "Here's the deal. You get me. And, Mrs. Dylan, I get you."

"You've had—"

"A taste," he murmured, and bent down. Slowly, slowly he captured her lips. Teased them, played with them. He waited for her mouth to part, to accept his sensual invasion, to return the touch, sweet motion by sweet motion....

Her arms wound around him, and he made love to her again.

So slowly. So sensually, teaching, exploring, discovering. Touching, laving, still tasting, whispering, having.... Becoming one with her. Bronze flesh against ivory, slick, fluid. Hungry. Creating a storm, a sweet tempest, bringing her with him until she writhed so erotically beneath him.

And when he finished, he captured her lips to keep silent the cry he had wrung from her being. She lay beside him, dazed, panting, flushed. Then she turned away.

"No!" she whispered.

"A month," he reminded her. His arms around her then, he pulled her to him gently. She was so warm, silken still. It seemed just as sweet to hold her. And she did not pull away. She paid her debts—

And kept her bargains, so it seemed.

Golden strands of hair softly entangled him. He lay awake, staring at the ceiling, wondering what he had done. A month. Had he cast them both into the fiery pits of hell...? Or the sweetest heights of heaven?

Chapter Six

Jessica woke early, as she was accustomed to doing, yet it seemed that her eyelids were heavy, that it was hard to open them. Her lashes fluttered. The first thing she saw was his hand. Large, powerful, long-fingered, bronzed, nails clipped, not manicured, but clean. It lay around her waist, holding her close against his body.

She closed her eyes tightly again, recalling the night, assuring herself that she must be absolutely horrible, yet not feeling that she was in the least. She had to get to the land, she reminded herself. She was determined to get to the land, and maybe she had been willing to pay almost any price to get there.

But…this price hadn't quite occurred to her until she had first seen McKenna. And no matter what she tried to tell herself, a certain fire had stirred and burned deep within her from that moment. He was beyond a doubt the most intriguing man she had ever seen. He was perhaps an inch or two over six feet, lithe, graceful, silent, his every movement one of perfect ease—startling in a man with such broad shoulders, such fine, taut muscle structure, she thought. He was straight as oak and hard as stone, his face something handsomely chiseled from granite. His sleek, thick, pitch-black hair and ebony eyes were a striking giveaway to his Indian heritage, while the hard planes of his face somehow combined white and Indian characteristics into a visage that was arresting, strikingly handsome, and still so very rugged. He had fascinated her from the first seconds she had seen him. When she heard him speak, she felt tremors steal down her spine. When he looked directly at her, she felt fire seep into her bones.

She'd never felt anything quite like it before in her life. Ever. She'd been in love, or, rather, she had loved, and perhaps there was a difference. Charlie had been a part of her life forever. She had known him so very well. It was circumstance that had come between them, war that had split them apart.

And yet... As much as she had loved Charlie, as much as she was here on his behalf, she had never begun to feel for Charlie what she did for this man.

A hard throbbing suddenly began within her heart. Well, she had won. She had lost...and then won. He'd told her that he'd come with her for a month. That was all she would need. But then, in a month...

She swallowed hard, not wanting to waken him. She wanted to rise and dress, to hide herself. Morning's light could be so harsh. She started trembling each time she remembered just how he had made her feel. Turning crimson, Jessica prayed that no one else in Mrs. Peabody's boardinghouse had heard how he had made her feel.

One month. She had him. He had her. Could he really want her so much? she wondered. He had been so damned furious with her innocence, or perhaps it had been her lack of expertise or—

No. He hadn't wanted an involvement, she reasoned, and men always seemed to think that any inexperienced woman had to be after more than she was willing to say.

He would never understand. She owed Charlie, she had to get to the land and stay there long enough to find his papers. And she would have done anything...with *this* man. She couldn't explain it. Couldn't explain what Blade had touched within her.

She drew away, easing from the bed. She winced somewhat as she tried to walk, hurrying across the room to the washbowl to drench and cool her face. She shivered in the brisk morning air, washing her throat, breasts, arms. She dropped the cloth at last, turning to open her trunk, which Shorty had brought by at dinnertime last night. She withdrew a corset, pantalets, a petticoat and a cool calico dress. Although it was cool now, she was certain the afternoon would be warm. She had just stepped into the pantalets when her eyes fell upon him. He hadn't made a sound or a motion, but his black eyes were on her and she flushed, suddenly certain that he had been awake, watching her, since she first had risen. They were enigmatic eyes, so Stygian dark, so piercing and demanding. She lowered her lashes quickly, trying to draw the dress over her head before she had tied the pantalets.

He laughed and came swiftly to his feet. She could feel him at her back, pulling up her dress, finding the lace on her pantalets and pulling it into a sturdy tie. She quickly smoothed the calico down, her cheeks still flushed. Eyes downcast, she murmured swiftly, "I have to pick up a few things I had ordered last night. My land isn't far from here. I'd like to start out right after breakfast, if that's all right. If—"

She hesitated. He was still at her back. She swung around and felt tremors all over again because he simply had such a beautiful body. Tall, bronzed, his chest devoid of hair, glistening even by daylight with taut muscle. She swallowed hard. "You, er, need to get dressed."

He nodded, offering her a dry smile that caused her to blush all over again. She had started all this by bursting into his bath. She shouldn't be dismayed by his nakedness.

"That is," she murmured softly, "if you haven't changed your mind. You—you did say that you'd come."

"Hmm. You've got me. I've got you."

She exhaled, a shaky sound of relief. Then she spun around quickly. "I'm just going to go downstairs—" She broke off, her eyes going wide. "The—"

"Bed next door," Blade finished for her. "Don't

worry, I'll go mess it up. I'm not too sure what we can do about this one."

"Do?" she murmured, then glanced at the sheets that gave away everything. "Oh…"

"I can just steal them," he offered politely.

"Oh, yes, that should go unnoticed!"

He grinned and laughed. "We'll put a bandage on your hand. You can say that you cut it opening a letter last night or something."

"Will it—work?"

"Better than nothing, I imagine," he assured her. He turned and left her, crossing through the door that connected their rooms, returning to hers with a swatch of clean, white linen cloth. She stood still while he wrapped her hand. She was painfully aware of his very natural nakedness once again, and she stiffened as she breathed in the sensual scent of him. His eyes were suddenly on hers. "What's wrong?"

"You—you really need to get dressed. You—"

"Look ready?" he suggested, laughing. She bit her lip, lashes sweeping over her eyes.

"There you go again, just dying to give me a good right to the jaw," he said.

She sighed. "I didn't say that you look ready to—"

"But I am—always," he assured her huskily.

Her eyes flew open. "Braggart!" she accused him, and he started to laugh again. He finished wrapping her hand, then suddenly drew her into his arms.

"Want to test me?"

"No!" she exclaimed. But, God, his touch... What was the magic? How could he be so fierce and so tender? Jessica pondered.

Such a stranger...while she was beginning to feel that she knew him so very well.

His lips touched upon hers. She struggled against him. "There's business—"

"Debts to be paid!" he agreed.

"Here—I mean, now?"

He laughed softly again, releasing her. She saw in his black eyes that he had been teasing her, taunting her all along. He didn't need to force anything. He had lots of time. That was the agreement. And she did always pay her debts.

"Go on down," he told her. "Do what you have to do. I'll be ready when you are."

Jessica spun around and hurriedly left the room. She met Mrs. Peabody on the landing at the foot of the stairs. "Good morning, Jessica, dear. Oh, no! Your hand, dear! What did you do?"

"Oh, it's just a scratch. I cut it with my letter opener. I'm fine. I'm afraid I was on the bed, though, and there are a few spots of blood." And she had to be the color of blood by now, too. Would such a lame story fly? What was Mrs. Peabody going to do, accuse her of lying? Of misconduct beneath her roof?

"Don't you worry about that at all," Mrs. Peabody said. "Jane will get them out with lemon juice. I'm just so concerned about your hand."

"It's nothing, really. I swear it." It *was* nothing—that was honest enough, Jessica reasoned.

"All right, dear, I won't press it. How did you sleep?"

"Wonderfully. I wish I could stay longer," Jessica said. Well, it wasn't a lie. Once she had fallen asleep, she had slept like the dead. And she did wish that she could stay longer. Mrs. Peabody had made a beautiful home out here in the wilderness. It was comfortable, warm. So incredible after what she had been through traveling.

"Why don't you stay another night before moving on, dear? I'm sure you'll hit problems and hard work aplenty once you leave. One day of rest might be just the thing you need."

One more night in this proper place with Mc-Kenna? She didn't think so. Just the thought made fresh color seem to fly to her cheeks. And she only had McKenna for a month. One month.

She shook her head. "I—I really can't, Mrs. Peabody, though I would love to."

"I understand, dear. You want to get going to your own home."

"Yes. But it's not even a full day's ride from here. I'll be back often enough. In fact, I'll be back next week for a few days to buy cattle."

"That's wonderful. I'll be expecting you."

"And Mr. McKenna," Jessica said softly.

Mrs. Peabody had begun to move her portly body when she turned back, smiling. "Pardon, dear?"

"Mr. McKenna has graciously consented to work for me for the next few weeks." Mrs. Peabody was staring at her. "I—I've had a great deal of trouble ever since I started on my way here. He bailed me out twice, so...well, I seem to need someone."

"But Mr. McKenna is working for you?" Mrs. Peabody repeated, astonished.

Jessica nodded. "What's wrong with that?"

"Nothing, nothing. It's just that, well, he's so much his own man, dear. I would have never believed that he would have consented to work for anyone else. And then again... Well, dear, surely, if ever there was someone in need... Oh! Here I go babbling. You just run around to the stables, right around the corner. Your wagon should be loaded, your horses ready. Everyone in this town was just pleased pink at the orders you gave. And," Mrs. Peabody added, "the gold you had to pay for them all!"

Jessica grinned. She liked it out here. She liked the honesty. She hadn't come West intending to stay. Now she began to wonder what it would be like.

"Thank you, Mrs. Peabody, I will just run around and check on the wagon."

"Coffee and breakfast will be on when you come back," Mrs. Peabody called to her.

Jessy stepped outside and walked around the corner to the stables. Her wagon was waiting right in front.

It was exactly what she had wanted, a big, flat wagon with a high box seat, the kind of conveyance fit for a ranch that was starting out. There were two roan horses harnessed to it already. The horses looked fine and strong, the harness well made and nicely polished. A man came out of the stables when she approached, a crinkled older fellow named Delaney. His eyes were bright Irish blue and his smile was broad. "Morning, Mrs. Dylan. We've got it all, every last speck of stuff you wanted! There's coffee in that bag, flour there, salt right over here. Let's see, there's the fabric you wanted, the grain, the jarred jellies and fruits, and Mrs. Shrewesbury even had some canned tomatoes, beans and turnip greens. She threw in a few of her fresh vegetables and fruits for you—she started out here herself from back East, and says she knows getting started is hard. I think you're just about all set, at least to get started."

"That's fine, Mr. Delaney. Thank you so much. What about the lamps?"

"In the back of the wagon. You've got some oil there, too, and a big box of candles. You should be just as right as rain. You've done ordered and paid for just about everything. Except one thing that's darned important," Delaney told her.

"Oh?" Jessica asked. "What did I forget?"

"You forgot that you're going out a day's ride from town. A woman alone out there might plum be a target for any no-account outlaw in the territory!"

"I'm not going alone," Jessica assured him quickly. "Mr. McKenna is coming with me."

"McKenna!"

Mr. Delaney seemed as startled as Mrs. Peabody had been. "McKenna has agreed to come with you?"

She nodded. "From what I've seen, he can probably outgun any no-account outlaw."

Delaney nodded. "Yes, well, damned right you'll be safe. Just—" He hesitated.

"What is it?"

"You watch out for him, too, Mrs. Dylan. There's some out there that believe he's a no-account outlaw, but there's some truths out here in the West, and one of them is that a man's got to do what a man's got to do…and Mr. McKenna, he only went after a vengeance that was rightfully his! But you be careful where you bandy his name about, Mrs. Dylan. You don't want to be the downfall of a damned fine man!"

Jessica stared at him, stunned by his vehemence. She didn't know what he was talking about.

I never said that I wasn't an outlaw… Jessica suddenly remembered Blade's words. Wasn't that what he had told her? Something very much like that?

"I'll be careful, Mr. Delaney," she promised. "He won't be with me that long. Only a month."

"Then you look hard and find yourself good help, and get yourself established in that time, young woman, you hear me? We're willing to do all we can from town here, you know."

She smiled. "Thank you."

"You go on and have your breakfast at Mrs. Peabody's. I'll have McKenna's horse saddled and ready when you are. Smart girl. I couldn't imagine how you could have forgotten how wild and lawless this land can be."

"No, I was really good, Mr. Delaney," she said wryly. "I was careful. I've bought—and paid for—everything." Including McKenna, she added silently. She offered Mr. Delaney her hand. "Thank you. Thank you for everything."

"Thank you. It's not often we're paid in gold by such beautiful young women out here," Delaney told her with a wink.

She smiled. "Thanks again." She turned and walked around the dusty corner to the wooden sidewalk, then hurried into Mrs. Peabody's. She found Blade already seated at the dining room table. There was a huge plate of ham and eggs and sausages and biscuits set before him, and he seemed to be enjoying them tremendously. Jessica sat across the table from him while Mrs. Peabody served her some coffee.

"Thank you," Jessica said.

"Everything all set?" Mrs. Peabody asked cheerfully.

"Yes, Mr. Delaney was wonderful, he pulled everything together."

Blade chewed on his biscuit, arching a black brow as he stared at her.

"Mr. Delaney said I ordered very well, and that I have everything I need."

"I hope so," Blade told her.

"This pot is empty," Mrs. Peabody said with a tsk. "Let me run out to the back, I'll be back shortly." She exited the room with a bustle.

"You're damned sure you've got everything?" Blade asked Jessica.

"Well, I had been," she murmured, "but now that I see how you eat..."

He grinned at her, unperturbed. "Spent a lot of energy last night. Made me really hungry this morning."

She blushed, picking up a biscuit.

"Don't you dare throw one of those!" he warned her.

She couldn't resist the temptation. She gritted her teeth and threw.

He caught it. Mrs. Peabody walked in. He started to butter the biscuit.

"Here's more coffee—" she began, but Blade was up, smiling, taking the pot from her.

"You sit down, Mrs. Peabody. I'm going to the buffet to get Mrs. Dylan a plate. She's going to have to learn to have a hearty breakfast like a Westerner, right? If she didn't acquire a good appetite last night, I'll just have to see that she does in the future. Of course, we'll have to hope that she can learn to be as good a cook as you, my dear *Rose!*"

He was at the buffet, heaping her plate with eggs and ham. She could never eat it all, even though she was starving. He set the plate before her.

She met his black eyes. "Thank you!"

"Grits! I'll get you a bowl."

"No, that's fine. Really, I've never eaten them—"

"This may be Indian territory, but it's damned close to Texas. Grits are a staple, you'd best get used to them. Easterners!" he said, black eyes on her. Then he added very softly, *"Northeasterners!"* He turned away from her suddenly, his tone changing. "Mrs. Peabody, this was delightful, as usual."

"Have more coffee, Mr. McK—er, Blade."

He picked up his cup, walking with it to the rear window of the room, from where he could see Mr. Delaney's stables.

"Things look about ready," he said.

Jessica sat back, sipping her coffee, studying him. She felt warm tremors assailing her once again. There was so much she liked about him. He was exceedingly handsome this morning in fitted dark trousers, a black cavalry-styled shirt and riding boots. His dark hair, cut to his nape, seemed exceptionally sleek, his face clean shaven but rugged.

Outlaw? He couldn't be. His manners were perfect. He could taunt her easily enough, but he was kind and courteous to Mrs. Peabody, the perfect gentleman. He was so obviously Indian, yet so obviously white. He had been well educated somewhere, but he seemed to live nowhere, with nothing but his beautiful bay and his saddlebags. And vengeance. The whole idea gave her goose bumps. And yet, he had his right to it, that was what Mr. Delaney had said....

He turned, his coffee cup cradled in his hand. "Eat up," he told her.

"If you're in a hurry, I don't have to eat—"

"Yes, you do," he said with amusement. "You're definitely going to need your strength."

For the ranch? For herself? For him?

She lowered her face quickly. Damn him, she had to stop blushing. She wasn't going to let him spend endless days and nights doing this to her!

Her hunger had been real; she ate everything. When she was finished, they rose, and she discovered that Mrs. Peabody already had asked her boys to bring Jessica's trunk out to the wagon. They were all set to go. Moments later, they both had said their goodbyes. She crawled up on the wagon, taking the reins. But Blade leapt up beside her, taking them from her.

"You're welcome to ride your horse—" she began.

"He's tethered to the back," he assured her curtly. Then his gaze was upon her for a long moment. "I've got to make sure I earn my keep, eh, Mrs. Dylan?"

She gritted her teeth, swiftly looking downward, aware that Mrs. Peabody and Mr. Delaney were still waving, watching them start their ride out of town.

"I do wish that you'd stop that!" she whispered.

"Why? You were the one doing the bargaining, the one who suggested the price."

"Because I would have paid anything—"

"For this land? I am dying to see it!"

"My husband left it to me!" she said icily.

"Your husband—the chaste Yank?" he said.

"The dead one," she murmured, looking away. Then she stared at him suddenly. "Does that bother you? That he was a Union soldier?"

"That *you're* a Yank?" he inquired, his gaze upon her again, a black brow arched. "No," he said after a moment. "Hell, no, the war's over, isn't it? Long over."

But there was a note of bitterness to his voice. The war wasn't really over. Not for him.

"I don't give a damn what he was, or what you are, Mrs. Dylan. Not so long as it doesn't affect our bargain."

She stiffened her shoulders and looked ahead. "If you're going to earn your keep, McKenna, start getting us there!"

He, too, looked ahead, and they rode in silence for a long while.

Morning turned into afternoon. They stopped at a stream, watered the horses, drank deeply themselves and moved onward again. Blade rode his bay for awhile, and Jessica took the reins. She soon learned why he had been helping her. In an hour, her hands were blistering.

"The trail is steep here!" he yelled at her suddenly. "You've got to control those horses!"

"I'm trying!" Damn the blisters. She took firm hold, and they moved through the trees. And then, with the sun setting and casting an incredible golden glow upon the valley below, she saw it.

Charlie's land. There was the house, a log structure, big and sprawling in an L-shape. There were corrals and paddocks before it, long stables and a huge barn. Even from this distance, she could see they were all in need of repair. Still, the spread below her was impressive.

"How much is yours?" Blade asked.

"Five hundred acres," she told him.

He sniffed. "Cattle land, trees, a stream passing through there…" He shrugged. "Maybe you're right. Maybe this place is worth fighting for. I haven't seen ranch land quite so fine since—"

"Since?" she asked softly.

"A different life," he murmured. "Let's get down there."

Twilight was with them even as they reached the house. They worked together in silence, getting the candles and lamps first so that they could see what they were up to. Blade cared for the horses, taking them into the stables he had swept out to give them water and grain.

Jessica began to sweep the house. It was filthy, years of grime and dust having accumulated on the furnishing. Nonetheless, it was a fine house. There was a kitchen with a sink and a pump that drew fresh water from the well.

Charlie had furnished the place. There was a big leather sofa that sat before the fireplace, two rockers at its sides. There was a knit rug on the wooden floor, and a dining table with six well-carved seats. Down the hallway there were four bedrooms, two of them fully furnished with cherrywood bed frames and dressers, and one even had a beautiful washstand with a marble top. The largest bedroom also had a screen that surrounded a big wooden tub, and Jessica promised herself that it would be one of the first things she cleaned in the morning. That night, she swept and scrubbed the floors and countertops, stripped the bed, plumped up the mattress, and put new sheets on it. When she turned, he was there. He stood tall and strikingly handsome in the lamplight.

"Horses are all taken care of," Blade said. "A hinge was off the front door so I took care of that, too." He smiled suddenly, watching her with a new interest. "Then I smelled something good from inside. Can you actually cook?"

"You didn't think I could?"

He strode to her, picking up her hand. His fingertip traced the bubblelike blisters, and she winced. "You've had servants your whole life," he said softly.

She wrenched her hand back. "Fine. Don't eat."

"I'm a gambling man," he reminded her.

She strode by him quickly. She'd set the ham and beans in a pot above the fire as she wasn't too sure about her stove yet. The mixture was bubbling, and she found two of the plates she had cleaned and filled them, bringing them to the table.

"I'll get some water," she said, eyeing him nervously. "The glasses are right there. They're washed. Or—I suppose you might want whiskey. The coffee is on now, but it will take a minute—"

"Never mind," he told her, "I bought something from Mrs. Peabody this morning myself." His saddlebags lay near the door. He pulled out a bottle of red wine and brought it to the table. "Will you join me, Mrs. Dylan?"

She nodded. He poured the wine. She sat down and sipped it quickly. Then, sliding a napkin onto her lap, she dipped into her food. Across the table, Blade joined her.

Warm, flushed and exhausted, Jessica quickly drank a glass of the wine. She could feel his eyes on her. He took a spoonful of the ham and beans, still watching her.

"Will it do?" she whispered.

"It's excellent."

"Thank you."

"What are you really doing here, Jessica Dylan?" he asked suddenly.

"You just said that it was good land. You said—"

"Good land. But you're rich. You must have had some decent life back East."

"I want to be here. Is that so difficult to understand?"

"Just difficult to believe," he told her dryly.

"And what about you?" she demanded. "Are you some kind of outlaw?"

"You tell me," he replied.

She drained a second glass of wine. It was getting to her tonight. Perhaps because she was so very tired. She set the glass down and stood uneasily. "I'll get the coffee," she murmured.

But he was beside her, a subtle grin on his lips, sweeping her into his arms. "I'll take care of the coffee. You—we don't need any."

He carried her into the bedroom, laid her upon the bed and started to take her clothing off.

"I can manage."

"You can't manage anything else tonight," he told her curtly.

Ah, yes! She owed him. The days were when he worked. The nights were when she paid.

Instead, she found the covers pulled up over her nakedness and felt his palm upon her brow.

"Good night, Mrs. Dylan."

He left her then. Alone. Untouched. She bit her lip, wondering if she hadn't been a disappointment to him, if he didn't want her with the same fire he once had. She should be relieved, she thought. Surely, she was. She was so exhausted. So she slept.

Not alone. In the morning, she awakened with the first rays of sunlight. They fell softly into the room. She started to rise, again realizing she was naked. And then she felt his touch, his fingers sliding down the length of her spine, curving over her buttocks. Her breath caught. His hand circled persistently on her hip, drawing her around to him to meet his eyes.

"Good morning, Mrs. Dylan."

She started to tremble. She was amazed. She wasn't afraid. She wanted him.

His lips found hers. He touched her, guiding her hands upon him. He kissed her mouth, her cheeks. He spent long moments laving her breasts, then, moving lower, creating hot fires between her thighs. He stroked her there, kissed her there and made love to her until she was crying out softly, arching, straining to meet his thunderous beat. She needed him, ached for him, longed for the sweet surcease she had so recently learned was within the magic of the world. Suddenly, it was hers. The sweet heat and lightning shot through her. She clung to him, screaming out. And there was no reason for him to still the sound with his kiss, for there was no one to hear them in their wilderness.

Later, the sun streaked in more fully. She turned to him suddenly, biting her lower lip. He groaned softly, caressing her side as he held her to him. "What now?'' he asked. "No more modesty, no turning away? No distress over what comes between us?''

She met his eyes, shook her head, and turned bright red.

He laughed out loud, as he stroked her cheek with his knuckles, then leapt from the bed. "Up, Mrs. Dylan! It's going to be a damned long day!''

Chapter Seven

To Blade, it wasn't so incredibly amazing that Jessica began to rise in the middle of the night, saddle and bridle her horse and begin to ride out. It was amazing that she really believed she did so without waking him!

Actually, it all began after they had been in the house about five days. They had been long, productive days. He'd forgotten how good it felt to work on the land. The satisfaction of repairing broken fences, fixing a house. A home. Jessica—who had seemed such a hothouse flower from the East—proved to be anything but. Maybe she'd just never blistered her hands before.

She had a knack for making a house a home, and in those first few days it seemed that he was living in some kind of dream of paradise. He'd work through the day, and at night, she'd always manage to make something tempting. There were warm, clean drapes up all over now, fresh hot coffee always ready—and even flowers on the table. At night, after dinner, they would spend a few hours before the fire, and he would tell her his opinion of the best cattle to buy, or how to judge a ranch hand once she was ready to start hiring on men.... It was downright homey.

Sometimes they even went a little further. They were two closed people, opening up just a little to give one another personal glimpses. He learned that she had been born in New York State, that her family had been in the country since the first Pilgrims had landed, that her father had made his money in steel and that she had been his only heir. Blade had been curious that anyone so wealthy and comfortable in the East would brave such hazards in the West. "Money is only worth the things that can be bought with it," she had said softly, staring into the fire.

"You could have bought a lot back East."

"Things only have value if you really want them. I really wanted this land."

That was as far as she had gone. On his part, he had told her that he had gone to school back East himself, to a Virginia military academy, and he even conceded that he had ridden with Mosby until the bitter end of the war. She'd heard plenty about Mosby's men, even in upstate New York, and he knew she was curious, staring at him, wondering why a half-breed Sioux would risk his neck so for the Confederate cause.

He didn't tell her about Quantrill. And though he easily described life with his mother's people—the warmth, the harmony that could exist within the tribe—he never mentioned the Sioux wife he had brought home to his father. He tried to explain to Jessica that some of the Plains Indians had formed deep friendships, while others were natural enemies, fighting one another since tales and memory could recall.

They both gave. They both held back. And still, the domesticity of their situation seemed to be swiftly entangling him. The days, the evenings, and the nights.

It was wrong. Wrong to have such a hunger for her, to hold her through the dark hours, needing her, demanding her. Wrong for her, wrong for him. But he couldn't let her go. He couldn't let this beauty slip though his fingers, couldn't fight the fascination of being with her and seeing her flower with each night....

She seemed to need him in turn, even hunger for him. Her delicate ivory fingers were so sensual upon his dark, bronzed flesh. It was wrong, perhaps. But it was a part of this strange paradise, and so the early days passed with a touch of magic.

Then it began. And perhaps what was most amazing of all was that she didn't realize he followed her.

Actually, the first night, she didn't ride. She rose, slipped on a robe, and went out to the barn. The first time she had started to rise he had asked her what was wrong and she had gone stiff, saying nothing and pretending to sleep once again. The second time, he had let her go. But he had followed her. And in the barn she had paced over the entire space, stomping in each stall. It went on at length, until she grew tired and frustrated and returned to the house.

He had slipped into bed just two seconds before her. He had almost demanded an explanation, but then he had decided to wait. *She* would tell *him* what she was doing.

She didn't.

The next night, she rose and dressed silently, slipped from the room, and headed for the stables. He followed her as swiftly as he could.

The moon was full. She could see easily enough, and she seemed to have an abstract idea of where she was going. They rode south along the corral and over a small hill to a clump of large, scattered rocks. The stream ran just behind them; he could hear the bubble of water even as he carefully lagged behind her.

She dismounted, looked about with dismay, then began to try to push the rocks. They were good-sized, to say the least, each weighing well over two hundred pounds. He might have pitched in and helped her. He watched her with astonishment instead.

When a rock or boulder seemed set in the ground, she gave up and started on a new one. In all, she managed to move perhaps two or three before she paused, looked at the moon, then looked around herself, shivering. She didn't see him because he'd been very careful to take a stance behind the grove of trees to the extreme south of her.

She was going for her horse, he realized. He swiftly

mounted his bay bareback, and easily beat her to the ranch and back into bed.

She joined him within a matter of minutes, anxiously watching his face to assure herself that he slept, crawling in very carefully beside him.

He waited, aware that she lay there, still as a candlestick, waiting for him. He kept his eyes closed, and at last, it seemed, she sighed and slept. Baffled, he lay awake.

They made plans the next day for a trip into Jackson Prairie for more supplies, for cattle and hopefully, a few hired hands. They would go at the end of the week.

That night, she rose again. And he followed her. And she tried to push stones. Once again, he beat her back to the house. And she slipped in beside him. And he lay awake, absolutely confused. What in God's name was she doing? And why the hell didn't she trust him?

When she slept, he came up on an elbow and studied her. She had curved against him already—naturally. Her hair was a golden sweep around the two of them, her delicate features so perfect and serene against her pillow. Her vision caught upon something in his heart. Even the touch of her flesh against his was newly evocative.

He was tempted suddenly to pinch her awake. To demand an explanation. Instead, he lay watching her.

He didn't pinch her. He swept his arms around her and held her closely to him.

But the next night, he determined, was going to be it.

It started the same. Stew for dinner, coffee before the fire. They were both rather silent. When her eyes touched his, he didn't say a word, just set down his mug, swept her up, and made love to her. Hard, passionate love, created by his anger with her silence. He drew from her a fiery response that evoked his ultimate tenderness in the end, and when she was captured gently within his arms again, he knew that he was in love with her.

The past still hurt. It was a huge void in his heart. He owed Mara, he owed his father, he owed his unborn child. But when that debt was paid, he would love the golden blond Yankee beauty, who might well be maddened by moonlight.

She rose again, just as she had the past two nights. He waited. He followed her. And she went back to shaking those damned rocks. He wasn't going to ride back ahead of her, he decided. Tonight, when she finished, he'd be here. Right here, in her path, waiting.

But even as he stood there, watching her, he heard a noise from the east, just past the spring, and was instantly wary. He blended against the trees and watched.

There was another man watching Jessica that night.

He had a scar across his face, starting below his eyes, continuing to his jaw. A big-brimmed hat hid his eyes. He was atop a charcoal gray horse, waiting silently, watching.

Then suddenly, he was moving toward Jessica.

He spurred his horse to gallop close, then suddenly leapt from the animal. Jessica had, at the last moment, seen him coming. She had drawn a small pistol from the pocket of the simple gingham skirt she was wearing, but the man had flown upon her before she could begin to fire the weapon. Blade heard her gasp and hit the ground, hard. Then he heard her scream, and suddenly fall silent, even as he was on his way to her. The man was talking to her. Heatedly. "I'll have those papers, Mrs. Dylan. The captain ain't coming back to haunt me now! I'll have his papers, and I'll have his wife, by God!"

She could fight. Jessica could fight. She was wild beneath the man—biting, clawing, scratching.

But he was stronger. And infinitely pleased to discover she was naked beneath her simple blouse and skirt. As he wrenched up the latter, Blade was upon him, silent as the night behind him, striking like lightning. Maybe he'd meant to kill from the beginning. Maybe he'd been so furious to see the man's brutality toward Jessica. Maybe it had just been that he was touching Jessica. Maybe it was just happenstance...

Blade pried the man from her. The stranger turned, snarling, reaching for the knife at his calf. Blade belted him in the jaw and the man spun around. He fell on his knife, dead even as he hit the ground.

Jessica cried out softly, trembling. She looked up, meeting Blade's eyes, swallowing hard. "Thank God—" she began.

"What the hell is going on here?" he demanded furiously, reaching for her, jerking her to her feet. She was still trembling. Maybe he should have given her a little sympathy, he chided himself. After all, she had come so close to rape, perhaps worse.

But Jessica had been in trouble since she had come here. This man had known who she was. She had needed a bodyguard. She had wanted protection from this man. She wanted more. And Blade was willing to give it. She was forcing the game, and she wasn't letting Blade play with a full deck. He couldn't give her the least bit of sympathy. Not one iota of tenderness. She'd just get herself into worse trouble.

"Blade, damn you, you have no right—"

"Oh, madam, you are wrong! You've given me every right—"

"You're paid for your services!" she cried wretchedly.

He was amazed at just how cutting the words seemed to be, how they tore into his heart. He grabbed her shoulders suddenly, wrenched her against him and shook her. "I'm not paid to be a fool, Mrs. Dylan, and maybe I'm just not paid well enough for your lies!"

"I've never lied to you!"

"You've never told me the truth!"

She fell silent, pulling away from him. She was still shaking. He gritted his teeth, then came behind her, shoving her along.

"What—?"

"Go back. Now. I'm going to bury this fellow, and then I'll be right behind you. And then you can tell me who I just killed and why. And I want the truth, Jessy. Damn you, I want the truth!"

She didn't seem to move very well on her own, so he picked her up bodily and set her on her horse. When she was gone, he looked around, then picked a spot in the grove and buried the man. Dirty, sweating and exhausted, he returned to the house. She was sitting before the fire in the rocker, staring at the flames. The whiskey bottle was at her side. She'd poured a shot for him. And one for herself.

She heard him enter. It was a moment before her eyes slid to his, then back to the fire again. He walked over to stand behind her, picked up the whiskey, swallowed it down. His hands fell on her shoulders.

"Let's have it, shall we, Mrs. Dylan?" he said softly. "No lies."

"I never lied to you. My name is Jessica Dylan, my money came from my father, and I was married to a Captain Charles Dylan who was..." She hesitated a moment, clenching her jaw. "He was my best friend all of my life. I loved him with all my heart."

Blade moved to the fire, staring at her from a position at the mantel. "You loved him so much. You married him. But you never made love with him?"

Her eyes rose to his. "You don't understand, maybe you can't understand."

"Try me."

She lifted her hands. "I was an only child. My mother was dead, my father was always away. Charles lived near me. He was older. He came to my schoolroom, he made snowmen for me. He read me stories. He gave me the world. At the beginning of the war, he finally asked to marry me. Things moved too quickly. We had a wedding, at which he was burning with fever. I sat with him through the night. Before he really recovered, they had ordered his troops to move, and he was sent West in an army ambulance. I would have come. He wouldn't let me."

"And in all that time, he didn't come back?"

"There was a war on. And it wasn't *all that time,*" she added softly. "He was killed at the end of 1863."

Blade lifted his hands. "All right, Mrs. Dylan, you've still got me, I'll admit. What does all this have to do with the man I killed tonight?"

She shivered, drawing her feet up on the chair, hugging her knees to her chest. She started to speak, but fell silent.

"Jessica, now!"

"Charles was worried. He was third in command of the fort out here, and, due to conditions back East, he was being sent a number of Confederate prisoners. They kept escaping, and Charles was being blamed. But he knew that there were two men, at least, who were aiding and abetting the escapes. One was an enlisted man, Manson Jenks—''

''The fellow I just killed?''

Jessica nodded, swallowing hard. ''I imagine. I never met the men, either of them, I just received letters from Charles about them. The other man was the commanding officer of the camp, Lieutenant Harding.''

''Harding!'' Blade exclaimed.

''You've heard of him?''

He shrugged. He'd heard of Harding. He'd outrun him once. ''He's a colonel now, I believe. He's still stationed at the fort. Still running it, I believe. But I don't understand. Why are these men after you?''

''Charles found some correspondence between them that proved they were taking bribes from the Confederates to release them. Charles didn't dare mail the letters to me, but he did let me know he had buried the proof on the property he bought. He—he loved it out here. He was fascinated by the different Indian tribes, even the Apaches. He loved the landscape, the vistas. He thought that I might, too. And so he bought this property.''

''And then?''

She shrugged. ''There was a major uprising among the prisoners. Someone had given them weapons and had helped them escape. Charles was killed. And even then, well, he was blamed for the whole episode. It's on his military records. I just couldn't leave it that way.''

"But you little fool! You were willing to risk your own life—"

"Don't you see?" Jessica asked. "He was my life. For years. And he was a good man. He deserved so much more. There was no one left to fight for him— just me. I had to come here, and I still have to find those damned letters and prove the truth!''

"Harding might well be after you now," Blade warned her.

She nodded. "I know. I have to find the letters fast.''

"Why didn't you tell me? Why the hell didn't you just tell me the truth and let me help you?''

"Well, you're not fond of Yankees," she reminded him. "And I was afraid that you—''

"That I would what?''

"That you might try to stop me. I have to do this. I can never go forward, never really live anywhere, until it's done.''

You're a fool, he wanted to tell her. Charles is dead and gone, and none of us can do anything for him. He turned away from her, facing the fire. "Go to bed," he told her briefly. She didn't move. He swung around on her. "We'll find the damned letters to-morrow night. I assume you have some idea of where you're looking and that you weren't trying to lift rocks for the hell of it?''

She nodded, her face pale. ''He had a cache in the stables once, he had written to me. But he mentioned the stream and rocks in another letter, so he must have grown worried that he might have been seen around the barn and moved whatever he had. I—I didn't just come out here blindly.''

''No, you just walked into outlaws and Apaches by blind fool chance!''

She stood then. ''And you!'' she reminded him softly.

He was silent a minute. ''And me,'' he agreed, turning to the fire. A moment later Blade heard her rising, approaching him. ''Go to bed!'' he repeated.

She turned and did so. He stared at the flames a while. He wondered why he was so damned mad when he understood.

Because he couldn't bear to see her in danger, hurt. He sighed and rose and went into the darkened bedroom. He splashed water from the pitcher into the bowl and scrubbed his face and hands, stripped off his shirt and scrubbed his chest.

He felt her delicate fingers on his back. He felt them touching his shoulders. He heard her voice, soft, entreating.

''Blade…''

He stiffened. ''Go to sleep, Jessica. Just go to sleep.''

Her delicate fingers withdrew as if his flesh had burned them. She was gone.

He finished scrubbing, grabbed a towel and dried himself, roughly. He threw down his towel at last, and crawled onto his side of the bed. He couldn't bear it any longer. She'd used him because she'd loved another man so deeply. Maybe that was what hurt, too. He really didn't know.

And it didn't matter anymore.

He groaned softly and drew her into his arms. He tasted her tears on her cheeks. "Love me, Jessy, love me!" he told her. His lips found hers. She responded sweetly, erotically, hungrily. She gave in to his demand...never knowing that what he demanded was emotion, and not just surrender.

Chapter Eight

They found the documents the next night.

Blade had been tempted to start looking first thing in the morning, but though they so often seemed to be alone at the ranch, he couldn't forget that Jessy had been accosted last night, and that it was amazing how quickly people could sometimes appear from a vista of apparent emptiness. They were both anxious now, but Blade decided they would wait.

It wasn't a long search. The night was light, with a full moon rising above them. Midnight approached. They could hear the calls of owls, the occasional howl of a wolf.

Blade had the strength Jessy lacked to lift the big stones, and after his fourth try, he found the leather satchel buried just beneath the surface. He wouldn't let her open it there. They hurried to the house, then searched through it. Letters and notes fell from it, and he and Jessy scanned them quickly. He found one from Harding ordering Manson Jenks to see that the prisoners were freed from any shackles, and another stating that Friday would be the right night to taste fresh air. There was a letter from Jenks, assuring Harding that "everything was in order, and should move

as smooth as silk,'' and that there were things in this
war that could "beat bootlegging.''

He wondered how Charles Dylan had managed to
get this correspondence, and realized he must have
done so very carefully—and with great courage and
determination.

The last of the letters he discovered was to Jessy.
It wasn't sealed in any way, just folded over, and he
opened it, having no idea of what it might say.

> Jessy, if you are the one finding this stash, it will
> mean that I am gone, and that you have braved
> tremendous rigors to come here. Bless you,
> Jessy. Take care of yourself. Your life is far
> more precious than my honor, so don't do any-
> thing at all dangerous. I'm very afraid these
> days. I don't know who to trust. I love you with
> all my heart, and pray for your happiness. Death
> holds no fear for me, only the pain of leaving
> you.
>
>   Ever,
>   your Charles

Blade hesitated a moment.

"What is it?'' Jessica asked worriedly.

He handed her the letter. She read it. He saw her
fingers begin to tremble and he turned away. He knew
that there would be tears in her eyes, that she would
be furiously trying to blink them away.

She had loved Charles. An emotion pure, sweet and

beautiful, and based on years of companionship. While what she felt for him...

Well, hell. He was a hired hand. One she had needed desperately. One she had been willing to pay well to keep. He'd been the damned fool to fall in love with her. Even when he had thought that his own heart had been broken and had turned to stone he was here helping her exonerate a man. Forgetting his own quest.... No, it was never forgotten.

She folded the letter, put it away in the pocket of her skirt. The others she stuffed into the satchel.

"I'll have to do something with these, now that we've found them," she said. She stood. "I guess—"

"Don't guess!" he warned her, aware that there was a harsh edge to his voice. "What you're holding now is dangerous evidence against a powerful man. Manson Jenks was here last night. He surely told Harding that he knew you had come, and just as surely, Harding is going to realize that your husband had evidence against him, and he's going to be wanting to make sure that you don't get your hands on it, either. When Jenks doesn't appear, Harding is going to be very worried. He's going to have to come after you."

"But I'll just see that someone else gets the letters!" she exclaimed.

"He's a colonel now, Jessy! We've got to go above him, we've got to find a general." He paused for a moment. "Sherman has been riding out here. After the Indians," he added wryly. "We'll go into town first thing in the morning, and you'll go in with Mrs.

Peabody, and don't you even think of moving out of her place until you hear from me again, do you understand?''

''But what—''

''I'm going to find Sherman,'' he told her.

''You want me to just sit and wait?'' Jessica asked.

''No. I want you to order more supplies and wait. But I don't want you away from Mrs. Peabody for a minute, do you understand?''

''I—''

''Jessy, damn you, you paid a high price for me to protect you, remember? Let me do it.''

Her chin set and her face paled. She stood up and walked across the room to the bedroom door. ''Good night,'' she said icily.

He nodded and watched her go. He stared at the fire, and at the leather satchel. He shoved the satchel under the sofa and stretched out upon it.

It suddenly occurred to him that, if he were caught, this might be his last night with her. He couldn't be caught. But there were still a lot of Yanks out there who knew him. It wouldn't matter he tried to tell himself. Not if he could take a few of them down with him.

No, if he were going to take anyone down, he wanted it to be the right men now. The war was over. He was tired of the fighting. He was even ready to make peace with an army ready to decimate his mother's people, he realized. He just wanted revenge on a few.

To help Jessica, he might never get that chance.

He rolled over. He couldn't hold on to the letters. Once they were delivered into the right hands, Jessica would be out of danger. He tossed on the sofa again, onto his back. He heard a sound in the night. His eyes flew open instantly.

Jessica. He half-closed his eyes and waited. She was wearing a soft, sheer gown. Her hair was free, newly brushed, cascading all around her in a rich golden fall. She hesitated by his side, and must have seen his eyes closed, he thought, because she started to turn.

He reached out for her, caught her arm, pulled her back. He swept her down beside him, held her, kissed her. He enwrapped her in his arms. He held her close and stared at the ceiling, praying. Please, God. Please, God. He wasn't even sure what he prayed for.

Just a life with which to hold her again.

Mrs. Peabody was delighted to see them. She was startled when Blade said that he couldn't stay to supper. "You're headed over to the saloon, I'll wager!" she chastised him immediately. But he smiled, and assured her that he was not, his eyes touching Jessica's.

"I'm not, Mrs. Peabody, I mean, Rose. I've got a ride ahead of me tonight." Jessica was standing next to Mrs. Peabody. Tall, slim, shapely, her eyes steadily upon his, so anxious while she tried so hard not to give away the emotion.

Blade tipped his hat to them both and turned, starting down the two steps to reach his big bay in the street. "I'll be back as soon as I can," he promised.

He mounted quickly and started to turn his bay for the westward course he needed to take. Sherman was traveling along the Washita, he had been assured by Mr. Delaney. The general was moving very slowly because he was visiting officers stationed at forts deep into Indian territory.

"Wait!" Jessica cried suddenly. She picked up her skirts and hurried down the steps, running to him. She came to a halt as he quickly reined in, and stood looking up at him, concern in her eyes. Liquid, shimmering, so beguiling. "You shouldn't be doing this! It's not your fight, not your problem, and I'm so afraid...."

"Afraid of what?" he asked her.

She moistened her lips. "You never said that you weren't an outlaw!" she reminded him softly.

He smiled. "I'm going to be all right," he told her. "Now let me move on while there's still a little bit of daylight left."

She stepped back. He started to ride. She ran after him once again. "Blade!"

He reined in. "Jessica—"

"I love you," she said swiftly. "Please, please, take care of yourself. I—I love you."

He nearly fell off his horse. He wanted to. Wanted to forget the damned letters, forget revenge, forget everything in life. He just wanted to hold her, and live with her, and know that he could wake with her every morning of his life. He wanted to grow old with her.

But it wouldn't be any good. They could never run from Harding. They couldn't run from his past, either. He reached out and touched her cheek and felt the dampness of her tears there. "I love you, too," he told her softly.

Then he spurred his bay. He dared not wait any longer.

He rode through the night. Thankfully, the moon was still nearly full and there was plenty of light. It was easy enough to follow Sherman's route along the river—remnants of camp fires along the way, broken branches on the foliage, heavy footprints along the trail. Blade could tell that there was a fairly large encampment moving west, for there were marks from many tents, little things that people lost along the way. A rag doll lay in the trail, a broken pipe, a strip of calico that had tied back some pioneering woman's hair. Army officers often brought their wives with them. Women cast into a hard lot, but an intriguing and adventurous lot, too.

He picked up the little rag doll and carried it with him. Maybe he could return it.

It was just at dawn when he came upon the camp. He saw the sentry by the river before the sentry saw him, and he called out quickly. Men had a habit of shooting first and asking questions later when a man looked as much like a Sioux as he did.

"Ho, there!" he called out, raising both hands in

a peaceful gesture to the very young soldier by the river. The man took a look at him and began seeking his gun—where he had lain it by a rock by the river— too late. "I'm looking for General Sherman!" Blade called out irritably. "And don't pick up that weapon because I don't want to shoot your damned fool head off!"

Maybe it was the warning. Maybe it had just been his very natural use of the English language—with a little bit of Missouri thrown into it—that advised the young sentry that Blade was not his enemy. Maybe the sentry realized he still had his scalp.

"The general is in camp, sir!" the sentry called out quickly. He had gained some dignity. He held his army-issue rifle, but did not aim it at Blade. "I'll call for an escort, sir!"

The sentry whistled, and a second man in cavalry blue appeared, this one an old-timer, one who quickly eyed Blade. He saw that the half-breed was alone and presumed he might be a scout. "I'll bring you into camp," the older man said, still watching him curiously.

"Thank you. I've letters with information I think he'll find exceptionally interesting," Blade said.

"Come with me."

Blade dismounted from his bay and followed the old man. They passed through the wakening camp, men rising, dressing, shaving, washing. They all paused to watch.

Blade felt their eyes. Felt them roam down his back. Did any of them know him?

They reached one tent with a middle-aged officer just pouring coffee in front. He paused the second he saw Blade. He had a haggard look about him.

Blade knew that look well. Most men had worn it after the war. Many men still did.

"Lieutenant Gray, this man has come to see General Sherman. Says he has important correspondence."

"It's an old matter," Blade said. "But an important one."

Lieutenant Gray looked at him, scratching his chin. "What's your tribe, Blackfeet?"

"Oglala," Blade replied.

"I heard about a fellow like you once," he said. "A half-breed with Mosby. Faster than lightning."

"Had to be," Blade said.

The lieutenant grinned. "The war is over," he said. He hesitated. "Though they did say this particular fellow had once been with Quantrill."

"Briefly, so I heard," Blade agreed.

The lieutenant turned, still grinning. Blade realized that he hadn't quite been breathing. He gulped in some air, then let it out.

"I'll find out if the general can see you," Lieutenant Gray said. "Help yourself to some coffee in the meantime."

Blade did so. It was hot and strong and black, and helped a little against the exhaustion he had begun to feel. But he felt something else, too—eyes upon him. Union army eyes. These were the men he had been fighting not so long ago. Now they were men with faces.

Lieutenant Gray returned. "This way, sir. General Sherman is quite curious."

Blade followed Gray into Sherman's big field tent. The general was behind his desk. He was a man of medium height and medium build, with a ragged face, helped somewhat by his beard and mustache. A little man, Blade thought, for one who had ravaged so much of a countryside.

A smart one—a brutal one, in a way. Hell, Sherman had sure helped to bring it all to a close. And now he was bringing his talents and energies against the Indians in the West. There was just no way he could ever be a man Blade would like, he decided wryly.

But at least he hated Indians openly, and he had made no bones about his plan to bring the South to her knees. He was the right man to bring Harding to his knees, as well.

Sherman stood, eyeing Blade curiously. "All right, so what is it that sends a half-breed ex-Reb into my camp?" he demanded flatly.

Blade didn't say a word. He handed the leather satchel of letters over to the man.

"What's this?" Sherman demanded.

"Letters, sir," Blade responded. "Read them, General."

Sherman sat at his desk. Blade realized that Lieutenant Gray was still behind him. Maybe they had been afraid that he intended to knife Sherman the moment he had been alone with him.

Sherman glanced through every letter. He looked at Lieutenant Gray. "We just met with a Colonel Harding at the fort, eh, Lieutenant?"

"That's right, General."

Sherman drummed his fingers on the desk. He stared at Blade. "What's your name? Who are you? What's your involvement in this?"

"My name's McKenna. I'm working for Dylan's widow. I've left her back in Jackson Prairie, at the boardinghouse there. I came as quickly as I could. I'm sure Harding will come after her if he even suspects she might have found the letters."

"Mrs. Dylan knew about these letters?"

"She came West to find them."

Sherman nodded. "Lieutenant, arrange a party to travel back to Jackson Prairie. See that Mrs. Dylan is safe, then move on to the fort and relieve Colonel Harding of duty. He'll be placed under arrest to face a court-martial." He studied Blade. "I'll assume you'll be accompanying my men."

Blade nodded. Lieutenant Gray hurried out.

"I heard tell of a half-breed Sioux with Mosby. Was that you?"

Blade hesitated. This was it. Mosby had been a legitimate member of Lee's army—not like Quantrill, who had been an embarrassment to the entire Southern command. Still… "Yes, sir, that was me," Blade said.

Sherman drummed his fingers on his desk. "Custer used to hate Mosby with a passion. Used to hang any of his men he could get his hands on."

"Yes, sir. Colonel Mosby was careful to hang only Custer's men in return."

"Sad state of affairs, eh, among civilized men? He was one hell of a raider, your commander."

"Yes, yes he was." Blade hesitated. "If you're going to put me under arrest—"

"Hell, sir! The war is over. I admire the man, and I bemoan our losses to him. That's all."

Blade started to turn. Sherman's words stopped him once again. "Though I must say, there was some rumor that Mosby's half-breed rode with Quantrill first. With boys like Bloody Bill Anderson. Men who dragged Union officers out of trains, stripped them, and shot them right in the back."

Blade felt his spine begin to freeze. "If you're going to hold me, General—"

"Oh, there was lots to the story. It was my understanding some Red Legs bushwhacking out of Kansas had mown down the half-breed's whole family. Father, pregnant wife."

Blade turned to him. "I didn't stay with Quantrill," he said softly. "Even after what I'd seen, I couldn't."

"There may be worse ahead out here," Sherman warned him. "The West is going to be a rough place with the war over. Custer didn't like Mosby. A lot of men don't like Indians."

Blade shrugged. "A lot of Indians don't like white men, but being a mix, General, I find that I really have to try to like myself. And if I'm not under arrest, I'm staying out here. No matter what."

Sherman leaned forward, studying him. "There's a

lot of bushwhackers straight out from Kansas in the army here. There were a number of them at that fort I just left.''

''So I'd heard, General.''

''You might have been looking for a few men out here right from the start, mightn't you?''

''I might.''

Sherman wagged a finger at him. ''You'd best be damned careful, McKenna. Harding needs to face a court-martial. You can't just ride in and shoot up all my men.''

''I have to—''

''Yes, Mr. McKenna. You go. Ride with my troops. They move quickly. They must be about ready to ride. Take care, McKenna. I like you, and I'll be damned if I know why. I hated Quantrill and I'm not all that damned fond of Indians, sir, but I admit, I do wish you the best.''

So Blade turned and walked out of the tent. The warmth of the sun struck him, and he smiled suddenly. A massive weight seemed to fall from his shoulders.

''Mr. McKenna!'' Lieutenant Gray called out from atop a handsome roan. ''Are you ready, sir?''

''Indeed, Lieutenant!'' Blade mounted his bay. And in the morning's light, they started to ride hard, back to Jackson Prairie.

The night seemed to last forever.

Jessica tried to sit still with Mrs. Peabody, sipping her sassafras tea. She tried to answer the woman's questions intelligently, tried to forget that Blade was running after the army.

At nine she jumped up and said that she was exhausted and needed to sleep. She never slept.

She paced the blue room for hours. She worried endlessly. Each time she closed her eyes, she saw him. He was so tall, dark and completely fascinating. She remembered his eyes, the way they could pin her to the wall, the way they could touch her with warmth and fire. I love you.... The words had just tumbled from her. Maybe she hadn't even realized it until then. Maybe she had known that he had given her something she had never imagined. But until she had seen him riding away, she hadn't known that she had really fallen in love with him, that their lives together now meant more than anything else. I love you, too, he had told her.

But though he now knew all about her life, she still knew very little about his. And she was so afraid. He had been taking chances to ride into a Union army camp. And if anything happened to him...

It wasn't even dawn when she rose and dressed. She slipped out of Mrs. Peabody's and hurried around back to see Mr. Delaney. He was already up and busy, brushing down someone's carriage horse. He arched a brow when he saw her. "Morning, Mrs. Dylan. Aren't you supposed to be waiting in the boarding-house for McKenna to come back?"

"Yes," Jessica said, looking at him intensely. "I've got to know what I'm watching out for, Mr. Delaney. I've got to know something about him."

Mr. Delaney lowered his head. "Seems like you've got to ask him, now, Mrs. Dylan—"

"Mr. Delaney, please! I need help. Blade is gone, and now I'm terrified that he might not come back. You've got to help me, please, Mr. Delaney. I—I swear to you, I'd never hurt him. I'm in love with him."

Delaney's eyes shot swiftly to hers. Then he shrugged. "Well, I guess there's lots of people who know the truth. I wouldn't really be telling tales out of school."

"So help me, please!"

Delaney shrugged again. "He was ranching with his father back in Missouri, back before the beginning of the war. His father took an active stance against the bushwhacking goin' on, and anyway, some Red Legs come down and killed the elder McKenna and Blade's wife.

"Wife, yes, ma'am," Mr. Delaney said in response to Jessica's gaping mouth. "She was expecting a little one at the time. Anyway, Blade done joined up with Quantrill and his men—until he seen what they did in a raid. That kind of brutal violence wasn't what he was after. He just wanted to kill the men involved. He couldn't find them what with the war beginning and all. He traveled east and joined up with Mosby. Fought out the war. And then came back."

"To find the men?" Jessica whispered.

Mr. Delaney hesitated a minute. "We'd heard tell that a lot of the men had joined on with the Union, and that they'd be in one of the forts in this vicinity.

I imagine that's why he was coming this way when he ran into you." He hesitated again, then said very softly, "Yes'm, Mrs. Dylan. That's why he'd ridden out here—to find the men."

"Thank you," she said softly. "Thank you." Jessica started to walk back to the boardinghouse, her mind reeling. He was an outlaw…. No, he wasn't an outlaw. He'd ridden with outlaws. And he'd had a wife killed. A pregnant wife. Jessica fought a sudden rise of tears. He'd never told her. He'd said that he loved her, too….

But not enough. And that was why he had ridden on. Sure, he wanted to make sure that she was safe— his end of the bargain. But then he was going to ride away again. After those men. She was so immersed in her own thoughts that she didn't hear the riders at first. And then…

Then it was too late. When she looked up, she saw a cloud of dust coming down the street. Then the men. Ten of them, armed, wearing blue, atop cavalry mounts. The first of them, a grim-looking man with dark eyes and mustache, leapt down and came toward her. "Jessica Dylan?"

"What do you want?" she demanded. She knew. Her heart was beating a thousand miles an hour. He'd told her to stay in the boardinghouse! Mrs. Peabody would have lied for her, found her a place to hide. The men could have ripped the place apart, but now…

"You're under arrest," the man told her, reaching for her.

She snatched her hand away, taking a swift step

backward. "Arrest! We are not in a state of military control here!" she cried angrily. "You can't arrest me. I haven't done anything—"

"We have reason to believe that you were engaged in traitorous activity with your late husband, a conspiracy that cost many lives during the recent War of Rebellion," the man said.

"You've no authority with which to arrest me. Don't touch me. I'll scream so damned loudly it will be heard all the way to Washington!" she cried.

His hands were on her. He wrenched her toward him. "I'm Colonel Harding, Mrs. Dylan. *Harding.* I want what you've got from your late husband, and I'll do what I have to in order to get it from you. Do you understand?"

"I don't have anything—" Jessica began.

"Lady, you're a liar!" Colonel Harding fired back.

She wasn't lying, she didn't have the damned letters, they were in Blade's hands as he crossed the plains. Right into the hands of the Union army. A man who had been with Mosby. With Quantrill.

Her mind raced. She didn't dare give Harding the least hint that someone else was holding the damning evidence against him. She had to let Harding believe it was still buried on her property somewhere.

She lifted her chin. "You're the lying, murderous traitor, Harding. You killed Charles, I'm sure. You probably shot him in the back once you found it was the only way to frame him. They say a Reb did it, but you and I both know. You killed him."

Harding lowered his head, his eyes burning into

hers. "All I can assure you, ma'am, is that I will kill his widow, slowly, if I don't get what I want."

"And how will you explain that?"

"I'll find a way. Come willingly now, or it will be the worse for you."

She stared at him, gritting her teeth. Then she began to scream. "This man is taking me unlawfully! He's a murderer, he was a traitor to his cause—"

Harding's hand slammed across her cheek. Stunned, she nearly fell. He lifted her. She gathered what strength she could muster and began beating him, fighting him. She found herself thrown, stomach down, over a horse, then gagged and tied there, like a beast ready for the slaughter.

Harding caught her hair, lifting her eyes to his. "We'll have time to talk, Mrs. Dylan. Lots of time."

He dropped her hair and hurried to his mount.

"See here!" someone cried. It was Mr. Delaney. "What do you think you're doing? You can't do that to a lady. What kind of officer are you—"

"She's part of a conspiracy, dangerous as a rattler!" Harding told Delaney.

"Bull crap!" Mr. Delaney announced indignantly. There was a crowd gathering around him. Jessica couldn't see the people because her hair was blinding her, but she could hear them. She heard Mrs. Peabody's voice.

"Don't you dare think to take that young woman, you barbarian! We'll have the law on you! We'll—" Mrs. Peabody shouted.

"Good day!" Harding roared. "Men, ride!"

And beneath her, Jessica's horse began to move. To walk, trot and gallop. Racing her out of town. And far, far away from Blade McKenna....

Chapter Nine

The sun was high, and it seemed as though they had been riding forever. Jessica had been barely conscious, but now she was suddenly aware of one of Harding's men speaking to him.

"We ain't taking her to the fort, right?" she heard him ask. "Colonel Harding, we're your men to the last breath, but if you take her back to the fort, some of the guys there just might not think it's right, they might feel some sympathy for her, they might just…well, sir, they might just protest!"

"Dooley," Harding said with a trace of exasperation. "I am not taking her to the fort."

"Then—?"

"We're heading back for her place."

"Her place?"

"The land Charles Dylan bought when he was out here and left her, Dooley. Where the hell else would he have left anything of value to him!"

Dooley fell silent.

Harding chuckled softly and continued. "No one will see or hear her there. She can scream until the sun sets and rises again, and no one will hear her."

They kept riding.

When they reached her property, Jessica was so

stiff from being in such an awkward position during the ride that she couldn't stand when Dooley came to lift her from the horse. She fell against the creature, her feet and ankles numb.

Harding didn't care. He quickly had a hand on her elbow and started to drag her to the house, calling orders to his men. "Tear apart the barn, the stables. See what you can find."

Jessica longed to tell him that he could dig from here to Kingdom Come and he wouldn't find anything. But she didn't want him to know or even suspect that someone might be riding away with his evidence. If he did start suspecting, he'd probably begin asking questions in town. God forbid if he found out Blade had the evidence…and that he had also killed the man who had never come back. But…but if Blade had found Sherman and managed to walk into the army camp, then maybe…

Then what? He'd come back to town. She wouldn't be there. Mr. Delaney and Mrs. Peabody would tell him what happened, and he would come for her.

Except that he wouldn't know where to come….

Yes, yes, he might! This was the logical place for Harding to have brought her. To the ranch Charles Dylan had loved so much, the place that was his, the place he had come whenever he'd had a few spare minutes away from the fort.

Could he come in time? Jessica wondered.

She stumbled up the steps to the front door. Harding wrenched her to her feet. He kicked the door, still dragging her.

The house seemed so strange. No fire burned in the hearth. There was no aromatic scent of coffee in the air, no feel of life today. Yet it was still different from when they had first come, Jessica realized. It was neat, it was clean, it had little touches of home in the drapes, in the afghan over the sofa, in the cloth on the table, the vase there. It was a house that waited. Empty, and a little cold because of that, but waiting for them. For her and Blade.

Because they had, strangely enough, made it a home.

Harding shoved her into the chair before the cold hearth, then gripped the edges of the hearth and stared into her eyes. "Where are they, Mrs. Dylan?"

She lifted her chin. "Where are who, Colonel Harding?"

"Don't get wise with me, Mrs. Dylan. They. The letters. My property. Stolen by your husband."

"I haven't the faintest idea of what you're talking about."

"No? Yet in Jackson Prairie, you called out to everyone that I was a murderer!"

"Charles wrote home, of course, Colonel. He told me that you were a vile traitor and murderer, and that some of the Confederates had the money to buy that break they made. That is why I know that you are a traitor and a murderer."

"Colonel!" Dooley called impatiently.

Harding forgot Jessica for a moment. He turned to Dooley—who had apparently been sticking his nose around the house.

Dooley threw a shirt across the room. One of Blade's. Harding caught it, and stared at Dooley.

"My husband's—" she began in exasperation.

"I don't think so. I think she's living here with someone," Dooley said. "There's a shaving mirror and a razor in that bedroom. Looks all nice and cozy and domestic. Seems the widow here is into a little bit of entertainment."

Harding looked down at her with a sardonic smile. "That's good. Why, I won't have to feel half so guilty now. Raping old Dylan's widow might be kind of a cruel thing. But since she's just some cattle herder's whore, well, then it won't be quite so bad. We can have lots of fun until she decides to talk, or before we get to the real violence. Dooley, you go ahead and start a fire. I'm going to question my prisoner a little further in the comfort of her bedroom. I do want her to feel at home. But I need some good hot pokers. If I can't gently persuade her to turn over the letters, she'll have to lose one eye, and then the other. Dear me, Mrs. Dylan! You are going to be a mess before I leave you. And such a beautiful woman! What a pity."

He reached for her. Jessica struck out, slapping him hard, her nails raking across his face. Harding swore, wrenched her up, and threw her. She stumbled for balance and turned to flee. He caught her around the waist, lifting her. She clawed at his hands, but he didn't seem to care. "Get the damned fire going!" he ordered Dooley.

She fought. She fought even as Harding dragged

her toward her bedroom. She gripped the frame to the door and flung her weight wildly around.

Harding shouted for Dooley again. "Get over here! Leave the damned fire for a minute and help me get this witch in here!"

Dooley obliged, prying her fingers away from the doorframe. She was a fighter. Blade had told her that. But she couldn't fight them forever. Her heart seemed to constrict within her breast. No, this was her home, her place. It was where she lived and loved with Blade. Where she had discovered hope and desire and happiness once again. Where she had even dared to dream of a future, here, in this wilderness. She'd fight for it even if it killed her.

"No!" she shrieked. She heard her skirt rip and saw Dooley reaching for her bodice. "No!" she shrieked again. And then, amazingly and suddenly, Dooley was gone. Plucked from her, thrown across the room. She followed the motion of his body, saw him crash against the far wall, eyes go wide, then close, all consciousness stolen from him in one swift second.

She looked above her. Blade. He had come for her. In time.

She stared at him, into his dark, passionate eyes. She touched his cheek, bronzed, handsome, so rugged, so very appealing and arresting. She ran her thumb over the tight pad of his lower lip, and thought his was the most noble face she had ever seen. "You made it," she whispered softly.

"The army made it, too. A troop is right behind me."

"And—"

She broke off as she suddenly heard gunfire from outside, and then a bullet whizzed by them both, making a very strange sound as it sank into the bedding.

"Roll!" Blade shouted to her. He was on top of her, rolling with her. They both crashed down to the floor on the side of the bed. "Stay!" he commanded.

Well, she would stay, all right, but she had to see what was going on. She inched up, gazing across the bed, watching as Blade leapt up, jumping, spinning, avoiding the next bullet Harding sent flying his way, then pitting himself against the man. The gun went flying. Blade lit into Harding, his knuckles crunching into his cheek. He raised his fist to slam it down again. Then he paused. "He's out," he said, and rubbed his fist. "Out cold."

Blade lifted him up, hiking him over his shoulder. He turned to Jessy. "I wanted to kill him," he said huskily. "I wanted to kill him for touching you. I should turn him over to Lieutenant Gray. Gray is a good man, and Sherman wants Harding to stand trial. It is best—it will clear Charles Dylan."

"Yes, yes! Turn him over to Lieutenant Gray!" Jessica cried.

Blade nodded, and left her. There had been a skirmish outside, too, Blade realized. Yet, by the look of it, it had ended as quickly as it had begun. The Union troops who had followed Harding had been quick to surrender to Lieutenant Gray.

Jessica rose stiffly and walked to the window. She could see Blade handing the man over to a good-looking man. Gray. He was in control. It was over, she thought. At last. All over.

And Blade was alive and safe, and she was alive and safe, and there was nothing left except—

"Don't make a move, Mrs. Dylan."

She had forgotten Dooley. Forgotten that Blade had thrown him across the room, that he had seemed to be as out cold as Harding.

"Listen to me. All that I want to do is get away, and fast. I didn't have anything to do with your husband's frame-up, lady, honest. I never wanted to hurt you, but I've got to get out of here. I can't let that crazy half-breed get a good look at me. Wave! Wave quickly. Let them see that you're all right. Then you've got to find some way to get me out back. I've got a knife against your spine. Feel it? I can slice right into you in a matter of seconds. You'll be dead before you fall. Do you hear me?"

She nodded. She heard him. She heard the death of hope, of life, of love.

Outside, Blade finished saying something to Lieutenant Gray. He turned to her. She tried to smile. She lifted a hand.

"I'll kill him," Dooley whispered suddenly. "I'll hurtle this knife at him the second he steps through the door. Then I'll throttle you. I won't go down alone, I won't let him get me, I won't let him get me!"

It was Blade! The man was terrified of Blade. She

swallowed hard. Blade had come here, Mr. Delaney had told her, because he had heard that some of the men out of Kansas were at the fort.

And Blade was staring at her. She was trying so hard to smile, to look normal! But he knew her, knew her so very well. He looked at Gray again. "I've a few things in the barn, Lieutenant, that I need for the general. If you'll wait here for just a moment..."

His voice seemed to fade away. Lieutenant Gray was obviously confused, but he was also quick, and he acknowledged Blade's request with a nod. Dooley, behind her, exhaled a sigh of relief. "Get me out of here now!" he commanded Jessica.

She nodded. She turned away from the window. "There's no back door. There's a window—"

"Get me there!"

She turned from the window and started to walk. She had barely taken two steps before she screamed, spinning at the sound of shattering glass.

Blade. Crashing through the window, his hands around Dooley's throat, was Blade. He wrenched Dooley from her, throwing him to the ground. He straddled the man, his knife drawn, a savage look upon his face.

"God!" he raged suddenly. "You!" He grasped hard at Dooley's hair, wrenching it up. He raised his knife. He was preparing to scalp the man. And then...kill him, in cold blood.

Jessica watched, frozen. The bastard probably deserved it. But somehow, that didn't matter. What mattered was Blade. "Blade, no! No!" Jessica cried.

Blade paused, his knife held high, hatred burning darkly in his eyes. "You don't understand, Jessy," he cried out. "He was with them. Three of them. They came on my property. They shot down my father. And they came after Mara. They killed her—and our baby. She was running and running and they just shot her down. And they thought they'd killed me."

"Blade! I *do* understand what happened, Mr. Delaney told me. But Lieutenant Gray will take care of him, the army will take care of him. The war is over, I swear, we can see to it that he's prosecuted, I know they'll see justice done. He's down, it's all right, we're safe. Blade, I know how you were hurt, but Lieutenant Gray is outside, right? Let's give this man to the army, let him face the law. Please, God, Blade!"

"This is him," Blade said softly. "Frank Dooley, worked for Lane back in Kansas, so long ago now, eh, Dooley? This is him. I saw his face. Saw him shoot down Mara, then he came for me. Lord, I've waited forever for this moment. I swore that I'd kill him slow. That I'd take his scalp before he was even dead."

"Blade!" Jessy cried, rushing to him, falling down by his side where he straddled Dooley so tightly. She gripped his arm. The arm with the knife. It was like holding steel.

"Blade, you can't! You can't. You've got to turn him over to Lieutenant Gray. You have to! Please! If you don't, you'll have to run again. They can't let you take your vengeance, even if they think you're right. Gray will be obliged to come after you. And more men will die. Let him go to trial. Let Lieutenant Gray take him. Blade, I love you more than I've ever hated anyone in my life, you've got to feel the same way! It's the only chance that we've got!''

"Listen to her!" Dooley cried out. "Listen to her! I didn't want to kill anyone. Lane sent us out. He said we had to clear your place, that too many men were listening to old man McKenna. And sometimes, we were threatened, too. If we didn't follow orders, we'd be killed ourselves. McKenna, please! The others are dead!" he said in a sudden rush. "Jake Morgan died out here in that Confederate break that killed Dylan. Quantrill killed Yancy Thomas not a year after your—after your place was raided. It's over, McKenna, it's over! Please, lady, don't let him scalp me alive, do something, please—''

"You shot down a pregnant woman!" Blade raged.

Jessica realized that she hadn't gotten through to him. He was standing so rigidly, so tensely. He didn't even seem to feel her touch upon him. Tears stung her eyes. She didn't mean anything to him, not at this moment. He had waited all these years to find and kill the men who had slain his family. Jessica was certain that Dooley was telling the truth. The others were dead.

Dooley was broken. And it was almost damned certain that the Union army would deal with him. He'd hang. They had to leave it the way it was! Dooley, grateful to die by the rope rather than inch by inch at

Blade's hands. And Blade, for his own sake, had to let him go.

And Jessy…had to have Blade. She had to gamble. It was her only chance. "Blade!"

He couldn't feel her touch, so she dropped her hand from his arm, standing, stepping back. "Blade, I love you, I want you to marry me, I want to stay out here and build a life with you, I want us both to let go of our pasts. Can you hear me, Blade? Please, give him over to Lieutenant Gray. I beg you. There's so much out here that's lawless, let us be part of the law. Worse will come, there will be more injustices. There will be battles ahead, but Blade, let us have peace together. I beg you, give him over to Gray. I—I can't stop you from anything, I understand your hatred and your heartbreak, I just pray that the love we can have in the future can be stronger than all the hatreds of the past. I'll—I'll be outside."

"Lady!" Dooley screamed. "Don't leave me!"

She had to leave him. She was almost blinded by her tears. She was so afraid. If Blade killed Dooley now, Gray would have to bring Blade in.

She opened the door and stumbled outside. It was cool, clean and crisp.

They were standing before her. Gray and all his men, with their prisoners—and the dead—thrown like cargo over their horses.

She could see Harding. He'd killed Charles. And she had thought that she'd wanted him dead, but now it didn't matter. He was going to face trial. The name of Charles Dylan had been cleared.

Yet that didn't matter so much to her now. What really mattered was Blade. She had fallen in love with him. She had lived blindly for a long time, getting the deed to her property, managing to ride out to claim it. Wanting only to prove Charles innocent. Then Blade had somehow forced her to see that there was so much more to life.

"Mrs. Dylan?" Lieutenant Gray was coming to her, his eyes anxious. "What—?"

She shook her head. "I—I don't—"

"Here's another one for you, Lieutenant!"

Jessica heard Blade's voice and spun around. He was standing there, holding Dooley before him like a rag doll. He lifted the man and threw him down at Gray's feet. "Lieutenant, take him, please! Get him away from me. Far, far away."

Gray nodded and two of his men rushed forward. Dooley was taken quickly away and mounted on a horse. He stared at Jessy and she shivered. She felt Blade's hands on her shoulders.

Lieutenant Gray saluted them both. He lifted his hat to Jessica. "It's fine land, Mrs. Dylan. Mighty fine land."

"Thank you."

"Thank you, Mrs. Dylan. And McKenna, thank you. You've our most sincere appreciation. And—" He hesitated. "And I think you might find this a peaceful place in the future. A place where you might raise a herd of cattle, do a little farming…settle down for a spell."

Jessy felt Blade's smile. "Maybe," he told Lieutenant Gray.

Gray's troops moved then, their horses riding out of the yard, slowly disappearing into the setting sun. A cool breeze brushed Jessy's hair about her face. She felt Blade's chin on her head. "When's the wedding?" he asked softly.

"Tomorrow? At Mrs. Peabody's! She and Mr. Delaney can be there that way. That is, assuming we can get our hands on a minister."

"I'll find one," he promised her. "I'll get my hands on one. Even if I have to ride back to the Union army to do so!"

Jessy laughed. "Seems to me like you never really were any kind of an outlaw. And if you were, you've been fully pardoned."

"That's how it seems," he agreed.

Then, shaking, he swept her into his arms. "If the wedding's at Mrs. Peabody's tomorrow…"

"Yes?" she whispered huskily.

"Think we could start the honeymoon at home tonight?"

Laughing, she ran her fingers through his ink black hair and fell in love with his ruggedly handsome features all over again. "I think so!" she whispered, and he carried her into the house. "I love you," she whispered.

"I love you. I never knew just how much until I nearly lost you."

She didn't know what to say, and so she kissed him.

"And to think!" he said softly. "I won you in a poker game. On a gamble."

Jessy smiled, stroking her fingers through his ink dark hair. "And to think! I kept you on a gamble!" she replied. She arched a brow and smiled again. "I love the West," she murmured. "I love the wild, wild West—and the wild, wild things you can find in it!"

"Oh?" Blade asked.

"Mmm. And I love you."

"Oh?"

"Want me to prove it?"

"Mmm."

They walked through the house. They both knew that they'd made it. Out of the fire, into life. And their future loomed there before them, wondrously in their Western frontier. They had slept together in the wilderness.

And then love had made it a home.

*   *   *   *   *

International bestselling author

JOAN JOHNSTON

continues her wildly popular Hawk's Way
miniseries with an all-new, longer-length novel

THE SUBSTITUTE GROOM
HAWK'S WAY

August 1998

Jennifer Wright's hopes and dreams had rested on her sum-
mer wedding—until a single moment changed everything.
Including the *groom*. Suddenly Jennifer agreed to marry her
fiancé's best friend, a darkly handsome Texan she needed—
and desperately wanted—almost against her will. But U.S.
Air Force Major Colt Whitelaw had sacrificed too much to
settle for a marriage of convenience, and that made hiding
her passion all the more difficult. And hiding her biggest
secret downright impossible...

**"Joan Johnston does contemporary Westerns
to perfection."** —*Publishers Weekly*

Available in August 1998
wherever Silhouette books are sold.

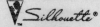

Take 2 bestselling love stories FREE

Plus get a FREE surprise gift!

The World's Most Eligible Bachelors are about to be named! And Silhouette Books brings them to you in an all-new, original series....

World's Most
Eligible Bachelors

Twelve of the sexiest, most sought-after men share every intimate detail of their lives in twelve never-before-published novels by the genre's top authors.

Don't miss these unforgettable stories by:

Dixie Browning

MARIE FERRARELLA

Jackie Merritt

Tracy Sinclair

BJ James

RACHEL LEE   Suzanne Carey

Gina Wilkins

VICTORIA PADE

MAGGIE SHAYNE   *Anne McAllister*

Susan Mallery

Look for one new book each month in the **World's Most Eligible Bachelors** series beginning September 1998 from Silhouette Books.

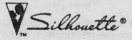

Silhouette®

Available at your favorite retail outlet.